THE CURSE OF SILVER AND SUNLIGHT

Riley Cain was born in Dublin in 1968. Following the success of his first book for children in 2020 - *The Halloween House: 31 Putrid Poems and Rotten Rhymes for October* – Riley returned in 2021 with *Banshee Rising*, an adventure novel for teens inspired by his love of ghost stories and Irish folklore.

The Curse of Silver and Sunlight is the first in a planned series following the adventures of the vampire Benjamin Blake.

Riley still lives in Dublin, and haunts the internet at www.rileycain.com

THE CURSE OF SILVER AND SUNLIGHT

BENJAMIN BLAKE BOOK I

RILEY CAIN

First published in 2023 by The Riley Realm
www.rileycain.com

ISBN: 978-1-7393718-0-7

Set in Linux Libertine 13/16
Cover and book design by Alba Esteban | Alestura Design
Illustrated by Alba Esteban

For Ben
'You are one of the lights, the light of all lights'
(Dracula)

A Warning for the Curious

So, you want to know about the vampire Benjamin Blake.

That's why you came to the theatre tonight, isn't it? To learn more of the legend, the story of the London vampire who comes each time Macbeth is staged here. You heard the tale and how I, Charles De Courcey, supposedly met him once in this very dressing room.

Or perhaps you came to see the production. Did you? Was I good? I haven't acted in the Scottish play in so very long. Ah, but I see the eager truth in your face. You want to know about *him.*

Well, the incredible truth is I did meet him, and more than once.

The first time? Gosh, that must have been fifteen years ago. He slipped quietly backstage after curtain call and gave me quite the fright when he introduced himself. I hadn't caught sight of him in my makeup mirror, you see. Well, I wouldn't, I suppose. I turned to the sound of his gentle voice and found him standing in the doorway, right where you are now. In my surprise, I blurted something silly about mistaking him for one of the theatre's famous ghosts. And he offered the funniest reply. He said, 'I've been coming to the Lyceum for over two hundred years and I've never seen a ghost.'

Well, we laughed at that, but do you know, that's when I glimpsed the truth. It was in the way the light caught the silver of his eyes and, of course, those teeth when he smiled.

And then he said something to really convince me. 'May I come in?'

There, I see it. You're thinking exactly as I did in that first moment. A vampire cannot enter unless invited.

But he can.

Entering a space quietly and uninvited is something vampires do very well, actually. Benjamin Blake learned long, long ago the trick of slipping through cracks and keyholes. Now he can do it almost without thinking.

Does that answer one of the many questions you have? Let me guess at some others. Sunlight, crosses, stakes, sleeping in coffins, billowing capes? What else?

What did he look like? Well, it's easy to forget Benjamin is nearly four hundred years old now. In the flesh, he is a boy of fifteen, the age at which he was transformed to 'the shadow world'; that's what he calls it. He is of medium height and build, though immensely strong. His hair is full and raven black, his skin smooth and quite pale and he has nails one might consider somewhat long and sharp for a boy. His eyes, when you can hold their intense gaze, are sky blue most of the time. But in the moonlight, or when a candle flickers, they reflect that silver sparkle of the undead.

He doesn't wear a cape by the way, at least he hasn't done since the 17th century.

Oh, his scars. I nearly forgot his scars. Across the back of his right hand, above the thumb, Benjamin has four small, crescent-shaped cuts. It's rather like looking at a cycle of the moon, which is ironic when you learn how he got them. And quite chilling.

For the most part though, Benjamin is just like any vampire in the world tonight. He is not even the oldest of his kind. But he is without question the most remarkable. That's because of the magical abilities he possesses, powers other vampires can only dream of. To understand why that is, you need to hear the full story of his coming to be. Trust me, slipping through keyholes will seem like a cheap trick after that.

It is only fair I warn you, however. To learn about Benjamin is to learn of a supernatural world filled with all manner of wicked things, including witches, and to know of *them* is to enter a dangerous realm indeed.

But you seem insistent still and eager to know

more, despite all. In that case, enter. Take a seat and I'll tell you what I know of my friend the vampire. It just so happens you have chosen the perfect hour for the tale of Benjamin Blake.

As Macbeth himself says, 'Tis now the very witching time of night...'

Are you ready to begin?

I

ut, oh, *where* to begin?

This is a vampire tale after all, and no one is born a vampire, so Benjamin Blake's must, naturally and supernaturally, be a tale of two beginnings.

The setting for both was the Essex village of Ravenhill, a small farming community some two days' ride from London. Here Benjamin had his first, mortal beginning, in the year 1630.

And, by all accounts, what a day that was! On the cold, clear October morning of his birth there was not a single person in the sleepy village indifferent to news that Catherine Blake was with child. Her babe's arrival had become the anticipated event of the year, the subject of months of breathless whisperings throughout the community. Why, such an episode had not been experienced in Ravenhill in living memory and it drove the villagers to the borders of impatience as they waited for the first cries from 'the Blake child'. The collective sense of excitement did not arise from some portent of greatness accompanying the infant's arrival, however, like a comet in the sky, or a thunderstorm to demonstrate Heaven's fury – though God surely *was* angered by the event. For the birth was one of scandalous mystery as to the identity of Benjamin Blake's father.

The unanswered question had from the outset inspired cruel and fevered speculation among the Blakes' neighbours. In place of facts and an honourable marriage to set things right, knowing winks and nods went eagerly with loose talk. A dark-haired soldier of ill-repute was one favoured figure of gossip, or a runaway thief the girl took pity on. But Catherine Blake held fast against all whisperings and hinted only that 'he' would return when his fortune was made, to make things right by her and the infant she named Benjamin. Her faith in a wayward love became one more reason for Ravenhill to look down its collective nose at the girl and her ill-begotten child.

That Benjamin's mother was not ultimately forced upon the road by pious villagers was due to her brother, Thomas. Whether through an act of familial kindness (sincerely doubted by all who knew that surly, grasping innkeeper) or a chance to penny-pinch a wage, the elder Blake loudly reminded the parish of its duty of care to neglected children before taking mother and child into the Straw Hall, his home and place of business across the Blackwater Bridge. There

Catherine would work in return for shelter and food, while Thomas counted his profits and grumbled of the shame and cost brought upon him by his sister.

It was the Straw Hall that provided Benjamin with his first clear memories of home and hearth. There are recollections of touch, the feeling of the wooden floor against baby hands where he crawled excitedly between the gigantic legs of chairs and tables. Vivid memories of his mother's laughter from above as she raced in chasing to cut off first one route, then another, peeking under a tabletop to call, 'Where's my Benjamin? There's my Benjamin!' And after play, resting in her lap, the smell of her skirts scented with lavender as he drifted to sleep by a newly prepared fire in the wide grate. Slipping off, watching the growing flame, he listened to the sound of her gently singing,

> *'Close thine eyes and sleep secure,*
> *Thy soul is safe, thy body sure.*
> *He that guards thee, he that keeps,*
> *Never slumbers, never sleeps.'*

Carried by her clear voice, the song would stay with Benjamin down the centuries. It was the strongest memory of his mother among so tragically few. He was barely three years old when she was taken by fever to her resting place in the churchyard of St Mary's, there to lie in a lonely corner neglected by the villagers.

After that, the child's remembrances became of those of a man who was neither father nor mother to him. Uncle Thomas proved instead a most reluctant guardian, complaining loudly and more often of his abandonment with an unwanted stray, a drain on his hard-earned coins through need of schooling and feeding. This was ever the refrain that followed Benjamin as he laboured in his mother's stead at the inn, never quite managing to do enough to curb Thomas's grumblings over meals he prepared or to avoid a whipping belt amid barrels he rolled. Yet, neither did he do so little to be turned out in favour of a paid hireling. Thus, Benjamin earned his nightly bed, there to push off the day's store of insults in favour of his mother's remembered voice lulling him to sleep with gentle singing, and the hushed assurance that his father would come, would surely come, and make things right. Her promise became Benjamin's fervent prayer every night to the time of his transformation from the waking world.

That, his second beginning, came fifteen years after the first, at a time when all England seethed in turmoil.

In 1645 the realm entered its third year of bloody war with itself. In pursuit of his divine right to rule, King Charles I and his Royalist followers set themselves against a rebellious people and their parliament, staking all for unopposed control of the nation. Stories reached Ravenhill of great armies moving from Oxford and London to challenge one another in fierce slaughter, some giving victory to the king's men, some to the citizen soldiers, the so-called 'Roundheads' who resisted them.

What a time it was to be a young boy intrigued by tales of war and fighting!

Benjamin was such a boy, of course, and whether through good fortune or a blessing from the god of war, he quickly found himself well-placed to hear the latest exciting news from the battlefield, all to the great envy of his friends in the village who craved stories of war and adventure in no less measure.

Living and working in the Straw Hall, Benjamin had access almost daily to the tales carried by travellers between London and Colchester. By day, tending to his work around the inn, he listened keenly for snatches of conversation in which the progress of the war was discussed. By night, when the day's chores were completed and young boys ought to be in their beds, Benjamin secretly joined the men of Ravenhill when they came to debate the conflict over tankards of ale. Perched above all in the shadows of the inn's gallery, the boy listened in thrilled silence to the stories of recent battles late into the night.

Each nugget of information gained by such secret watching sent him creeping to bed with the map books Uncle Thomas possessed and a candle, by whose light Benjamin sought out the battlefields of Edgehill, Grantham, Newbury and Marston Moor. How he delighted in discovering each one and measuring the distance from it to Essex and his little village, so often no more than a finger's width on the page. By dawn of day, he would perch on his toes on the small hill behind the Straw Hall in vain hope of spying flags and pike-tips of regiments on the march just over the western horizon. There he imagined distant fields covered over with musket smoke and lines of pikemen clashing with charging cavalry. And among them, his mind's eye found a great and powerful warrior, his father, a captain of the guard, cutting a swathe through his enemies astride a mighty steed as he unleashed a deafening war cry.

This last part Benjamin kept to himself in the daylight hours, when the boys of Ravenhill gathered by the Blackwater and demanded every lurid detail of his eavesdropping. Benjamin would shrug and shake his head to tease with a hint of 'reports from Warwickshire' or 'an advance on Oxford'. Only after much pleading would he supply more colourful elements, remembering, of course, his audience's desire for precise descriptions of bloodletting and ripped guts.

Then, one drinking night in late spring, news of a different kind and more exciting to a young boy's imaginings, came to the Straw Hall.

'Witches, I tells you. Witches.'

Armstrong the weaver banged down his tankard sharply in response to the mocking laughter for his report. He had that evening returned from market at Colchester, bringing with him tales of sorcery and covens, of dark magic in the misty forests along the river Stour, tales to make Benjamin's skin prickle in his hiding place.

'Three of them I saw myself, led off to the town jail,' Armstrong insisted to his fellow drinkers, 'there to await investigation by the witchfinder Hopkins. What do you say to that?'

'I say you've had enough of my ale,' Uncle Thomas called from the bar to more raucous laughter all round.

'I say I haven't had enough,' Armstrong shouted back. 'But I tells you certain sure, the land about is filled with incidents of witches and the devilish arts. The witchfinders are kept busy this season.'

In frustration at the increasing volume of merriment greeting his statements, Armstrong shifted his attention to the village blacksmith who cradled his own measure of beer by the fire. 'You tell them, Bolton,' Armstrong demanded, 'tell them I'm speaking in me senses.'

Shifting awkwardly in his seat, Bolton rubbed a meaty hand thoughtfully through his beard. Finally, with the weight of all eyes on him, he nodded slowly and sombrely.

'I've heard talk myself of witches,' he admitted, and the laughter began to fade away.

'What talk?' The call came from Billy Preston the farm labourer, scoffing from his usual card-covered table in the corner. Benjamin watched the young man offer a playful nudge for his gambling partner, Jem Canning, and the pair waited with mischievous glee for more stupidity from old men.

Bolton drank long and deep. 'A gentleman rider from the north stopped in with me two days back,' he said when the room at last came to full quiet. 'I shoed his mount while he offered a tale, of two women held on charges of sorcery. The one, he said, was a widow over at Haverhill. She had promised her soul to the Devil for the power to sicken a neighbour and steal her husband. The other, well, she's held now in the magistrate's house at Manningtree. Caught in the act of casting spells at a midnight crossroads for some wicked purpose or other, she was. The gentlemen rider said he heard himself her confession in open court, of conjuring for the power to use evil spirits. "Familiars" she called them.'

'Familiars,' Armstrong interrupted quickly and with an urgent thrust of his tankard. He faced the listeners as he remembered the word. 'The people in Colchester spoke of them too. They said a sorceress questioned by the witchfinder Hopkins out Langham way had revealed to him her "familiars". Dark-of-night creatures with silver eyes they were, and they appeared at her calling and terrified all present until sunrise drove them off.'

This time no one laughed at his words and more than a few supped deeply.

Listening on, Benjamin's imagination blazed to tales of magic in places but a few miles' distance from the village. Silently he vowed to hunt across the pages of his uncle's maps into the small hours, setting aside battle sites in favour of Haverhill and Manningtree. And he would rise earlier tomorrow, long before chores were due, and turn his hilltop gaze north for the spires of Colchester, certain he would catch smoke across the fields, not from farmhouse chimneys but from witch-burnings!

But even as the plan thrilled him, Benjamin cursed his own faulty memory and disregarded his scheme. Tomorrow he would be in no fit state to rise early for a witchhunt. It was dark of the moon tonight and that meant dark work for him.

2

The smugglers came after midnight.

Through a pallid mist rising on the fields, their cart trundled slowly towards the main road from the east, where the miles ran back to the Channel coast and its many hidden inlets.

Benjamin knew well the routine. For as long as he could recall, Uncle Thomas had worked his profitable sideline to inn-keeping. Once each month he played host to the rum-runners, storing their illicit barrels among his own and making a pretty penny from the illegal trade between Colchester and London. And since turning of an age to work, Benjamin had been assigned his dual roles in the night trade as dogsbody and watcher.

He watched now as the cart driver steered to the lee of trees hemming the main road, there to stop a safe distance from the Straw Hall. Benjamin sensed the men aboard looking to the inn and towards his place in the upper window. There were four of them, always four. And always they paused in the trees and strained through the dark for signs of ambush, for the candle that Benjamin had set winking, his signal the night was clear of magistrates and revenue men.

'Get down here, boy.'

Benjamin moved obediently to his uncle's far-off summons. At the foot of the main stairs, he found the inn's rear door opened in readiness. Likewise, a lantern's gleam beyond the bar revealed the cellar hatch set on its hinges. Shadows played up through the light and betrayed Thomas's presence down there.

Descending, Benjamin looked between cobwebbed stacks of barrels and casks to where he knew his uncle would be. Sure enough, at the farthest end of the cellar, where the space gave way to a tall work-bench set against one wall, Thomas worked quickly on the final barrier.

With grunting efforts, the man forced himself between the bench and a stout barrel, there to fumble along the wall behind. Straining hard, his tongue popped stupidly between wet lips as he concentrated until, with the softest of clicks, the latch he sought was lifted. Thomas allowed himself a satisfied smile as the bench released from its fixing to a rattle of tools.

At the man's impatient direction, Benjamin grasped for wood and pulled in time with him, and with the sliding aside of the furniture, the Straw Hall's secret was revealed. Through a low doorway so neatly obscured, the cellar ran on to a hidden store of lesser dimensions. Within this darkened space, Benjamin spied the trove of smugglers' casks.

'Back to your watch,' Thomas instructed gruffly and Benjamin hastened to comply.

He had barely climbed two steps when a shadow fell from above and his way was blocked. With a nervous swallow, Benjamin retreated as a masked and caped form decked all in black came slowly on, gloved hands close to the pistol and sword he wore.

'Ready?' the secret man demanded. He gazed warily about the cellar before looking directly to Thomas in search of an answer.

Thomas agreed quickly, anxiously.

'Ready, Captain Hazzard.'

Not trusting the innkeeper's assurance, Captain Hazzard scanned around once more before angling his hidden face upwards. A soft whistle issued from behind the mask and the boards above creaked to an advance of hasty footsteps.

At their coming down the steps, Benjamin slipped between barrels to watch the smugglers work. Two men, their faces similarly hidden, moved awkwardly beneath the weight of a crate they bore. Their masks puffed to labouring breaths and muttered curses as they struggled to fit the long rectangular box through the narrow hatch and guide it along a precarious angle to the foot of the steps. There the men paused briefly to renew their strength before heaving the coffin-shaped cargo on to the secret store with more bitter mutterings for the low doorway.

Uncle Thomas looked on the work and frowned at the passing of such an unusual crate. He offered Hazzard a confused glance. 'No brandy or rum tonight?' he asked.

Even behind his mask, Hazzard's displeasure at questions was evident.

'Muskets,' he said then, testing the innkeeper with the word.

In his place, Benjamin thrilled but saw fear rise in his uncle's face.

'Muskets?' Thomas gasped. 'But-but who for?' He blinked against terrible alternatives. In a time of divided loyalties, brandy made money and friends but muskets made only enemies.

Hazzard cocked a mischievous brow. 'Who would *you* sell them to?' he challenged. He fixed unblinking eyes on Thomas as a hand slipped visibly towards his pistol. Only when Thomas spluttered fearfully enough for amusement did Hazzard give up on games. He bypassed his weapons and snatched a purse of coins from his belt. 'Calm yourself, Blake,' he ordered, 'I know you serve coin and not king.' He cast the purse to the sweating man. 'Your share is increased for this shipment. Three crates for two nights; no more than that. And no more questions.'

The mention of an increase was enough to settle matters. Benjamin watched Thomas gleefully play the purse between his greasy fingers before looking on its shiny contents with relish. 'No more questions,' his uncle agreed dreamily.

'And what about you?' The question shot between the barrels to Benjamin's heart. When he looked, he found Hazzard's eyes set on him.

Benjamin eased from cover as the second crate was carried past. Up close it looked even more like a coffin.

'I do as I'm told,' he said, and stood for what felt an unending time beneath Hazzard's appraising glare. Finally, through crushing silence, he felt compelled to look to that portion of the smuggler's face he could see, as though to perceive the man's thinking. But there was nothing to read in those staring eyes, sky blue and sparkling in the lamp light.

'Good,' Hazzard said, and after a further pause to inspect the boy, he turned away to talk barrels and crates again with Thomas.

Relieved, Benjamin took his opportunity and made for the steps, eager to be back on watch in the upper window, far from the cellar and Hazzard's gaze. Certain those piercing eyes were on him again as he climbed, he quickened his steps, almost tripping into the bar as he fled.

In his room, he did not look on smugglers again until the slamming cellar hatch caused him to jump and he set the flickering candle dancing with a startled breath. Only then did he slip from his post in favour of the gallery, there to hold to shadow and watch the men depart wordlessly through the back door.

Hazzard paused in following his companions into the pressing night. He lingered instead with Thomas by the hearth to issue final whispered instructions. Their conversation ended with nods of agreement and Hazzard turned away. But all at once he halted his stride and turned to peer sharply up to gallery shadows.

Benjamin froze in his place, seized by an intensity of fear in his gut. Had the last light of the dying fire betrayed him between the rails? He held taut his muscles, limbs and breath, and offered a silent prayer against Hazzard and his pistol. But the smuggler did no more than look and at last dropped his gaze to stand a moment longer, as though in contemplation, before turning away to sweep into the night.

With a deep sigh of relief, Benjamin set the night and smugglers behind him to creep gratefully to his bed.

3

'You, sir, shall not pass.'

With this dire warning issued on the warm summer air, Benjamin paced slowly across one end of the Blackwater Bridge. He kept a watchful eye on the figure peering back and waited for the advance that must surely come. Just as slowly, his opponent mirrored Benjamin's slow steps and boldly held his gaze. When Benjamin halted, he halted. When Benjamin walked backwards over his route, he reversed too, and when he raised his sword menacingly, his opposite met the challenge likewise.

'Aside, I say,' the enemy called sternly. 'I am Lord Buckingham and I will bring my message to Oliver Cromwell himself.'

Benjamin sighed wearily and lowered his sword. 'You can't be a lord if you are for Cromwell,' he protested. 'Cromwell is for the people, not the king.'

Lord Buckingham, played so well till now by Jack Harker, the glover's son, advanced across the sunlit span, his weapon held ready.

'You lie, Royalist dog,' he barked dramatically, 'taste my blade.'

Benjamin held fast and threw up his sword against the first swinging blow. Blades came together with a loud wooden *clack!* and battle was joined.

Having blocked the first strike, Benjamin parried with a slice at Jack's guts. This killer blow the boy avoided with a quick leap backwards and a triumphant 'Aha!' His fighting arm whipped over his head for a fresh assault. Benjamin turned to block, anticipating the angle of attack, and swords were halted in mid-flight as they slapped together.

'Cede to me,' Buckingham-Jack ordered through gritted teeth as they pushed one another in a tight circle.

'Never,' came Benjamin's defiant grunt of reply. 'No quarter sought, no quarter given.'

'Then the Devil take you, sir,' Jack cried as he leapt from the circle. Drawing back, he built up to a fatal jab.

Benjamin spotted the boy's intention and deftly side-stepped. Jack, overextending his thrust, stumbled past into the space created. As he did, Benjamin threw a shoulder into him. The force of the blow took both off balance and onto the grass. For a moment the boys seemed to hold, suspended between Heaven and Earth in a final struggle until gravity sent them tumbling headlong down the riverbank, in a great knot of arms and legs.

Benjamin was luckier in the dusty, shuddering fall. He had Jack to land on.

'Get off,' the boy demanded breathlessly when their descent ended just short of the water.

'Yes, my good lord,' Benjamin replied. He rolled aside, laughing.

Jack did not share the joke as he sat up in haste.

'Oh no,' he exclaimed and fumbled quickly beneath his rear as Benjamin watched with a frown. 'I think I sat on my sword.' He drew out his weapon and despaired at the wooden blade, splintered into a limp V-shape where his weight had snapped it.

The friends gave in to laughter at the ridiculous outcome of the battle, and their voices rose to the bright sunshine of the morning to ring clearly across the village.

'So,' Jack said at last, 'what news do you bring from the inn today?'

Benjamin shook his head for the question. *Smugglers and criminal trade?* There were some things he did not share with anyone beyond the Straw Hall, even his best friend in life.

'You first,' he insisted to divert the boy. 'I know your father returned from Colchester last evening. Did he bring stories?'

As a craftsman, Jack's father travelled regularly to the market in Colchester to offer his leather goods for sale. More than once this year already, he had returned with dark reports, tales to confirm rumours of wicked magic, causing the men of the Straw Hall to drink in silence as they pondered the trouble brought by witches for cattle and crops.

'I have better than stories,' Jack assured with a broad smile for his role as news bearer.

'Another witch trial,' Benjamin gasped, hungry for more.

'And better,' Jack teased with a grin. He reached into his tunic and drew out a slim booklet which he offered his friend.

Taking the document, Benjamin unfolded the covering page. He caught a breath at what he read. In bold black ink, the booklet announced itself ominously:

A Most Certain, Strange, and True
Discovery of a Witch

Below the title, a printed illustration gave hint of the dreadful story within. The picture focused on a witch in the act of conjuring. A hooded and sharp-nosed hag, she stood on the outskirts of a town and at the edge of a circle of raging fire. Around its flames, evil beasts raised on two legs joined with horned figures in dancing for the wicked celebration. Overseeing all, the witch stretched out a hand as though directing the ceremony while in the other, she held a book of magic symbols: her secret spell book to summon the dancing demons.

'She was discovered in Barnston at the beginning of the month,' Jack explained as Benjamin eagerly thumbed the pamphlet.

'And goes to trial this week,' Benjamin noted, scanning the details of the case with nervous excitement. The report described how a young woman of Barnston caused suspicion among the people of her village through strange nocturnal habits. Suspected by neighbours of practising black arts during night-time wanderings from home, the woman was at last seized…

'In the churchyard,' Benjamin gasped.

A search of her isolated dwelling was ordered to put an end to all rumours, and there proof of diabolical pursuits was uncovered when searchers reached her foul cellar. In that dank and dripping place, the villagers came upon twin chalked circles on the floor, containing between them unearthly symbols. While at the centre of the wicked art, candles melted about a large cooking pot, wherein the final damning evidence was uncovered. Benjamin's skin tingled as he read aloud.

'Human bones!'

'Father says her guilt is beyond question,' Jack said.

'Human bones,' Benjamin repeated weakly, his head growing light.

'If you are set to be sick,' Jack warned with a laugh, 'turn away from me.'

Not wanting to touch the booklet and its grim report any longer, Benjamin returned it, though its tale of not-so-distant magic lingered yet in his mind. Barnston, Colchester, Langham, Haverhill, all so much nearer than Oxford or London and yet still so far from the experience of Ravenhill. In a moment's irritation, he tossed his sword to the Blackwater and watched it ride with the flow beneath the bridge.

'What did you do that for?' Jack enquired.

'Don't you see?' Benjamin asked but, of course, he knew his friend did not. He sighed. 'In the space of this one afternoon, that wooden stick will travel farther from Ravenhill than I ever have. Or probably ever will.'

'Where's the harm in that?' Jack said. 'We have a nice village.'

'Don't you want to see a battlefield or a witch trial?'

'No thank you very much. I'll be happy to stay here and never see the likes.'

'And become a glover like your father before you?'

'It's a proper trade,' Jack said defensively, 'and so is an innkeeper. Think on that, Benjamin. You'll inherit the Straw Hall one day and all its pretty pennies.'

Benjamin's teeth ground at the thought. *Pretty pennies.* That he should ever become a money-grabbing man like Thomas Blake made him fume.

'My father was no innkeeper,' he grumbled. 'He was a soldier.' He felt instantly the awkward silence from Jack for that and glanced at the boy's features.

'What?'

'Nothing.'

'What?'

'Nothing.'

'Tell me,' Benjamin demanded.

Jack shrugged. 'It's just that, well, most in the village believe your father was, well, a gypsy thief.'

Benjamin's flash of anger was enough to send him to his feet, and with a look so fierce it drove Jack scrambling backwards over the grass.

'My father was no such thing! He was a soldier. That's why he left. But he's coming back and when he does, I'm going to see Oxford... and Cambridge, and London!'

The scorn he felt for gossiping villagers poured down on Jack, pale and wide-eyed at his feet. Only slowly did his anger subside until embarrassment at his actions sent him into retreat. He dropped to sitting by the water and, with sharp motions, sent plucked grass flying into the river.

'My father will come back.'

Looking at the heat-shimmering fields about and hearing nothing but songbirds in thickets, part of Benjamin agreed with Jack's assessment. Ravenhill *was* a good place to be. This was home and life, such as it was, was here. But then he looked on the sparkling water sweeping under the bridge on its way to a coast he had never seen. A mere stick would be there before moonrise. And he would still be in Ravenhill, waiting with nothing but tales of witchcraft and far-off battlefields.

The final thought jarred a memory of untold news and drove off the last of his gloomy mood.

'Oh, I suppose you are right, Jack,' he said with mock weariness, 'what is the use of troubling ourselves with tales overheard at the Straw Hall? They are exciting, true enough, but not for us in our happy village.'

Jack sensed the teasing in the boy's voice with fresh anticipation. He crawled rapidly to sit by him. 'You do have news, I *knew* it. Tell me.'

'Oh,' Benjamin sighed again and now with a dismissive wave, 'I was all set to tell you this morning, but after your talk of a quiet life, I don't see the why of sharing.'

'Tell me!' He punched Benjamin in the shoulder for good measure.

Benjamin's grin became a broad smile as he turned to relate the story: a conversation overheard between Uncle Thomas and a guest newly arrived that morning. 'News of a coming battle. One that will settle matters once and for all, and a new army to do it.'

'For the king or the people?' Jack asked earnestly.

'A new army for the people,' Benjamin reported.

Jack savoured the words as though tasting some new and exotic food for the first time. 'A new army,' he whispered breathlessly. 'What else?'

Benjamin told all. The London government had finally created an army that would best any force of the king. Fourteen thousand fighting men had been trained in the use of pike and musket and would march behind no fewer than thirteen thousand cavalry versed in the newest battle tactics.

'Somewhere to the west they are seeking the king's men right now and spoiling for a fight,' he concluded excitedly.

Jack's lips flapped like those of a stranded fish as he tried to envisage the scale of numbers.

'Thirteen thousand horses? Thirteen thousand!' he gasped eventually, scratching his head as though the figure was hurting his brain. 'I haven't seen even *thirteen* horses together!'

'That's because you live in Ravenhill,' Benjamin reminded him with a playful smirk. He eased to the river and scooped a handful of water to quench his thirst from storytelling.

The world reflected below was a beautiful and inverted painting on smoothest glass. Clouds of pure white sat upon a sea-blue sky and the bridge clung to the green fields above, while upon it, and appearing to hang like a roosting bat, a caped man silently watched.

4

'Hello below,' the man called as the boys leapt up. Of middle years, the man was round-faced and wore a jolly expression under a dark and unruly beard. His whiskers, combined with clothing and a cape that had seen better days, gave the impression of a wandering beggar. Though when he addressed the friends again, his speech was cultured in its delivery.

'Good morrow to you, my fine young masters,' he said waving heartily, his smile growing as Benjamin and Jack scrambled up from the riverbank to join him. 'If it pleases,' he said when at last they stood before him, 'my companions and I seek directions. Might you offer assistance?'

The companions spoken of comprised a small band of figures packed into a covered wagon trundling under the power of two ragged horses towards the bridge. The vehicle drew up lazily and the boys watched as the passengers descended to stretch weary limbs with groans of relief for this pause in their bone-rattling journey.

'Where are you bound?' Jack asked.

'Could you inform me if we find ourselves at the fair village of Ravenhill?' the man asked. 'We hope to reach there by nightfall.'

'Yes, sir,' Benjamin responded. Turning on his heel he pointed along the road past the bridge. 'Ravenhill lies before you.'

'Excellent, excellent,' the man proclaimed, thrusting his fists excitedly. 'But tell me, if I may press ye further, do the inhabitants of Ravenhill welcome entertainments?'

'What sort of entertainments, sir?' Jack asked. He peered suspiciously where one of the travellers, freed of the wagon's confines, began to perform toe-pointing dance steps across the road, while another began to juggle stones plucked from the roadside.

'Why, the very best entertainments,' the man insisted. He cast a hand wide to present his companions. 'Ye find yourselves, noble sirs, in the presence of the Greenwich Players, veterans all of the London stage and the finest exponents of the dramas of Misters Shakespeare, Dekker, Marlowe and Jonson. We are, I am sad to relate and despite our rare talents, set upon the highway by the forced closure of London's theatres. How the war blights our times. But!' Here he held a determined finger to the sky. 'What London has lost, all England shall gain as we bring our productions and

fine talents far and wide to villages such as yours. I am
the leader of this merry band. Janson De Courcey...
Perhaps you have heard of me.'

'No,' the boys replied innocently as one.

'Oh,' the downcast De Courcey responded. 'No matter. After tonight's performance, the Greenwich players will live long in the memories of the good people
of Ravenhill.'

'What performance?' Benjamin gasped, excited by
the prospect of an evening's fun.

'Why, a play,' De Courcey said, 'a play to entertain
and thrill the senses. I'll wager Ravenhill has not seen
so fine and dazzling a performance as can be staged by
the Greenwich Players.'

'What play?' the boys chorused excitedly.

'What would you like to see?' De Courcey asked.
'Choose a play of your own liking as a reward for your
kind directions to us. We are equal to the challenge
you set.' With a dismissive wave to the air, he sniffed
haughtily. 'Anything of the wordsmiths I have named,
we have played them all. I'm told my Hamlet is par-
ticularly good.'

'A play with fighting,' Jack suggested and De
Courcey pursed his lips in deep consideration.

'One with mystery,' Benjamin prompted and De
Courcey stroked his bushy beard in pondering yet
more deeply.

Suddenly inspired by his inner muse, the man jumped back from the boys and whipped his cape over his shoulder. With exaggerated movements, he drew an imagined sword and thrust at each lad in turn as he boomed. 'Once more unto the breach with noble King Henry, perhaps.' In a moment his sword was forgotten and De Courcey shifted his body to bent and cruel angles. 'Evil King Richard and his treacherous plots, perchance?' Next, and with a proud stomp, he drew a wing of cape across his chest and stood tall and proud. 'Or would you prefer the bloody tale of Julius Caesar?'

'Can you be a witch?' Benjamin challenged.

'Aha,' the player exclaimed with a nod of appreciation. His cape flowed slowly across his head and his body hunched forward, his face screwing to a pinched mask as fingers gnarled to skeletal hooks. His voice when it came was made high and creaking.

'What about three witches?'

5

The trio of hags gathered to circle the bubbling pot, and chanted incantations to the red-rising moon.

'Double, double toil and trouble, fire burn and cauldron bubble,' they cackled and circled again the steaming concoction. In unison they reached forward to drop "fresh" ingredients from spindly fingers into the brew. The action brought a hissing smoke which drew up to join the coven's slow, eerie dance of conjuring. Behind the snaking cloud, two of the forms slithered back to shadow, arms aloft in listening to their wicked sister recite the foul recipe.

'Eye of newt and toe of frog, wool of bat and tongue of dog,' she breathed with a gleeful wiggle of fingers. 'Adder's fork and blind-worm's sting, lizard's leg and howlet's wing, for a charm of powerful trouble, like a hell-broth boil and bubble.' Her list complete, the witch swept forward to offer a smile of blackened teeth to the onlookers.

Crammed into the stable yard of the Straw Hall, the audience offered gasps of horror for the witch's staring features. High on his father's shoulders, the blacksmith's son hid behind his hands and peeked nervously between chubby fingers. Billy Preston put on a bold show but mopped his brow, while pretty Kate Tindall was distracted by fear, and Mistress Taylor of Hilltop Farm drew her shawl across quivering lips to stifle an emerging scream.

Delighted by the fearful reactions they inspired, the three evil sisters glided nearer the stage's edge and reached theatrically with clicking nails to drive terror to new and colder heights. But, on the very cusp of panic, at the exact moment it seemed the audience would turn and flee, the heroic figure of Macbeth – De Courcey bedecked in regal cape and sword – strode from the wings to boldly confront the coven.

'Ha-ha-haa! How now, you secret, black and midnight hags!' he bellowed, diverting witches' stares from the grateful audience.

The villagers' relieved cheers rose high and drifted to the inn's upper windows to find Benjamin and Jack comfortably placed with the best view of the night. No less horrified by the three hell-visions now clawing the air before brave Macbeth, they watched in rapt silence as the hags revelled in the telling of their murderous crimes and the working of their plot to destroy the unwary Macbeth.

'I'll not sleep tonight,' Benjamin confided to his

friend. His eyes remained fixed on the hags, now prowling about the stage to introduce spirits with stage thunder and lightning, again prompting whimpers of fear among the wide-eyed audience.

'I'll not sleep for a week,' Jack admitted with his gaze locked on the horror unfolding below.

So it was the mesmerised boys neither heard the approach behind nor sensed the presence of the creeping arrival until it was too late. Heavy hands fell on their shoulders and a grim voice growled, 'You will sleep foreverrrrrr!'

Twin screams blended seamlessly with those rising from the audience for another on-stage fright and the boys spun to meet the dread presence. Spilling to the floor in a terrified jumble, they discovered Uncle Thomas standing over them, wickedly amused at the shock he had caused.

'That shook you,' he snorted. 'You'll not sleep for *two* weeks!'

'Master Blake,' Jack croaked in breathless relief.

'Yes,' Benjamin said dryly, 'Uncle Thomas the jester.'

'Watch your tone,' the man warned gruffly, no longer amused. 'Don't lose yourself in merriment too long; you have work clearing up after those daft play-actors are done. The Straw Hall will be supped dry tonight, I'll wager.' With that, he left, finding his own entertainment in a vision of good business.

Benjamin and Jack shared muttered curses for the man's notion of a joke – and for adults in general – before hurriedly regaining their spot to catch up with theatrical events.

Settling back into the action, Benjamin took a moment to cast an eye across the faces of the rapt villagers, their features palely illuminated by lanterns burning about the yard. As he did, his attention was caught by something beyond the lights, the movement of an indistinct shape on the roadway, approaching through mist in the south. Slowly he perceived the form of rider and horse quietly nearing the inn. So silent was the advance that when at last the rider drew up at the yard entrance, the spectators nearest him remained oblivious to his presence. Under the brim of a broad hat, the mysterious horseman raised his head a moment to study events in the yard, offering Benjamin a chance in turn to examine him.

Tall and in his middle years, the man was dressed in fine garments and a cape, with tough riding boots in addition to his black hat. Beneath dark eyes watching the players on stage were the clipped moustache and beard of a gentleman and, on his hip, the tempered sword of a soldier.

What it was that held Benjamin's close attention on this traveller, he could not reckon for sure, but as the man steered his mount towards the front of the inn out of sight, he was drawn to abandon the play and steal across the landing to his own room and the over-looking window there. Close to the leaded pane he peered down for another examination of the stranger but was surprised to find the horse alone and already tied at the hitching post.

Benjamin moved quickly to alert Uncle Thomas to the possibility of a paying guest.

At the head of the stairs he spotted the rider below, standing just inside the inn's doorway and quietly sur-veying his surroundings as he removed dusty gloves.

'Good evening, sir,' Benjamin said, descending.

The man turned and set a gaze on Benjamin that was immediately piercing in the candlelight. Taking time to examine the boy, the visitor seemed to inves-tigate him deeply and Benjamin felt his very soul probed. Only when gloves were folded and tucked into his belt did the horseman speak.

'Tell me, have I reached Ravenhill?' A simple ques-tion, yet to Benjamin it seemed weighted with gravest importance.

'Y-yes, sir,' he stuttered, still trying to steady him-self under the power of that stare.

The traveller nodded, pleased, and the heaviness he communicated eased a measure. He looked from Benjamin to his surroundings. 'Then this must be the establishment of Master Thomas Blake.'

'It is, sir,' Benjamin confirmed. 'The Straw Hall. My uncle's inn.'

'I see,' the mystery guest said. He took to studying the boy closely once more. 'Are the rooms comfortable?'

'They are, sir, and the food is excellent.'

The man's features softened for the boy's salesmanship and he moved to smooth his moustache delicately as though to hide the slightest smile. 'Perfect,' he declared. 'I will stay here to await my friend.' After a moment's further consideration, he considered his host again. 'What is your name, youngster?'

'I am Benjamin Blake, sir.'

'Benjamin,' he repeated. 'A fine name. Be so good, Benjamin, as to announce my arrival to your uncle. A room for the night and stabling for my horse, once the entertainment ends.'

'Gladly, sir,' Benjamin answered. 'What name should I give?'

The rider drew off his broad hat at the light of the fire and the weight in his tone returned with the answer.

'I am Matthew Hopkins. I am the Witchfinder General.'

6

The Witchfinder General! In Ravenhill! The Witchfinder General in Ravenhill and in the Straw Hall!

Long before the conclusion of the night's performance, the name of Matthew Hopkins had swept through the audience, tripping from mouth to ear on waves of amazement. No sooner had De Courcey choked his last dramatic line than the men were ushering the women and children home and racing one another to the bar, vying to gain the best seats close to the famed visitor. Where they could not sit, they stood, forced together in cramming every corner of the inn and every step of the stairs to the upper floor. Their pretence at casual drinking failed woefully as they gave in to nudges and stolen glances towards the figure brooding alone at the hearth. Here was a crowd far larger than any Benjamin had ever seen in the Straw Hall and, without doubt, the quietest ever to grace a drinking establishment in England.

So hushed was the scene that even high above in the shadows of the gallery, Benjamin and Jack could hear clearly the fire snapping in the grate as Hopkins consumed his evening meal. He bent hungrily to his plate to cut portions of meat with his own bejewelled and silver blade, seemingly oblivious to the multitude focussed intently on him. But each time he lifted his head to sup from a large tankard, he peered over its rim to examine some of the watchers with those piercing eyes, studying carefully until more than a few looked uncomfortably away. With a wry smile for his obvious reputation among them, Hopkins lowered his drinking vessel.

'You have witches in these parts?' he said, in a tone that was at once a grave statement and a question.

Some of the crowd shuffled awkwardly, each man waiting for another to find courage and address the witchfinder. At last Billy Preston, sneering in his corner, dared take on the role of spokesman. 'None that we are aware of,' he said. His answer was met with a muttered assent from the gathering.

'Then you are a rare parish in these times,' Hopkins responded. He sipped his ale again while men took to murmuring.

'We are a God-fearing village,' Billy said in return, slyly testing the older man with his gaze while the villagers nodded eagerly for the truth of his statement.

'Perhaps we are favoured for our faith.'

Hopkins smirked.

'Perhaps you are blind! Spell-weavers are tireless in their pursuits, forever subtle in their wicked business. I know men of the church struck down by dark magic for all their prayerful ways; men of goodness laid low by servants of the Evil One.'

Matthew Hopkins fixed all the power of his glare on Billy Preston, and while the men looked nervously to him for more, the young man faltered and turned to his ale with a muttered curse.

It fell to Uncle Thomas to break the grim silence.

'We should perhaps be thankful there are men such as you, good Master Hopkins,' he offered humbly for the witchfinder's benefit. Tankards raised in ready salute for that while Billy Preston supped and grumbled secretly with Jem Canning.

The witchfinder smiled, pleased at Ravenhill's acknowledgement of his importance.

'Tell us of witches,' a quavering voice in the crowd prompted and thus emboldened, the rest broke their silence to lend weight to the request, urging Hopkins to share stories with them.

'Yes. Tell us.'

'We hear rumours and tales.'

'Sorcery and spells.'

'Curses and charms.'

'Tell us. What is the truth of it?'

By way of response, Hopkins raised his empty drinking vessel towards the men. 'Refill my tankard and I will tell all,' he promised, drawing a cheer from the men who surged to the bar, each for the honour of refreshing the witchfinder and a replenished measure of their own.

In the shadows above the melee of thirsty men, Jack poked Benjamin's arm. 'Now we'll hear tales to give sleepless nights,' he whispered, his voice shaking with nervous expectation.

He heard Jack's words but Benjamin did not once take eyes off Matthew Hopkins. Thus, as coins rattled to shouted demands for ale, he alone saw the witchfinder's hand slip into the folds of his tunic to produce a small leather pouch which he worked to conceal in his palm.

Slowly, a hush fell again on the inn. Men sipped their drinks and settled to hear Hopkins speak. For his part, the witchfinder passed the quiet interlude staring into the blazing fire. Only when a sloshing tankard was placed on his table did he take his cue. He drank deeply, as one steeling himself for a dreadful task, and brought the drained cup down hard upon the table.

'Have you ever seen the Devil?' he asked, still peering hard into the flames as frightened murmurs denied the question. 'I have.'

The witchfinder's hand darted to the fire, and the secret pouch released a cloud of fine powder to the grate. The plume swirled across licking flames and erupted to a blaze of dazzling light and rolling smoke. Men cried out and pushed back from the explosion, and began to gag and cough as a foul stench reached their nostrils.

Moments later the malodorous mist seeped between the bars of the gallery. Too late, Benjamin and Jack clapped hands over their mouths and nostrils against a cloying reek of sulphur. Benjamin looked to his friend and saw him retch against the disgusting smell, even as his own stomach churned. He shook his head in warning against Jack's frantic need to cough out the foul air, and together they laboured to suffer through in silence. This was no time to be discovered and scolded to bed.

'The Devil's stink, men of Ravenhill,' Hopkins loudly proclaimed, 'Hell's own perfume!' Standing before his captivated audience, he held up the pouch for all to see. 'This wicked concoction was taken from a witch just two months past, an ingredient she combined with others to summon her dark master as I and John, John Stearne my faithful deputy, wrestled with her power for our very souls. She spoke in tongues to confound us, uttered incantations to wound us, recited spells to murder us, and finally... finally, when all other magic failed, she summoned protection and the Dark One came.'

Here he paused as though unable to bear the memory and stared in wonder to the middle-distance as he recalled the horror of it all.

'What-what did he look like?' a voice croaked through the cloudy atmosphere.

'Like all your nightmares come to life,' Hopkins gasped. He relived the infernal encounter while young boys listened. 'He formed up from blackness to the dimensions of a man, but a man-shadow deep and terrible, with eyes that were hellfire coals burning in the dark. To see that gaze was to feel holes burned in one's soul. But even with the courage to look, we witchfinders could not secure the terrible vision, nor catch it in the light of our blazing torches. It dwelt in shadows and took strength from them to assail us. One moment it towered above, the next behind. After that it rose to the ceiling as though to fall and devour us. The next, it loomed on either side so quickly at once. All the while striving with curses and bestial howls to reach his pathetic servant bound in her place, restrained between me and Stearne. Only by the smell, that choking evil surrounding him, could we track Lucifer's motion in the recesses.

'Prayer! Prayer was our one weapon against the onslaught of jabbering cries, loud enough to shake the walls and make men mad. But we held and, through our prayers, we drove him back to the outer darkness. His mission, to pluck his witch to her hellish reward, failed with the day's blessed dawning and, with a shriek of defeat, he fled back to his fiery domain. We sent the accursed witch to the gallows that very day for her sins.'

His story spent, Hopkins dropped into his chair as though exhausted by the very act of remembering. He reached once more for his ale and drank long while he surveyed the faces around him, all drawn and terribly pale.

For the longest time no one stirred, none daring to break the awed silence, not even to sip a drink against throats parched by fear. The mood of wonder was broken at last from the heart of the gathering. The actor De Courcey surged forward, applauding vigorously in his appreciation for Hopkins. 'Bravo, sir! Bravo!' he cried, and he clapped until others followed suit and the entire bar was applauding a new-found hero.

That was when it happened.

With the joyous clamour at its loudest and cheering grown to a deafening pitch, the door to the inn burst aside, propelled by a figure looming without. The dark, black shape of a man formed in the frame: a man-shadow, deep and terrible!

Crying out as one, the men succumbed to earlier fears and tumbled from the dread vision. Jem Canning fell blubbering from his stool and crawled under a table. Blacksmith Bolton called on the Almighty and toppled behind the bar. Gripped by terror, the farmer Mackey spewed a measure of ale to drench the scream-ing De Courcey, and men crushed one another in rear-ing back from the awful thing in the doorway. Only Hopkins advanced as all others fell away. He rose boldly from his seat to meet that which stepped across the threshold into the inn. Drawing on from darkness, the night visitor moved into the lamplight, revealing itself as no more terrible a being than a mortal man.

The new arrival was tall and gaunt, head and shoul-ders above the men of Ravenhill where he moved among them, his spurred boots chiming on the boards as he walked. From behind wild hair falling under a broad hat partially concealing his features, he met each stare upon him with indifference, yet boldly. Before all, he removed his gloves and swept the dust of riding from his clothing. Dressed in a fashion similar to Hopkins, in breeches and cape, like the witchfinder, the man also bore a fine sword on his hip. And it was to Hopkins he shifted his attention finally, his thin lips breaking into a smile on seeing him approach.

'Matthew, my friend,' the man declared, striding forward to embrace the witchfinder.

'Well met, sir,' Hopkins replied happily, return-ing the grip. Turning to the staring ranks about, he declared, 'Good folk, this is the brave John Stearne of whom I spoke.'

Much relieved, the men raised trembling cheers and made way for the two witchfinders at the bar where a fresh tankard was made ready for the weary traveller.

'We were just hearing of your exploits, sir,' Uncle Thomas informed him as Stearne gratefully quenched his thirst.

'Indeed?' Stearne cast a questioning eye at his fellow witchfinder.

'I related the tale of the Stowmarket witch,' Hopkins reminded his colleague with a conspiratorial wink. 'You remember that terrible episode... the one with the Devil... our long struggle.'

'Oh. Aha,' Stearne said, nodding in quick agreement. 'Why, yes, a dour business indeed. But I bring a darker story tonight.' John Stearne drank again before proceeding.

'The king's army is defeated.'

7

'News of the war!'

Jack's loud cry of excitement would surely have meant discovery had the fierce clamour of voices below not drowned it out.

Ignoring the multitude of shouted questions and demands for more information, John Stearne made his way amid pressing men towards the fire. There he took time in warming himself, leaving it to Hopkins to urge silence by raising his hands over the crush.

'Tell us all, John,' Hopkins prompted his friend at last.

Stearne faced the crowd. 'The battle was fought two days ago. The field was at Naseby.' The name rippled as an excited whisper through the assembly. 'First intelligence states the king's forces were overrun by Cromwell's cavalry. The Royalist army is scattered, smashed asunder.'

Benjamin was forced to hold Jack from jumping excitedly from the shadows as the details unfolded.

'Did you hear?' the boy gushed in a whisper. 'Did you hear? Cromwell's horsemen have thrashed the king!'

'Yes!' Benjamin hissed at him. 'And if you don't keep still my uncle will thrash us!'

'What of the king?' Billy Preston called out.

'Fled the field,' Stearne replied. 'News from London says he is missing but not captured. That is all I know.'

The men fell silent as they considered the gravity of the report. Could it be the war was at last decided, finished by this engagement at Naseby? No one present was willing to declare outright this to be the case, and instead, the gathering fell to debating the consequences of the battle. The men broke to clusters to argue among themselves, setting aside talk of sorcery and leaving Hopkins and Stearne to their own sombre conversation by the fire. Some left soon after to bring word to the village and, in a short time, only a handful of customers remained to hear Thomas call time on the proceedings.

'I am for my bed,' Jack admitted as the men below were encouraged one by one into the night. 'Though I doubt I'll sleep after this.' He wished his friend good-night and stole away.

Benjamin remained, keen to continue his close study of the witchfinders and in hope that some more information on their trade would be forthcoming. He was to be disappointed, however; as the pair fell to speaking in hushed tones with forceful gestures by the dying fire, and its failing heat did not hold them long.

Pausing only to arrange a fresh room for Stearne, they bade Thomas goodnight and climbed the stairs to their beds. With nothing more to see, Benjamin began to move stealthily towards his own room.

'Come down here,' Uncle Thomas ordered sourly.

The boy's heart skipped in fright. How had his uncle known? He was concealed in almost complete darkness beyond the reach of the candles below. Yet when he looked to where his uncle stood, the man's scowling gaze was fixed directly at Benjamin's place in the shadows. Realising there was no use in continuing to hide, he nervously gave himself up to the light and plodded down the stairs.

'How did you see me?' he asked as he reached the bar, curiosity outweighing the fear of any punishment.

Thomas shook his head, despairing of the boy's ignorance.

'Do you think you are the first boy to hide up there?' he scoffed.

'What did grandfather do when he discovered you there?' Benjamin asked in certain dread of the answer.

'He paddled my behind with a thick branch for getting into adult business,' he said ominously. His nephew's look of dismay brought a grunt of cruel satisfaction. 'I'd do the same to you but there's work to be done. Start clearing tables.'

'Yes, sir,' Benjamin said obediently, despairing of

the labours ahead but glad to avoid the branch. He set about collecting tankards while Thomas delightedly gathered his earnings at the bar.

'Have you ever known a night as exciting as this one?' Benjamin asked.

'No. I confess there have been few nights at the inn to compare to this. And none I recall where the news was so serious.'

'Do you mean the talk of war or witches?'

Thomas shook his head and sighed. 'Fool of a boy. Put off that smoke and guff from Master Hopkins. I know a man playing to an audience when I see one. No, the war and this turn of events at Naseby is what concerns me.'

Benjamin was downcast to hear his uncle dismiss the witchfinder's tale so easily but he did not show it. 'The end of the war is a good thing, is it not?' he asked instead.

Thomas rolled his eyes. 'Have I taught you nothing?' He jangled a bag of coins as proof to an idiot. 'War is good for trade. The men of Ravenhill are gossipy like the nags they married but they come here to do it over tankards of ale. This war has sold more ale than I can tally, and every battle has meant more money behind the bar. And all the more when you add our latest stash below. How can that be bad?'

Benjamin was aghast at his uncle's words.

'It was bad for the men who died in those battles.'

'They weren't customers of mine,' he sniffed and shook his head once more at such reasoning. 'So much like your mother you are. She was always looking at the world the wrong way up and thinking of others before herself. That's why she never spoke up to reveal your father and kept the burden of their foolishness for herself.' He sighed. 'I took his portion of hardship, all the same, didn't I?' And he filled another bag of coins noisily.

'I'm sorry my mother and I were a drain on your profits,' Benjamin shot at him. 'I'm sure my father will compensate you when he comes.'

Thomas guffawed. 'See what I mean? Just like your mother, looking to dreams and notions instead of the real world. It was always tomorrow and tomorrow with her. Sickened her to an early grave it did. Get it into your head, boy: your papa didn't come back for her and he's not coming for you.'

'He *is* coming!' Benjamin barked against lies. Through his anger he felt the solid weight of a tankard in his clenching hand. Without pause for thought, he drew back and flung the vessel at Thomas. Flying wide of its target, the tankard clattered across the bar and struck a bag of coins. Split by the collision, the bag dumped its contents loudly to the boards.

Thomas looked on his tumbling wealth with bunched fists and a cry of horror. The sound became a snarl of anger as coins rolled about his feet and fists loosened to unclasp his belt, as he turned to fix Benjamin with dangerous intent. 'Pick it up,' he ordered, forcing the words through tightened lips.

'He's coming,' Benjamin repeated and stood his ground.

With practised skill, Thomas swept his belt clear to deliver a strike against the boy's shoulder. Benjamin recoiled from the stinging lash and the cruel sneer lighting on his uncle's face. The belt swung again, this time to catch legs, and Benjamin was sent to his knees with a cry of frustration and pain.

'Pick it up!' Thomas howled and struck the boy's back once, twice, three times. 'Pick it up!' and arms and legs suffered fresh burning torment. 'Pick it up!' and Thomas raised his arm high.

The belt whistled on the air once more, this time to reach Benjamin's arm, raised in defence. A fierce burning stabbed at his wrist where leather struck, and a lick of fire slashed his cheek as the weapon coiled about the limb.

Thomas issued a whoop of malevolent delight and delivered fresh blows with his belt until Benjamin was driven into a huddle against its torture. There he lay, enduring the blows in determined silence until, as ever, his uncle became winded by the effort and staggered back, his rage spent in red-faced huffing and puffing.

'One more year,' he grumbled breathlessly, 'one more year of war and I could have been rid of you to the recruiting sergeant. Now what's to be done, eh? I'm stuck with you unless I kill you myself.' He smiled at the thought and gathered up his coins with a grunt from the effort. 'The village might even thank me for that.' Cradling his money close, he stared on its glitter with an affection to melt consuming fury. At last, blinking against shifting emotions like a man waking from a dream, he looked distractedly about the inn. 'Your work's not done, boy,' he said and turned to go.

Helpless in his agony, Benjamin uncoiled with gritted teeth and lay alone amid tables and chairs.

8

Ravenhill's night of excitement lasted all too briefly.

The morning's golden dawn crept over rooftops to reveal Janson De Courcey and his Greenwich players already preparing to depart. The actors reloaded their crammed wagon and took to the south-bound road, singing a ditty in praise of summer as they trundled away. Never one to miss a chance at performing, De Courcey danced along the roadway behind the vehicle, his head and limbs decked with coloured ribbons, all to the amusement of a small cluster of village children who turned out to wave farewell.

Benjamin watched from the yard gate until first the wagon and then De Courcey, with a final salute to the laughing children, disappeared around the turn in the road. With that, it was time to get back to the inn's everyday routine and those tasks set by Uncle Thomas under threat of another whipping. Benjamin worked in silence and with lips pursed by pain lingering in his bruised arms and legs.

With Masters Hopkins and Stearne finishing breakfast in the Straw Hall, Benjamin prepared the horses for their eventual journey. Leading the two saddled mounts from the stables, he was in time to meet the witchfinders in the yard where they pulled on wide hats and riding gloves in readiness for the road.

'Well, young Benjamin,' Hopkins said cheerfully as he took charge of his steed, 'are we made ready for a long day's ride?'

'Yes, sir,' Benjamin agreed. 'There is bread and cheese stored for you and your bottles are filled.'

'Excellent, most excellent,' Hopkins proclaimed, hauling into his saddle. Pausing to dig beneath his cape, he produced a gold coin for Benjamin's consideration. He played the disc through the air, allowing the sun to catch its dazzling surfaces. Without warning he flicked the coin to the startled Benjamin and smiled at the boy's efforts to grasp the prize.

'I thank you, sir,' Benjamin said, examining the coin's bright face.

'And I thank you,' Hopkins returned, 'both for your assistance and honesty. The rooms were indeed comfortable and the food was most excellent. Farewell, young Benjamin.'

Together the witchfinders spurred their horses forward and trotted to turn north along the road.

Benjamin followed as far as the gate and called after them. 'Where are you bound?'

Turning in his saddle, Hopkins shouted back.

'Into the mouth of fear! Pray for us, Benjamin Blake!'

The riders whipped up their horses and galloped away, throwing up a storm of dust into which they quickly vanished, leaving Benjamin to wonder if the excitement of the day and night past had been just some fanciful dream from which he would now wake, and whether the Straw Hall would know such excitement again.

Distracted once more by his gold coin, he made two important decisions at once. He would add this bounty to his secret store: the purse in his room Uncle Thomas knew nothing of. The money he would take along when his father came for him. But first, he would speed through his daytime chores for the promise of fun later. Yes, he would double his efforts and then seek for Jack, simply to astound him with the hypnotic sparkle of his new gold coin. How the boy would marvel at it in the sunshine while Benjamin held it just out of reach. Thoughts of teasing his friend were a further balm for aching limbs.

The remainder of the morning was thus spent in sweaty physical labour undertaken with speed and enthusiasm, much to the unspoken satisfaction of

Uncle Thomas, who quietly celebrated his parenting skills as he eyed Benjamin hastening about the inn. A mountain of tankards was rounded up from all corners and brought for washing in the great tub in the yard. The cleansed vessels were next set and ordered in their neat rows behind the bar, freeing Benjamin to turn his cloth to tabletops and chairs before raking the grate for a fresh evening fire. Rest came only when he had he swept out the bar in preparation for another night's trade. Leaning on his broom, he took time to admire his work: the spotless evidence of his worthiness to be an innkeeper one day. Benjamin's moment of joy was overshadowed by that gloomy thought.

His duties done, the boy sought Uncle Thomas and, saying nothing of his gold reward, begged leave to make along the road to Ravenhill, there to find Jack. And though Thomas looked for reasons to quibble with the completed tasks, he could find none and so released Benjamin with a scowl and a warning to be back by nightfall.

The sun was reaching its highest as Benjamin hurried along the village road. The countryside about was bathed in glorious heat; bees drifted lazily amid the summer blooms and birds pronounced the majesty of the day. After the Straw Hall's murky interior, his skin tingled in the burning light and the tightness in limbs melted away with each happy step.

The Blackwater Bridge came into sight through the haze, its gentle crest obscuring all but the village rooftops as he drew near. But rising higher came sounds of some great commotion beyond, at odds with the peaceful day, and Benjamin quickened his pace in curiosity to cross the span into Ravenhill's main street. There he froze mid-step and gazed open-mouthed upon the origins of the clamour.

The street was filled with soldiers!

He counted twenty, no, thirty armed men. Arrayed in metal helmets and breastplates that gleamed in the sun, the soldiers idled in small groups across the roadway. Beneath a host of colourful banners declaring these parliament's men, the troops shared food and drink while their horses rested and drank wearily from the water trough at Bolton's smithy. One smaller group of men conversed heartily with the blacksmith as he admired a sword of polished steel. At this, Benjamin's gaze fell to the other weapons the soldiers bore so casually. Hands rested on pistol butts and swords, or cradled long muskets and fearsome pikes.

'Benjamin!'

The calling of his name jerked him from staring and he spotted Jack, trailed by his younger brother William, where they sprinted between the military men towards him.

'What is going on?' Benjamin managed to ask.

'Have you ever seen the like, Benjamin?' Jack babbled in jittery excitement. 'It's not thirteen thousand horses, but just look at them! I saw a musket, this close.' He held his finger and thumb almost touching as he skipped about.

'I held a sword,' William boasted.

'No, you didn't!' Jack scoffed.

'I touched the handle when the soldier wasn't looking.'

'What is going on?' Benjamin repeated, feeling a full measure of the boys' enthusiasm growing in his chest.

'You haven't seen her,' Jack realised with a gasp and he swung to his brother. 'He hasn't seen her!'

Benjamin despaired at keeping up with the hectic flow of Jack's chatter. He grabbed the boy firmly by the shoulders.

'Who have I not seen?'

'Why, the witch, of course!'

Benjamin was struck light-headed by the word. How could so much drama be visiting upon Ravenhill in just two days of summer?

'Where-where is she?' he heard his voice ask from miles off.

William enthusiastically pointed the way.

'Over there.'

Benjamin followed the brothers, weaving amid the leather and metal of the military gathering. At a place beyond the crowd, he spotted for the first time something he had overlooked while caught by the spectacle of the soldiers. Far back to the convoy's rear stood a wagon. Benjamin saw upon the vehicle a cage of black metal: a moving prison for captives, though he detected but one prisoner huddling within. He looked with a surge of dread on that dark and ragged form beyond the bars.

'She's really creepy,' Jack warned, relishing the moment. 'William ran away when he saw her first.'

'I did not!' the younger brother protested. He sought to cover his embarrassment in a display of knowledge. 'The soldiers were patrolling in search of Royalists when they caught her up at Langham Moor. They came this way hoping to meet the Witchfinder General for his examination. They said she kissed the Devil on the—' Here the boy clamped his lips against dreadful profanity and jerked a thumb at his backside.

Listening coldly to all, Benjamin angled his head to the grim cage in the hope of a clearer view of the bundled form.

'Hey, you boys!'

The friends jumped at the challenge and spun to a burly soldier walking towards them. He carried along a wooden bucket and a small bread loaf.

'We weren't doing anything,' Jack said quickly, 'sir.'

The man considered the claim with a dubious frown

and eyed each boy in turn. His face softened for the natural curiosity of simple country boys, and he thrust his chin towards the cage. 'Interested in our prisoner, are you?'

'Yes, sir,' Benjamin agreed.

'Well then,' the soldier said with a wink, 'why don't you have a closer look?' In a flash, the man thrust the bucket to Benjamin and the bread to Jack. 'You can feed her.'

The day became somehow unnaturally cold in a moment as the boys exchanged wary glances for the offer, so tantalising and fearful in the same instant. Conflicting desires to retreat and advance were settled only when they looked to William and saw in his face a keen readiness to mock cowards – for at least a month – if they backed down now. Thus, a silent understanding was reached, negotiated through a series of awkward shrugs and nods, before the boys joined at the shoulder for a nervous advance on the barred cart.

The frightful cage and its human cargo filled their vision. At the boys' first step, all remained still within the tiny prison. At their second, the briefest grating of metal on wood caused them to hesitate for the sound of her heavy chains shifting against the cart's floor. One more step and the crouching figure began to grow, rising to expose a head of lank black hair which fell to obscure the entirety of the witch's face, and the final shared step was tracked by cold eyes beyond the matted veil.

'Who comes?'

The voice, so soft and clear, was at odds with the nightmare vision kneeling behind the bars.

For the longest time, Benjamin and Jack silently willed the other to speak and so take the witch's dour attention. Jack was quickest to offer a sharp nudge to Benjamin's ribs.

'Food,' Benjamin stammered weakly, 'we bring food.'

'So kind,' the feminine voice sighed.

The witch reached from beneath her cape and the hand she offered was bony white, beneath layers of dirt smearing to fingernails long and chipped.

Jack faltered at the sight and his nerve melted with a groan. Fixated on the skeletal limb he staggered back and flung the loaf blindly towards the cage, somehow managing to pass the food cleanly between the bars. He continued his retreat as the prisoner clawed up the bread and ate noisily.

Held in place by amused guffaws from the soldier watching Jack's retreat, Benjamin stood firm. With a steadying breath, he pushed the bucket to the bars. The thump of wood against metal stopped the witch's feasting and her concealed gaze fell upon him again. Benjamin sensed the cold, tickling caress of her eyes from in there; he *felt* it!

'Thank you,' said that same soft voice and her white hand drifted between the bars to cup water.

'What is your name?' Benjamin ventured cautiously. He scanned the veil of dark hair as she slurped her fill.

The unseen but seeing stare came again and held for the longest time to silence. 'I am Adefina Corvus.' The hand scooped another portion of water. 'Who are you?'

'I am Benjamin Blake.'

'You are a kind boy,' she whispered.

At Benjamin's first unguarded smile for her words, the witch struck. The hand reaching so dreamily for water lashed between bars to enfold his face in a steely grip. He tried to cry against it, only to receive a taste of grime on his stifled lips. Wide-eyed he dropped the bucket to an eruption of water and clasped defensively the attacking wrist as its unnatural strength drew him towards the cage. Casting desperately about for escape, his sight fell on his attacker's free hand where it gripped a prison bar and, in a moment's wide-eyed madness, he beheld the ring she wore there. It was a band of glittering silver, thickly fashioned to present the shape of a leering skull on her knuckle. The instant passed as clawed fingers bit Benjamin's cheeks and he was pulled hard to the bars where the witch's hidden face thrust to his. The motion parted a line of soiled hair and one cruel and red-veined eye fixed him.

'You will sleep with the dead, Benjamin Blake!'

He was cast off by flicking fingers. Staggering back, he brushed against the soldier who moved with a warning strike against the bars to drive the attacker away. The witch slithered from reach to a corner where she flung shrill laughter at the world. Her crazed shrieking chilled Benjamin but, all too quickly, it served to replace fear with anger, and his hands thrust for the bucket. Driven by a burning humiliation, he hoisted the container high and launched its remaining contents at the bars to soak the foul prisoner.

Adefina Corvus cackled hysterically at the gesture and rolled about the cage. In dramatic fashion, she waved her wet hands for all to see. 'Oh no,' she screamed through hitching laughter, 'I'm melting, melting, meeeelting!'

Her jubilant screams pursued Benjamin as he was ushered away.

9

Benjamin scrubbed his face hard in the river and spat curses for the witch. He could still feel the prickling marks her nails had left and, despite swilling mouthfuls of water, could still taste her.

'She touched you,' the revolted Jack said for perhaps the tenth time. He shivered and rubbed his arms at the delicious horror of it.

'Does that mean you're cursed?' William asked casually. He yelped when his older brother struck his arm for silence.

Benjamin grumbled through tainted breath and washed out his mouth again, sloshing water vigorously between teeth before spitting the memory of Adefina Corvus and her clammy grip. But still the vile taste remained and it was a stew of ash and graveyard dirt on his tongue.

Jack examined his friend's face as though hoping to find the scorched outline of the witch's hand.

'What was it like?'

'I don't think she washed for a year,' Benjamin said

simply, not wishing to endure a stream of questions.

'That's why you gave her a bath,' William chortled in remembering. 'That part was funny.'

'Yes,' Benjamin agreed and smiled for the first time. 'I wanted to make her presentable for the Witchfinder General.'

William sniggered the harder at this and the others joined him, the tension of the encounter fading under their growing amusement until all were rolling on the riverbank, lost in gales of laughter.

A shout rose from the direction of the village, quickly followed by the sounds of massed activity. Horses whinnied and hooves clattered loudly on the road. Dust clouds plumed over those rooftops the boys could see from their place.

'The soldiers are leaving,' Jack exclaimed, leaping to his feet.

They raced to the bridge in time to meet the first rank of cavalry crossing at a trot. Under streaming banners, the riders sternly led the column, its onward passage coming in a deafening storm of metal. At last, the prison cart rumbled across, flanked by a close guard of four horsemen for the dangerous captive. The black form of Adefina Corvus clung to the bars with those whitened hands and surveyed the world still, through masking hair. Her head turned in time with the cart's passing to keep the boys in sight until the convoy turned by the Straw Hall and disappeared along the road to the north.

'What did she say to you?' Jack was prompted to ask just then.

You will sleep with the dead, Benjamin Blake.

'Nothing,' Benjamin said as he watched thunder clouds gather for the column in the western sky.

* * *

The summer storm that broke over Ravenhill did little to keep drinkers from the Straw Hall that evening. Thunder and driving rain could not dampen a taste for reports of soldiers and witchcraft, and the bar crowded early with many keen to offer their own details to the telling. Uncle Thomas kept busy tongues wagging with his ale and drinkers competed late in offering the juiciest stories.

Bolton the blacksmith felt himself the best informed of all, having dealt with a steady queue of soldiers bringing seven horses, a bent spur and five dull swords.

'Such blades,' he marvelled. 'Straight and true and once sharpened...' he blew an ominous breath, 'indeed 'tis little wonder the king's army fell at Naseby.'

'The soldiers warned that some of that army might flee this-aways,' Billy Preston added to Bolton's report. 'There was talk among the soldiers of rewards for the

capture of Royalist officers, with a king's ransom for…
well, the king!'

The men chortled at Billy's words and continued the
friendly sport of outdoing one another with increasingly tall tales.

None, of course, could offer an experience to rival
Benjamin's unsettling meeting with Adefina Corvus.
Among the customers, only the baker Merton could
relate how close he had come to the prisoner and
not too close at that, he added, lest she bewitch him.
Listening in his gallery perch, Benjamin grew bored
with puffed-up accounts and he determined early to
slip off to his chamber, where riotous conversations
seeping through the boards put paid to any hope of
early sleep.

Ah, but it wasn't just raised voices and hearty
laughter that kept him awake long into the night.
For each time he closed his eyes in search of slumber,
memory played its part in reminding him of an oily
touch on his skin, that grimy taste at his lips and the
cruellest of voices warning that he *would* sleep, but it
would be with…

Benjamin tossed and turned and cursed again for
wicked witches.

IO

Adefina Corvus knelt in the rain and watched her guards.

Soaked to glistening by teeming water, she remained an unmoving black shade within her cage, peering through dripping bars to the surrounding night, ever watching.

And patiently waiting.

Light from cooking fires in the nearby camp did little to illuminate the sodden hollow where the wagon stood, and it was by sharp lightning flashes on polished armour that she tracked the soldiers' routine on their late watch. She counted four, slopping to and fro behind the curtain of rain as a fresh crack in the heavens betrayed them, trudging and cursing the booming storm.

Thunder would prove useful soon.

Another flare across the sky revealed one of the men as he broke off from his rounds to march across sloshing mud to the wagon's rear gate. A round face, in a thick beard speckled by raindrops, pressed through the downpour to regard Adefina sourly. The soldier reached to the gate's thick padlock and tested it with a loud rattle.

'All right, princess?' he jibed. 'Just making certain your quarters are snug and secure.'

'You are a kind man,' she returned in that same soft voice, so whispering and dreamlike.

The guard offered a contemptuous snort and stepped away into the downpour.

The thunder rolled, the lightning flashed and Adefina Corvus eyed the guard's progress in rejoining his colleagues. She gazed upon the silhouetted forms of her three surviving guards and smiled beneath her hair.

It was begun.

Lightning reflected on helmets turning about in a sudden and urgent search. Muttered words were exchanged: confused, serious, but not alarmed. Not yet.

As the search for the missing guard commenced, Adefina followed the movements of the tallest soldier now approaching to her left. She picked him out as he stepped farther from his companions, and that was why she picked him. Isolating himself from the others like that was foolish and he would suffer for it. She probed the black woods deeply with a sense of anticipation.

The tall soldier proceeded cautiously, nearing the line of trees and the veiled spaces that swallowed rain and light between. He moved slowly, more from fear of tripping on the slick earth than anything his imagination could picture lurking in the dark. The long musket he held at the ready gave him a useless confidence as he stepped on.

Foolish.

The shadows came alive to a burst of violent motion. Faster than the soldier could react, the darkness seized his weapon. Through panic, the man's grip tightened on the musket as his defence, and to the trigger, as he was hauled from his feet. The explosion of shot was drowned in thunder as he was snatched through the rain into consuming depths.

Things moved quickly now. The two remaining soldiers called out for their missing comrades and Adefina fed on the cold anxiety in their voices. She watched with a sly smile how they levelled weapons as though to stop what was coming up through the black of night. The bearded guard stepped ahead and turned to urge the other on. In the motion, he was in time to see his companion swept backwards through the rainfall, his musket tumbling to splash the muddy ground where he vanished between the trees.

With a terrified cry, the bearded soldier fired wildly into the night, the crash of his shot resounding through the hollow. He wasted no precious time in trying to reload and instead cast his spent musket down in favour of the spare weapon at his feet. Scooping it quickly from clinging muck, he held it ready and kept his finger clear of the trigger while he searched for a visible target. But he saw nothing.

He heard.

The sound that came seeping between raindrops was a hiss of poisoned breath. It issued on all sides and from some terrible place in the heart of the woods. It found the soldier in his place and whispered monstrous things to his imagination. The man drew back from awful possibilities and, as he took a further step, the lightning came again to show him the thing in the woods.

The flickering light presented her demonic form: a shadow on the edge of the treeline. Stooped and poised to strike, the devil hung against the night, glaring at the soldier with eyes that offered a silver reply to the lightning's dance and the wickedest vampire smile set in a face shaped for nightmares.

The soldier reeled, shrieking from the creature and the passage from Hell it had surely followed to reach him. He tumbled backwards, blinded by fear and the absence of illumination. His back struck hard on something and he whirled about with another scream as the lightning returned. This time, to find the glaring features of Adefina Corvus at the edge of her cage, peering on him with serpentine glee.

In the moment's hypnosis, witch hands plunged between bars and clamped on the soldier's head. Nails bit deeply and dragged him to witness the full maniacal intensity of her face. He railed frantically for escape from those unforgiving features and the more, as the first burning of his flesh began under her grip. Cascading rain turned to steam on his skin and the witch rose through thunder and lightning, hauling the soldier impossibly from his feet until he danced puppet-like on the air to her torturous bidding. An eternity of burning passed only when she allowed, and she cast the stricken man through the air to splattering mud.

The injured soldier whimpered pitifully and sent hands flying to his cheeks and neck to ease wounds that sizzled yet. Through clamped teeth, he summoned anger to push him to his knees, and to standing, with his musket made ready. He shouldered the weapon and released a howl of rage as he triggered his shot at Adefina Corvus.

Click!

The hammer fell on wet powder.

The attack swept in from the trees, too fast for mortal perception. Only a path cleaved momentarily through the rain gave any clue that something had passed across the soldier's line of sight. Only the slightest jerk on his musket signalled a collision. The soldier's furrowed brow gave way to wide wonder as the leading half of his gun barrel fell away, severed neatly from the rest to splash into a puddle. The man looked to Adefina where she leered at him through the bars and, too late, he heard the onward rush of a fresh onslaught from his right. He turned to perceive the briefest flash of silver eyes before he felt the sharpest cut and then there was nothing more to see or feel. The soldier collapsed to a burst of mud.

Adefina hastened to the cage gate, there to work amid growing sounds from the camp rousing to the disturbance. Sweeping a hand from her cape, she made the necessary motions for the next part. A thumb pressed briefly to one little finger and from there moved to repeat the action on her third finger. In time with these movements, the sorceress whispered softly and thrust her hand through the bars to grasp the padlock. Light and smoke came instantly at her magic touch and the metal of the lock hissed, melting against the rain. With the softest click, the mechanism yielded and fell free. Adefina flung the gate aside and stepped into the night.

Dropping to the slick earth, the witch approached the darkest shadow within the hollow and stood before it. She peered into that inky black space and stretched forth her hand, and the silver-eyed phantom hidden there crept forward to pay homage, scraping low to reverently lick her hand with a rasping tongue.

'Ilemauzar,' the witch said fondly.

'My lady,' the she-demon acknowledged with a hiss.

'Where are the others?'

The figure drew back with reluctant eyes. 'We should depart; more soldiers are coming,' her empty voice said.

'The others,' the witch demanded.

'Four of your slaves are fled,' the spirit reported, 'but they are pursued. I came for you.'

Adefina nodded at the information unperturbed, little surprised by it. 'They are fools,' she declared, 'and they will be punished.' She turned to go.

'There is something else,' the dark devil ventured. The concern in her tone drew Adefina instantly back and a dangerous suspicion in the witch's face caused Ilemauzar to shrink to the comfort of deeper shadow.

'What is it?' the witch asked. 'Speak!'

'The four,' Ilemauzar offered hesitantly, 'they have taken your book.'

Adefina's rage surged up. It flowered in an instant to uncontrolled boiling in her eyes. Every sinew of her being locked in fury against the truth, and lips quivering for curses parted to reveal grinding teeth. Fingers strained in search of dread punishments for thieves and clawed together to a sparking magic as soldiers descended on the hollow, their weapons drawn towards her.

Thieves!

She spun on the advancing men and saw nothing but *thieves!*

To a piercing scream, Adefina conjured, and the storm tumbled back from the fire she raised, and the lightning and thunder were as nothing to the power she unleashed.

II

The scream brought Benjamin reeling.

Kicking against bed covers, he came from his nightmare on a wave of fear, moving without conscious thought to be free. For a breathless time, he searched about for the terrible images and sounds that had pursued him to the very borders of waking. The chamber stood silent and black, though he chilled at the sight of a form hulking in a shadowed corner until his addled brain recognised the harmless shape of his clothes shelf. A hidden sound startled him to gasping and he strained to detect the skittering of a mouse behind the walls of the slumbering inn. With a sigh for safety and familiar surroundings, he fell back in the dark and listened to the rapid pounding of his heart, as he recalled the vision that had come with such dreadful clarity.

The girl had been running in his dream. Though the form was in blackest shadow and he could not make out the features, he was certain it was a girl who charged through a night forest. Springing from a place of fearful darkness, she travelled beneath a cape that billowed with her hair and blocked the stars, though the moon sailed in pursuit where she pounded along tracks beneath clawing trees.

Behind, surging up to add unbearable measures of fear, another sprinter appeared. And after him a third, and then a fourth ran into view! The night played host to a dread race of phantoms plunging at breakneck speed through storms of withered leaves and swirls of mist.

The girl set the pace, bringing her demonic partners on. And somehow, Benjamin had known, in watching from his dreaming place, the journey of the foul four was not one towards a sinister destination, but away. Away from something grim and terrible behind. These charging forms were engaged in a desperate attempt at escape.

Like the one who led them, the runners' faces remained obscured by night. Only one common feature could be detected, and that was so slight as to be doubted. By a strange trick of palest moonlight, there appeared a curious and irregular twinkling of silver where the fugitives' eyes should be. Through this unsettling phenomenon, the running figures somehow communicated an air of determination in their flight.

As the breathless charge continued, the girl cast a sparkling glare back towards her companions. Seeking to spur them to greater efforts, she opened her mouth in the shadow of the whipping cape to issue a shout, revealing to the moon a pair of incisor teeth, long and sharp as a lion's!

Her shout passed between the fangs, but the voice reaching Benjamin was not one of bold urging. That shout was lost to the disjointed landscape of dreams as the shrill scream of a woman enraged came in its place, and the fury it carried had been of a power to drive Benjamin so violently from sleep.

The night stillness pressed round as Benjamin eased his breathing and tried to shake off unsettling images in favour of rational explanations. An excess of excitement witnessed these past days had been the cause of his sleeping terror, he decided finally, nothing more. Soldiers on horseback had conspired with witches and their familiars to haunt the back roads of his imagination. Taking comfort in this reasoning, he wilfully set aside the stuff of dreams and slowly drifted towards sleep once more.

What caused him to stir next, he could not say, but from the early depths of a cosy slumber, he roused sharply to... what? Had there been a noise? Seeking answers, he worked through those night sounds so regularly a feature of the sleeping inn. Were the mice in the walls again on the move? Had the snapping of a log in the fireplace downstairs caused him to stir, or perhaps a night bird settling in the thatch above?

He lay still and listened hard in the hope of some explanation to the mystery disturbance. And there, it came again. There *had* been a sound, momentary and indistinct but sufficient to betray some activity outside. Benjamin crept quickly to his window and peered out.

The moon bathed the world in ghostly light and the illumination proved enough to catch the silhouette of a figure in the lee of the inn. The man, somehow familiar to Benjamin's eyes, held the reins of a pair of horses, and worked to calm the beasts while peering nervously towards the door.

Shifting in his place, Benjamin searched about outside for sign of the man's companion but found no one besides. But all at once he pulled from the window, his ears catching muffled sounds of activity through the boards beneath his feet. The unseen horseman was inside the Straw Hall.

Benjamin moved rapidly from the window to raise the alarm. His room was but a short step across the upper corridor from his uncle's. But as he reached his chamber door a shifting on the boards outside caused him to halt sharply. Catching a breath, he held rigid as the sound drew nearer, finally to stop just outside. Benjamin watched with growing terror as the latch of the door slowly lifted. A manic cry tickled his throat, but an instant before he could scream out, Uncle Thomas appeared in the doorway.

Barefoot in his nightshirt, Thomas held up a hand to urge silence and waved Benjamin to him. The boy approached and saw a pistol in his uncle's hand, loaded and primed. The man leaned close to whisper in his ear.

'Thieves. Downstairs.'

Benjamin's blood grew cold. Thieves in the Straw Hall! What was to be done?

Apparently reading his nephew's nervous thoughts, Thomas indicated that Benjamin should remain and he began to steal towards the bar. He gained the head of the stairs and paused, and the boy watched as his uncle took a moment to level the pistol, drawing to aim at a target below and beyond Benjamin's sight. With the weapon held ready, Thomas whispered to himself, 'They'll not have my coins.'

Straining on his toes in the doorway, Benjamin quickly lost sight of Thomas where he descended. Reluctant in that moment to be alone in the dark with woeful imaginings of events below, he darted nimbly through the shadows to his hiding place on the gallery.

Uncle Thomas had already reached the bottom of the stairs. In the night gloom between tables and chairs, he pointed his weapon towards a shadowy form behind the bar.

'Stop!' he commanded, and the shape whirled to his voice. 'Come out here!'

By the light of fireplace embers, Benjamin watched the figure slowly obey and he gasped on seeing the one who stepped, with arms raised, into the light.

'Billy Preston,' Thomas scowled. 'You have no business here.'

'We mean you and the boy no harm,' Billy tried softly. 'Some coins, that's all I want.' He took a cautious step forward only to jerk back as Thomas stabbed the pistol threateningly at him.

'Stand fast there,' Thomas warned, 'no tricks from you.'

'You have money enough for you and the whole village,' Billy argued, unable to hide the bitter spark in his voice. 'One small bag and I'll be gone. I swear it. After all I've spent in here, you can spare me that much for a new life away from Ravenhill. I know you can.'

'You'll not have my coins,' Thomas snarled. His pistol grip tightened dangerously.

Billy raised hands higher in submission and he backed away, but not along his original path.

From his gallery position on high, Benjamin saw Billy Preston's terrible design in a moment of fearful clarity. With subtle steps, the man eased to one side, drawing Thomas's view from the bar door, where the latch was already lifting, and the door slid quietly to admit Jem Canning and the pistol he carried.

Benjamin lunged unthinking for the head of the stairs, already drawing up a shrill warning cry. But the shout was overcome in that same instant by a pistol's crash and flash, and the deafening report filled the inn as Jem Canning's shot took Uncle Thomas squarely in the back.

In the moment's chaos, Billy Preston's hand swept to draw his own hidden pistol. He levelled on Benjamin and tracked the boy to the foot of the stairs as he watched Thomas crash to the floor.

Jem came babbling through clearing smoke. 'He made me do it. He did. He was going to shoot you, Billy.' He searched for belief in his friend's eyes.

But Billy Preston ignored Jem to focus on Benjamin. 'Where is my money?'

Drawn up from staring on the dead man at his feet, Jem issued a cold gasp at finding Benjamin in the room.

'He's a witness' he warned, 'he's a witness, Billy. He'll go king's evidence and watch us hang.'

'Shut up!' Billy barked at him and he demanded again of Benjamin, 'Where is the money?'

'We must get away,' Jem insisted. His eyes cast about madly for an escape route. Abruptly he clawed at Billy's arm. 'The shot will have been heard by the whole village.'

Billy wrestled free and shoved the addled fool aside.

'When we have what we need,' he snapped and turned again to the boy. 'Where is it?'

Benjamin stared hard on the villain. 'Go hang,' he said.

With a scowl, Billy brought up his pistol. Benjamin heard the soft click of its hammer drawn back.

'For pity's sake,' Jem exclaimed, 'do it, or it's the rope for us.'

Billy heard Jem's frightened words and saw Benjamin's determined face, and somehow, between the two, his mind brightened to a new plan.

'A deal,' he offered suddenly. 'Half your uncle's money. That's fair; isn't it? You'll have that and the Straw Hall. And we'll take our share and leave you in peace. And in return you'll not dish us up to the magistrate.'

Benjamin listened to the man's lies as he searched with his mind across the floor for his means of salvation. His uncle's unused pistol had fallen free to the right, he remembered, so must now be lying somewhere close by the foot of the stairs. But even as he plotted desperately, something in his demeanour betrayed his scheming to Billy Preston, for the young man's features lit to an amused grin as he read Benjamin's intentions.

'Do you fancy your chances against me, Benjamin Blake; is that it?' he taunted. 'You think you can draw and fire so quickly? Go on, then; enter the game. Go on!' With a free hand he gestured to the floor. 'I'll make it easy for you. Your weapon lies just beyond your toes, primed and ready. Look.'

Benjamin allowed his gaze to shift and found the weapon indeed within reach, inches from his foot. But he held fast and made no attempt to seize it. He was not so foolish as to believe he could move swiftly enough to beat Billy's readied pistol. Forcing down a boiling rage, Benjamin glared at him and remained still.

Billy scoffed. 'You're a stubborn pup, aren't you?' Lowering his weapon, he turned to go, but in the act of stepping away, he abruptly swung back and struck the boy hard across the face.

The blow was enough to send Benjamin to his knees. Falling through dizzying pain, his hands swept out to steady him and fingers brushed blindly to the metal length of Thomas's pistol.

'We've wasted enough time,' Billy told Jem, and Benjamin saw the nod he offered his friend: the unspoken reassurance there would be no rope for either of them.

Now Benjamin moved! Tensing body and knees in time, he scooped up the pistol in a moment and jerked up to draw aim on Billy. The man's form passed squarely along the sights of the weapon and Benjamin sought frantically for the trigger. But even as he hauled on the hammer, he realised how the murderer had clearly anticipated the move and was already spinning back. Benjamin still sought his target as Billy Preston found his.

A sunburst of flame erupted to a deafening blast and a burning wind tore at Benjamin's body. Gunpowder clouds plumed and he was driven into the heart of a storm that came to assail all senses. And the storm carried with it a blazing agony that punched through his stomach. It was a blow of such power that it lifted the boy off his feet and sent him spinning. The inn became a tumbling scene where he flew like a discarded rag among chairs and tables to crash at last beneath the stairs.

Exhilarated, Billy came after, kicking furniture aside as he made to reload his pistol. His triumphant sport was far from ended. But Jem Canning lunged forward to intercept him, his patience finally spent.

'We have no time for this!' he shrilled.

Caught in the heat of the moment, Billy shifted his rage between Jem and the injured boy, reluctant to listen to warnings, to flee unrewarded. Only slowly, and with grinding teeth, did he relent. 'Bring the horses up,' he instructed and sent the man racing to do as ordered.

Benjamin fought through waves of agony as Billy came to stand over him. Through a haze of delirium, he watched a smile break on the man's lips as he judged his own marksmanship and was satisfied with the lethal injury inflicted.

'No need to waste another ball on you,' Billy mused aloud, 'you'll soon be with your maker.'

The image of Billy Preston's smirking face twisted as Benjamin's vision swam to darkness, chased by his killer's laughter as he swept from the inn to leave the boy to his slow fate.

I2

Agony.

Pain like Benjamin had never known clawed his body, streaming from a thousand daggers piercing his stomach. Every fibre longed to scream in anguish but the pistol ball had robbed him of voice as well as strength. He could raise neither a cry against torment nor a hand of comfort to the ghastly wound that seeped blood through the rags of his nightshirt. Icy needles prickled his skin as shock and blood loss worked to hold him down.

At first there was only the horrified realisation of what had happened.

Shot.

Benjamin's fevered brain jabbered the awful truth over and over as it sought a measure of logic in the painful madness running through his limbs.

I've been shot... I've been shot!

Passing through the moment of panic, he slowly accepted his reality and the overwhelming sensations that pinned him, somehow finding a place among the anguish to gather his wits.

Someone must have heard the firing. Even across the distance to Ravenhill, surely the clamour had punched through the sleeping night to draw someone from their bed to investigate. How long, he pondered fitfully, how long before rescue came? Could he last that long... how long? Or could he endure the hours remaining until dawn, when someone from the village would come on business? What day was this? Yes, he realised suddenly, desperately. Just after dawn on this day, the baker Merton would come from Ravenhill with loaves for the inn and the widow Gibbons would visit to offer fresh cheeses. There was hope, if only he could hold till the dawn.

A false hope, Benjamin Blake.

The voice intruded on his thoughts, dark and whispering, like a demon in the shadows. You are not meant to see the dawn, it taunted.

You will sleep with the dead.

Beset by pain and despair, Benjamin fainted.

A renewed tide of agony in his gut brought the boy once more to waking, but after how long, he could not guess. He clenched teeth against fire twisting within and hissed against its ceaseless torture. He blinked rivulets of sweat that blinded and tried to focus his vision.

The inn was yet in darkness; the embers of the fire extinguished long since. Only a pale shaft of moonlight through the open doorway pierced the near-crushing blackness. Having sailed farther west in the period of his insensibility, the patch of light cut sharply across the floor and between scattered furniture to settle on the prone form of Uncle Thomas. He lay on one side, his back to Benjamin, as though sleeping in the moon's glow.

The sight brought a weak groan from Benjamin's parched throat, and with it, a fresh bout of agony to assail his body. He fought against passing out again, casting around with tattered senses for something, anything, to focus on and remain awake.

It was hearing that at last provided the stimulus. Wheeling and spinning again towards unconsciousness, he detected a sound and immediately seized upon it, just as one who is drowning grasps for a board in the flood. He identified a soft raking, a scratching which at first he mistook for the mice. Quickly, however, he perceived his error. This sound was not coming from within the inn but from without, from a spot beyond the doorway. Something there was scraping slowly along the wall, drawing closer, approaching the entrance.

Blinking droplets of sweat away, Benjamin fixed on the doorway and fearfully prepared for the appearance of the nocturnal visitor.

It arrived in a final clicking advance and Benjamin, wide-eyed and awestruck, looked on pale fingers with bladed nails that came spidering around the doorpost.

Terror more fierce than mortal agony, colder than physical suffering, exploded through him. His weakening heart surged as though to burst forth and flee the dreadful spectacle filling his vision.

The Devil had beaten the dawn.

A bent form, born of darkness and swathed in its hooded folds, crept into view to hang as a spectre in the doorway. Pausing there, it sniffed the air: an infernal beast wary of traps. Only then, and slowly from amid the blackness it seemed to possess for itself, did the creature extend another human-like hand, a limb as pale and awful as the first. With the gentlest flick, the unwanted guest propelled the door fully open and with one last careful step, it entered.

Straightening, the shadow beast rose to consider the inn. Cloaked as it was, nothing yet of features could be seen and Benjamin was coldly glad of it. Another step forward and the shadow form's caped head began to examine more, roving first along the bar and up to the gallery, and across the floor to where Thomas sprawled, then at last, in a slow turn, to the upturned tables and chairs behind which Benjamin lay. That final slow rotation revealed in a dreadful instant a pair of twinkling spots of silver beneath the hood.

Had Benjamin the strength he should have screamed to the heavens for deliverance in that dread moment. But fear and pain constricted his throat and he could do nothing to dispel this nightmare. He waited helplessly for the demon to approach and claim him.

To his surprise, the creature made no such advance but instead gazed back to the door, and the boy dared hope in that instant the foul visitor might have overlooked his presence. Perhaps the creature of the night, this gloomy soul collector, would creep back to the shadows and steal away empty-handed. But it was a foolish hope. Rather than making to depart, the figure did something very strange indeed for a devil. It whistled softly to the night. And in response, the others came.

Benjamin looked on as the summons was answered by fresh movement in the doorway and another black form peered in with silver gleams, only to be joined by another, and yet another! The boy's fevered brain shrieked against madness as the three new devils passed noiselessly over the threshold to join the first.

Wordlessly, the lead figure drew attention to the innkeeper's body and together the phantom assembly moved forward to surround it in grim silence.

Benjamin's mind swam in confusion. Had the demons come for Thomas? Could this be the truth of the scene he watched, or would the visitors dismiss his body and turn yet in search of him? A surge of fear raced to his heart at the prospect and the paralysis gripping his body was shaken off just enough for his throat to loosen. The weakest protest slipped between unguarded lips.

Three of the shadowy forms appeared to hear nothing of Benjamin's voice and did not alter from their grim vigil. But the fourth, the fourth jerked up to the sound and cast attention to its source. Twinkling silver probed the room's darker recesses deeply, through its lingering shadows. Stepping away from its companions, it began to approach, seeming to glide across the floor, so silent were its footfalls. Only the briefest whisper of a short sword drawn into the half-light reached Benjamin's ears. The boy pressed harder against the wall and prayed against what was coming.

Weaving carefully between tables and chairs, the armed form came on until it rose over Benjamin to blot out moonlight and hope. Save for those twin spots of glittering light in the face, all was blackness. The sword hovered close as the figure knelt and reached towards the injured boy with a free hand. Cold fingers probed the bloody wound to draw weakened groans. The sword raised once more and, in one swift move, plunged to return to its scabbard.

'Who did this to you?' The voice beneath the hood was gentle and it was the voice of a girl.

Confused by a human tone from so demonic a form,

Benjamin looked for the hidden features of the 'devil'. Forcing dry lips to move he said, 'Two men... thieves. Help me, please.'

Peeling bloodied clothing aside, the girl-shadow examined the wound further. She paused, wavering silently as though lost in deep thought. Finally, she gazed upon him once again and asked softly, 'What is your name?'

'Benjamin,' he said numbly, 'my name is Benjamin.'

She considered the name awhile.

'You're dying, Benjamin,' she announced, 'I can hear your heart slowing.'

The information struck like a hammer blow. Dying! He was dying! Yet, even in that instant, weighed upon as he was by knowledge, Benjamin's mind struggled desperately with the girl's words. From her place over him, she claimed to hear his heart. How could this be? What manner of being could detect a faltering heart and even perceive its changing rhythm?

'Please,' he begged tearfully. 'Please don't leave me. I don't want to die.'

'There are worse things than death,' her light voice replied.

'Don't let me die,' he pleaded, weakened more by the effort. And despite those hidden features, Benjamin sensed a moment of uncertainty in her then, a conflict, as her own heart examined different courses of action.

She looked briefly towards the distracted others and Benjamin suddenly feared her departure even more than he had her first arrival. 'Please,' he whispered one final, desperate time.

Prompted by the words, the girl sprang to determined and rapid action. Hands of mighty strength seized Benjamin and he was swept up, his head tumbling towards those glittering eyes. He rested helplessly in the girl's cold embrace as she looped an arm behind his back as though to cradle him. His head fell back under a cold, pressing grip and she plunged towards his exposed neck. Benjamin had just a moment to behold a pair of sharp white teeth bared in the gloom – *sharp as a lion's* – before pain exploded at his throat. The girl was... she was biting him!

He struggled against the attack and the agony she offered, but to no avail. Her strength, so inhuman, could not be opposed and she crushed him to her. He fought with the little power he had left until suddenly, and in a breathless instant of change, all fears and thoughts of resistance washed away. Pierced by twin needles of fire, a tide of magnificent heat raced through Benjamin and he was stilled. Beneath his skin every vein coursed to an unknown power racing along the pathways and through his system, to explode in fingers and toes. His scalp tingled as tongues of liquid fire lapped his skull. Muscles and tendons raged aflame and his very bones felt scorched. Carried on the inferno, his body seemed to become light as air and he felt he floated from his own body, free of mortal agony. From afar, a great rumbling reached his ears, crashing over and over in his head, and he realised he was listening to the sound of his own heartbeat, hammering with the strength of a war drum. The darkness of the inn vanished in a storm of light erupting through the whole of his being. A tempest cracked and arced across the hemispheres of his brain like the birth of the world. Overcome by its beautiful raging, he surrendered to it. He became dimly aware of his hand spilling limply towards the floor, falling for an eternity and finally striking the wood with an explosion that seemed to shake the Straw Hall to its foundations. The thunderous sound was matched by the power of a single bolt of lightning, flaring to overcome all sight.

And in a blinking, everything was changed.

As though sensing the alteration in Benjamin's form, the dark girl released him and backed away, frightened by the transformation she had wrought.

Benjamin's body flexed as strength enough to crush mountains flowered within. Fists that could smash through bolted doors pushed him up and onto legs that could in an instant launch as high as the gallery above, and higher still if he willed them. He felt sharp prickles in hands whose power could bend metal and beheld nails grown sharp enough to cut through glass with ease. Every line and pore on those hands stood out distinctly to a vision that rejected darkness and rendered everything as by the light of a hundred suns.

The slightest of sounds nearby drew his attention to the waiting girl and Benjamin spied the revealed face of his maker.

Similar in years to him, her features were kind but with a clear strength of experience. Beneath flowing hair, raven dark, angular cheeks gave way to rounded lips set to a winsome smile. And with that smile, eyes of silver tint shone deep and piercing with a twinkle of mischief.

'How do you feel?' she asked with soft care.

'Like I have never felt,' he replied, and he examined her closely yet.

'Good,' she said. She gestured to Benjamin's stomach. 'How is your injury?'

Alarmed by the question, Benjamin cast his hands to the forgotten wound. He pulled at the ragged and bloody hole in his nightshirt and searched across the skin beneath, only to find the smooth flat line of an undamaged belly. He looked in confusion to the girl again. 'How...? What did you do to me?'

Amused by his wonder, her smile widened and Benjamin saw something there to make him forget his miraculously cured body. In the clear white line of the girl's teeth, he spied the pair of sharp incisors that had pricked so deeply. Prompted by the sight, he sent his tongue flicking from one side of his mouth to the other and, with a new chilling fear, he detected his own dagger-like fangs.

'What did you do to me?' he asked a second time, in a voice shaking with dread. Instinctively he reached for his neck in search of a bite already healed.

'Calm yourself,' she said, holding hands up to soothe him. 'I prevented your death.'

'But how?' he demanded. 'Who are you? *What* are you?'

In response to Benjamin's questions the girl offered a short and courteous bow. 'My name is Juno. That is who I am. *What* I am, well, I expect you are beginning to guess that, aren't you, Benjamin?'

Her twinkling gaze held him, and he knew; he knew full well what she was, and in that same moment of recognition, Benjamin knew what *he* had become.

What he *was*.

With a choked cry he retreated from her, stunned by the blow of horrific knowledge. He shook his head to deny it and held hands out to prevent it.

Attracted by the disturbance, the rest of the group joined the girl named Juno, lining out beside her to regard the curiously staggering boy in questioning

silence. One of them, a wild-haired boy also possess-
ing a set of dangerous fangs, examined Benjamin with
a mixture of bewilderment and rising anger.

'Oh, Juno,' he groaned at her, 'what have you done?
What have you done?'

13

Benjamin sat quietly while vampires argued.

Vampires. The very word strained his mind to the limits of imagination. Who believed in vampires, save for the very oldest people in Ravenhill with their talk of sprites and goblins and will-o'-the-wisps? Yet, right here around him, were those very creatures of fireside tales come to… life? It was beyond all reasoning, too impossible to accept. But how was Benjamin to dismiss his current state of being, free from injury and possessed of an unnatural sense of vitality? He held hands before his face and flexed them against the possibility of dreaming as the vampires raged on.

'This is perfect! Just perfect!' Wild-Hair ranted, marching back and forth through the bar. In spite of his words, it was very clear he considered *nothing* perfect about this current situation. He rounded sharply on Juno. 'We are running for our lives and you do this!' He waved a furious hand at Benjamin. 'What were you thinking?'

'He was dying,' Juno shot back, her tone more measured than the boy's. 'I saved him.'

'And gifted him our curse,' Wild-Hair snapped.

Juno glared but remained silent.

Into the moment of bitter silence, another of the vampires stepped quickly between the arguing sides. Though dressed in a cape like the rest, unlike his companions this boy wore beneath it a monk's simple garment, secured by a rope at his waist. 'Sister Juno, Brother Darach,' he implored gently, 'we have not come this far to fight among ourselves.'

Seated at a table nearby, where she toyed idly with a set of strange playing cards, the fourth undead visitor, a short-haired girl, petite of features, scoffed. 'Amen to that, Varney.'

'Be quiet, Brill,' Juno ordered.

Card-Girl Brill offered her companion a dismissive shrug and returned to flicking her deck, which Benjamin now saw was decorated not for gaming, but for the art of tarot-telling.

Wild-haired Darach leaned against the bar and gestured to Benjamin. 'What do you intend to do with him?' he demanded.

'My name is Benjamin,' Benjamin interrupted, annoyed at the group discussing him as though he were a farmyard dog.

Darach flashed an angry stare which Benjamin met defiantly.

'He comes with us,' Juno announced in answer to Darach.

The boy fumed. 'Are you out of your Roman mind? We are barely ahead of the hunt!'

'Is that wise, Juno?' Brill cut in. 'I mean, is it not dangerous for this young fellow to be drawn into our tribulations?'

'He might not survive alone,' Varney cautioned in return, his fingers set prayerfully togcther.

'He might not survive with us,' Darach shot back.

'I'm responsible for him,' Juno stated firmly. 'He comes with us.'

The boy flung up his arms in despair. 'This is ridiculous.'

'I think you're jealous, Darach,' Juno teased.

The boy exploded to fury at her words. Flinging a table aside, he seized to draw the long sword he wore and advanced. Juno reacted with dizzying speed to produce her own weapon for the challenge. Brill, meanwhile, fuelled by panic, scattered her cards in leaping to clumsily fumble for the slim rapier she wore.

The boy-monk was quickest of all.

Faster than Benjamin's new sight could follow, Brother Varney plunged hands beneath his cape. In a flash he brought forth not one but two swords, unlike any Benjamin had ever seen. Each weapon had grips fashioned to dragons, with blades following the gentlest curves in cutting the air. The weapons were identical save for the size of one being almost exactly half the other.

Spinning in a precise move, Varney brought his swords slicing down to strike the readied weapons of Juno and Darach. The ringing of metal still hung on the air as he levelled his weapons on each warrior's throat. 'Enough of this,' he snarled, his earlier placating tone replaced by one of stern admonishment.

With an eye to the young monk's blade, Juno stepped aside and faced Darach.

'I shouldn't have said that,' she offered and bowed, 'I beg pardon for my offence.'

'The chase has made us tense,' Varney said, 'and it tests even the best friendships.' He waited for his words to fully douse the rage in Darach's face before withdrawing his weapon to offer a suggestion in its place. 'What say you all we divert ourselves for a short time in answering the many questions Benjamin must surely have?'

The idea was met with shrugs and silent approval from the gathering and, as swords were tucked away and comfortable seats taken, the young vampires faced Benjamin again in his place. For his part the boy peered mutely back, caught by expectant faces, and completely lost for words at this... this committee of the undead.

'Well?' Brill prompted. 'You must have questions.'

Certainly he did, but where to begin in the light of a new and incredible reality? Benjamin wrestled against a storm of confused disbelief to plunge at last for the best first step: the simplest clarification of his situation. But even giving voice to it felt a bizarre, ridiculous action as he made to speak.

'I am a vampire?' he half-asked, half-stated.

'You are,' Juno confirmed.

'So,' he went on through a rising dread, 'by the end of this night, I must drink human blood.'

The group burst into helpless laughter. Brill chortled and dropped her cards to the floor again while Darach roared at the ceiling and slapped his knee over and over. Juno held her chest against the strain of her laughing as Varney shielded his amusement behind a modest hand, but laughed as heartily as the others.

'Forgive us, Brother Benjamin, forgive,' Varney struggled to say, 'the myths that surround vampires never fail to entertain.'

Recovering her composure quicker than the rest, Juno wiped away tears and explained.

'You do not have to drink blood, so rest easy. The bite of the vampire is not for sucking blood. It is designed to poison. Bitten once and briefly, a vampire's victim becomes extremely ill but does not die. Bitten over and over, night after night, and death will surely come. But mark this: the power of a vampire's bite is such that when offered in a single long attack to the point of death, it creates another vampire, just like you. But you don't have to go creeping in at windows to feed on the innocent or visit misty churchyards to ambush the unwary.'

'Nor fear crosses or holy water,' Varney said and joined his hands in prayerful thanks.

'Garlic,' Darach cut in, 'nothing to worry about there either.' He poked idly at the fire's embers as the others nodded their agreement.

'Sleeping in a coffin?' Benjamin added.

'Only if you want to,' Brill responded with an impish grin. 'But I hear they're not very comfortable.'

Frustrated, Benjamin changed the line of his questions. 'What *are* the rules?'

Juno leaned forward in her chair and set a twinkling gaze on him.

'The rules are simple but important, Benjamin,' she said. 'Tonight, you gained eternal life. Do you understand? You will live forever as you are: young and strong. Your senses are sharpened beyond all measure; your strength is greater than the strongest mortal. Your reflexes have become faster than any living eye can follow. You will walk through fire and emerge untouched. But there is a price for it all. Two things can destroy you and, for the whole of your vampire existence, you must respect them above everything else.' Here she paused to emphasise her message by raising fingers one by one in counting out the threats. 'Silver. And sunlight.'

'Never be caught by the rays of the sun,' Darach warned.

'And do not let silver pierce your heart,' Varney added. 'Your death, tonight interrupted, comes with silver and sunlight.'

Benjamin nodded mutely, as though the action might help him accept the information more readily. But even now he wrestled with a greater part of himself, seeking to wake from madness. Mortal sense, undimmed fully by the vampire's bite, demanded other than silver and sunlight. It needed a reality other than this space between life and death. More nightmares, it suggested abruptly, born of fright and delirious injury, that's what this was. But when he sought to locate his mortal body lying yet under the stairs, he found the space empty.

'Wrong, wrong, wrong.'

It was not Benjamin's voice breaking the silence but Brill's, where she muttered darkly under her breath and shook her head.

'There is something else?' Benjamin asked.

'There are three things to fear,' Brill answered, 'not two.'

Darach rolled his eyes. 'Not this again.'

'I am not wrong,' Brill insisted with a stomping foot. She returned her attention to Benjamin. 'There are three things. Beware silver, sunlight, and hellhounds.'

Darach snorted. 'You and your creatures of super-nature. I have yet to see evidence of werewolves in the mortal or supernatural worlds. Stick to facts and don't frighten Benjamin with campfire tales, Brilliana.'

The girl fumed and dragged splinters from the table as she fixed the warrior boy with glaring silver fire.

'Don't. Call. Me. That.'

Darach realised his mistake in an instant and somehow grew paler in his vampire skin. He offered hands in apology and against his friend's dangerously boiling anger. 'Brill,' he corrected, 'Brill.'

'It is no tale,' she continued firmly. 'Mark my words, we are tracked by the grimmest of creatures.'

'What follows us is dangerous enough without a need for adding hairy beasts,' Darach muttered.

Brill gave up. Swatting the air for his lack of belief, she leaned back in her chair and sulked.

'Following you?' Benjamin echoed Darach. 'What's following you?'

The vampires eyed one another uncomfortably, uncertain how to proceed.

'The foul answer to that,' Varney said finally, 'lies in

the understanding the role of vampires in the supernatural world. Do you know what a familiar is?'

'Yes,' Benjamin said, eager to demonstrate his rec-
ollected knowledge. 'A familiar is a witch's servant: a
demon she summons and uses to do her work.'

'Not a demon,' Juno corrected, 'a vampire. A familiar is a once-living person, summoned from the grave
by a witch and transformed to her undead slave. Once
in her power, the vampire is sent to do her midnight
bidding, to attack her enemies by biting to sicken
them, or their livestock, or... their children. That is
what a vampire is.'

The drinking stories of the Straw Hall came flood-
ing back. Benjamin remembered Matthew Hopkins
and his telling of the silver-eyed creature summoned
from shadow by his imprisoned witch.

'You are slaves?' he gasped.

'Once we were slaves,' Juno agreed. 'But we escaped
our witch.'

14

'She is called Adefina Corvus,' Juno said.

Benjamin felt a chill in his unbeating heart.

'Accursed is the name,' Varney whispered. He crossed himself fervently and recited a passage Benjamin recognised from Reverend Harrington's Sunday preaching. *'Upon the wicked He shall rain snares, fire and brimstone. This shall be the portion of their cup.'*

'Adefina Corvus,' Benjamin breathed. He looked again through bars in his mind and shivered. 'I have seen her. She was brought through Ravenhill by soldiers just this past day.'

'Mark the name well,' Darach instructed, 'and know that it stands for the darkest power.'

'Who is she?' Benjamin asked, dreading to hear the answer.

'That you should tell, Juno,' Darach said. 'Of us all, you are the longest her slave.'

In response, Juno shrugged uncomfortably and rubbed hands together as though suddenly, impossibly, cold. The others watched her ponder the best way to explain. 'Even I don't have the whole story,' she admitted. 'Adefina's past, before she called us, is a fog of mystery and whispered tales.

'Once upon a time, she was the youngest daughter of a respected family of Manningtree. They possessed money, land and titles, and Adefina wanted for nothing... and yet she always wanted more. Living quietly on a country estate with every wish fulfilled was not enough for her, not when her own dark imagination suggested greater things.

'What I do know for certain is she first discovered an answer to her restless spirit in the books of her father's library. Ancient volumes stored on shelves higher than those containing poetry and romances. It was in the candle-lit pages of these works that Adefina came to learn of dark forbidden arts and a coded language to make real her wildest dreams. She came to believe she could wield magic beyond imagination and even gain immortal life through sorcery.

'Deciphering the codes came first. Night after secret night she read and translated, double-checking until at last the first spell was possible. She chalked symbols on the library floor between circles of power. Bell, book and candle were set in place. Foul incantations were spoken aloud for the ears of terrible beings waiting in the dark until, and at last, success.'

Varney covered his ears.

'Preserve me, O God, for in Thee do I put my trust.'

'What happened?' Benjamin asked with a shudder.

Juno stared on flames made jubilant in the grate. 'The Devil came to Manningtree. The town records tell of a great fire at the manor house; a consuming inferno rose up and destroyed the structure, and took all lives inside but one.'

'Adefina.'

'Adefina. To the astonishment of townsfolk answering the fire bell, she stumbled from the blaze completely unscathed. In her arms she carried a large book, untouched by flame. But this was a volume never seen in her father's library and to which she clung fiercely, even as the women of the town sought to tend wounds they could scarcely believe she didn't have. "How did this terrible thing happen?" they asked of her, and she made reply, laughing hysterically as she pointed back into the fire. "He did it," she wept and laughed, "he did it."

From her mystic deck, Brill flicked the Devil card as Juno continued.

'That was the beginning. The year turned and a winter of growing suspicion came. More animals than usual died on farms around Manningtree and an air of dread settled on the town. Night travellers passing the derelict manor house brought reports of dancing lights and high laughter in the ruins. In the churchyard, the

Corvus family tomb was forced open, the bones disturbed and rearranged into strange patterns on the floor between melted candles. People began at last to whisper about Adefina, who had taken to sleeping late in the day and walking abroad long after dark. Then, one October night, a child cried of a dark figure with silver eyes who peered through the window of her bed chamber.'

'You?' Benjamin asked.

'No!' Juno snapped. At once regretting the anger in her voice, she eased her tone. 'I would never hurt a child. Not me, another.'

'Adefina's first slave,' Brill said, 'one of two servants who remain loyal to her.'

'The hell-sent Ilemauzar,' Varney whispered, and Benjamin watched angry fingers tighten to the handle of one exotic sword.

'They fled together,' Juno said, taking up the tale again. 'As the townsfolk moved to act against Adefina, the dark woods swallowed up the witch and her familiars, Ilemauzar and the barbarian Rok. None dared follow and Adefina's name was lost to memory, except when spoken at comfortable fires around Manningtree, or as a fright to keep children close to home.'

Darach flexed his fists as Juno reached the worst part.

'Out of sight and mind, Adefina grew in her capacity for wicked magic. Her knowledge increased thanks to the closely-guarded book of power, the *grimoire* of spells she had been gifted through the flames. But so true to her nature, it still wasn't enough to satisfy. The witch wanted more and needed servants to gain it. So, one after another, she called on us.' Here the girl passed a hand across the gathering, indicating each in turn.

'Darach the Oak, warrior of the Celts, drawn from his rest at Tintagel. Brother Varney, missionary to the Orient and the land of the samurai, forced from his tomb at Whitby. Brill, young spy and adventurer, called back after her execution at the Tyburn gallows.'

Brill grinned sheepishly. 'I was very naughty,' she admitted, and was amused by her memories.

'And you?' Benjamin asked of Juno.

His maker smiled for memories of her own. 'Juno Strix, daughter of Rome's famed General Tiberius, warrior scourge of the Suebi. In life, I witnessed Caesar's immortal victory words, "Veni, vidi, vici." In death, I was summoned from my grave at Londinium.'

Benjamin calculated rapidly. 'Six vampires. Adefina must be a powerful witch.'

'She is the most powerful witch in England,' Darach grumbled.

'Was,' Juno corrected. 'On Midsummer's Eve, Adefina was surprised in her spell-weaving by a patrol of soldiers. They caged her for the journey to Colchester and examination by Matthew Hopkins.

For her slaves, it was a chance at last for escape and we took it.'

'You didn't defend her?' Benjamin said, confounded. 'But why did she not summon you to fight for her or to free her?'

'She couldn't,' Brill said through a wry smile. 'Varney, show Benjamin the book.'

Benjamin sensed the mood grow sombre among the vampires as Varney stood. From the folds of his cape, the monk drew out a satchel, and its very touch appeared to unsettle him as he carried it to a table. The others assembled silently about and it seemed some foul rite demanding hushed attention was set to begin.

'Open it,' Darach instructed. The warrior crossed his arms as a comfort against fear.

With an air of loathing for what lay within the wrapping, Varney began to slowly unfold the package, revealing corner after corner of a large dark book. He stepped back from the uncovered volume and, rubbing the feel of it from his hands, he announced its presence.

'The witch's book of spells. The Grimoire Adefina.'

The book of grand dimensions was quite unlike any Benjamin had ever seen. Its covering all over was of a rough brown material that offered an unpleasant sensation as his fingers reached to trace across it. The spine binding all together was a series of great knobbed rings that grated against one another as he opened the cover and began to examine countless wrinkled pages that turned with a dry cracking.

More curious yet was the strange writing those pages presented. Every inch of the book, its covers, spine, and pages, was etched with a confounding array of symbols both bizarre and unearthly. Back and forth, up and down, lines of indecipherable text ran to every corner, making it impossible to perceive a beginning or an end to the text, or even to extract a single coded word.

'We had hoped to turn Adefina's own magic against her,' Darach said. 'We seized the book on the night she was captured and looked for a spell that might free us. Our plan failed at the turning of the first page.'

'After that, all we could do was run,' Brill sighed. 'Adefina's loyal slaves raced to betray our rebellion, so we got away.'

'And now running is the only hope left,' Juno added. 'The book is everything to her and she won't stop until it is back in her hands.'

'But she is imprisoned,' Benjamin said. 'I told you; I saw her.'

Saw? The memory of her vile touch returned to stain his tongue.

Varney shook his head ruefully. 'No prison or army will hold Adefina Corvus long. She will escape if she has not done so already. Heaven help those who cross her path.'

'Then why not destroy the book and free yourselves that way?' Benjamin asked.

'Try,' Darach invited. He gestured to the grate where the fire danced hungrily.

Benjamin lifted the mysterious book and walked to the hearth. There, and with a final nod of encouragement from Juno, he cast the volume in. The fire surged and fell upon the offering, pulling it from sight in a hissing red plume. Benjamin strained to witness the fiery destruction that was surely taking place amid the rolling flames.

Varney moved as though to better watch the burning. But after a few moments' pause, he reached forth and calmly placed a hand into the heart of the fire, there to rummage among sparking logs. When he withdrew, he held the book. Just like his vampire hand, it was completely intact. He held it forth for Benjamin's renewed consideration as he explained.

'Legend tells that the Evil One, in his hatred for all creation, penned this grimoire and others like it to spread dark magic over the surface of the world for mischief's sake. Look closely, Benjamin. These covers were fashioned from the skin of soul-sellers and cannibals cast down to him. The spine was formed from the bones of those damned to his care. Every symbol was etched in the blood of the wicked. No fire or device of man can destroy such an infernal book.'

Benjamin's stomach twisted to the monk's description. Happily, he made no offer to touch the volume again. Returning instead to the table, Varney flung it there to lie smouldering on the wood.

'We have considered everything,' Darach said. 'But what can we be sure of? If we bury it, Adefina will drag it up. A witch will always be drawn to her book. If we cast it into the deepest lake or ocean, her servants might still reach it. So, we run and hope to stay beyond her reach forever.'

'And we won't do that unless we move on again,' Juno said, turning to Benjamin. 'How soon can you be ready?'

The boy was stunned by the question. 'Ready for what? I'm not going anywhere.'

'Yes, you are,' Juno corrected him. 'Listen to me, Benjamin; your existence here is ended. You have become a familiar. Even if you could avoid Adefina somehow, or another sorcerer's call, you can't remain here as a night spirit. In a village so small, the people who were your friends will surely discover you; they will seek and destroy you. To them, you are a witch's slave: a demon in league with evil. You have no choice but to come with us.'

'No...' he argued, reluctant to yield to the ultimatum, unwilling to be carried off like... like a stick carried on water. 'I'm not ready to go. I mean, I can't leave Ravenhill. I can't. I have to wait.'

'What do you wait for?' Darach asked.

Varney was more perceptive than his friend. 'Who do you wait for, Benjamin?'

Benjamin struggled to give voice to the answer. The vampires would only scoff at the desperate hope of a lonely boy. They would weigh facts against dreams and try to convince him of things he did not want to hear, a truth long burrowing itself into his resistant mind. 'No,' he said again through gritted teeth.

'If you do not join with us, you will be destroyed,' Brill warned. 'Adefina is coming.'

'What is it that holds you, Benjamin?' Juno asked, her tone softer than the rest.

The voices crowded in, battering his mind, and demanding the explanation he had clung to for so long, far too long to abandon hope in it now. His father was yet to come; he *was* coming!

'No!' he cried. 'I cannot leave Ravenhill. I won't leave.' Desperation prompted a frantic plan. 'Why can't we remain here? We could make a stand against Adefina. In time we might even understand the book and its uses. We could turn her magic against her, like you said. We could summon others to help.'

'Do not say such things!' Varney exclaimed, horrified at the suggestion. 'It is not for us to raise the dead.'

'But what use is power if we cannot use it?' Benjamin challenged him.

'Dress quickly; bring coins if you have them,' Juno ordered, ignoring his words. 'We travel light.'

'You cannot make me,' Benjamin responded. He backed away from the vampires, angling towards the door. He would run, run into the night and... and... lose them in the fields. He knew the land better; he knew its hiding places and... he would hide... and...

Brill vanished.

Vanished. With his eyes right on her, and not even blinking, the girl simply disappeared. The chair obscured by her form but a moment before stood as empty as Benjamin's understanding. The tarot cards she had played lay undisturbed by the breath of air that came to brush his face.

'Stop and think, Benjamin,' she urged from somewhere behind.

He swung to find her standing in the doorway, casually blocking his escape.

'How did you do that? How did she do that?'

He fell back, tripping over his feet and, though plans of flight drowned in confusion, he staggered blindly towards the yard door.

Varney disappeared.

Benjamin cried out and whipped around, knowing already the monk would somehow be at the exit when he looked. And he was, standing there with his sainted smile.

'Take a moment,' the monk advised gently.

Darach vanished. At his place by the fire, his form turned to nothing, but this time Benjamin saw not just the vanishing but the warrior's reappearance on the stairs. And in between, he saw the slimmest fleet disturbance of space caused by Darach's passing. Benjamin heard his own whisper. 'You ran.'

'Reflexes faster than any living eye can follow,' Juno reminded him.

'I saw what you did,' Benjamin whispered, oblivious to the girl's explanation as he made connections in his own reeling brain and allowed something much, much deeper to guide his feet to the required stance. 'I saw what you did.'

Brill offered a titter of anticipation. 'He's going to do it,' she gasped to the rest.

'He can't,' Darach scoffed, 'not yet. He'll fall over his own feet.'

'I'm telling you,' Brill warned, relishing the moment.

In a blinking, Benjamin vanished.

15

He plunged into his run.

Between Brill and the door, and the door and its frame, he ran. Inside became out in one exhilarating moment, firelight to starlight, as he swept on. The very night seemed to bend to his passing and blurred at the edges of his flight. Only the centre held, crystal clear to his sharpened vision. The roadway streamed like a river between whipping hedgerows; the stars in the vaulted sky trailed comet-like. As he regarded them in dizzying wonder, he did as Darach predicted. With a cry, Benjamin fell over his own racing feet.

His flight became a high-speed stumble, reeling off course to a place where thick bushes waited. With a shout against the inevitable collision, he threw arms to his face. He careered through in a burst of foliage, tripping on as split branches clawed for him. Feet snagged and his body pitched down a leafy bank, in a heavy roll to a crashing stop.

Dazed, Benjamin came to his knees on a woodland

floor amid falling leaves. And as the curtain settled, he looked with awe on the new world his eyes beheld.

The crescent moon filtered through the canopy, each of its pale beams a shaft of glittering silver that probed the forest below. Once shadowed spaces, so feared by living men for their vapours and night sounds, shone magically alive. The very trees shimmered and only those places of deepest pitch between held fast to their secrets. Nocturnal creatures, thinking themselves concealed, stood out clearly for his viewing pleasure. Badgers foraged near a track; bats hunted and played on the air, and above, a staring owl, with vision barely a match for Benjamin's, watched him through night mists swirling languidly across the ground.

'It takes a little getting used to, doesn't it?'

Startled, he found Juno standing near, casually admiring the night. The girl smiled softly and offered her hand as moonlight played on sharpened teeth.

'Come back to the inn,' she said.

He reeled from her. Staggering with a choked cry from her outstretched hand, he turned to his run and swept between the trees, blindly on until sharpened vision revealed a track he knew led to the village.

He regained the road to Ravenhill and sped on. Already he could see the village rooftops and the sparkling roll of the Blackwater between.

A shape in the middle of the road surprised him. A black bundle hissed at his approach before darting, too late, from his path. Benjamin felt the cat pass between his feet and heard its furious shriek blend with his own alarmed yell.

The roadway filled his vision. Up became down in an instant of uncontrolled tumbling. Benjamin fell to a headlong slide of supernatural momentum. He cleaved a path through gravel and dirt, the earth dragging him back to the slower rhythm of mortal night, until at last he came to a dusty stop. Stunned by the fresh impact, he lay on his back beneath the pinpricked sky and discovered he had sprawled at the approach to the Blackwater Bridge.

Juno was already there. A mere silhouette sitting on the wall, she looked on him with amused curiosity behind starlit eyes.

'You learn quickly,' she said. 'Quicker than others.' She slipped between shadows, a ghostly form approaching like mist to kneel by him. 'Let me teach you more.'

The hand she offered again was pale and gentle but Benjamin flinched from it. He sprang back wordlessly and gained his feet to race across the bridge.

But where was he running to? The emergent certainty of his vampire mind was overcome by a lingering mortal doubt and he slowed, faltering at last under the windows of Ravenhill. He searched frantically within for an answer while glancing behind for signs of Juno. The quiet way back to the bridge lay deserted. And yet...

He ran again, his instincts alive to something unknown close by: a following presence, unseen and unheard, but sensed. He swept the lingering voice of his mortal mind aside and sprinted for the bell tower of St Mary's where it rose to touch the night.

He leapt over the churchyard's stone wall with uncanny ease and passed through a ghostly hue of headstones in the black. Within sight of the church's arched door he stopped again. There amid the dead he stood, eager to enter the holy building, yet suddenly fearing to try. His vision wandered over silent markers and blind windows for any sign of welcome but found none. Was the pressing silence a warning to the undead against approach? Could a vampire enter this place without harm and hope to reach the ear of God with pitiful prayers?

A movement to his right swept all questions away. At the churchyard's perimeter, Juno's silver eyes betrayed her stealthy progress along the stone wall.

Benjamin fled, skirting the edge of the church, using its covering shadow as he moved quickly on towards the dwelling houses of the village. There he must surely find shelter with someone.

Jack! In a flash Benjamin realised his friend's house was closest of all. He aimed for it, approaching quickly from the rear where the bedchamber the boy shared with William was located. Looking up, Benjamin spied only darkness beyond the diamond frames of the window.

'Jack,' he whispered harshly, 'Jack.' He waited impatiently but the call was met with silence from above. Frustrated, he bent to scoop up a pebble and, with careful aim, lobbed it upwards, watching the stone bounce off glass to clatter against the wooden eaves, dreadfully loud. Somewhere in the village a dog barked into the night, roused by the sound. But no sign of response came from above still.

If only there was a way up. Benjamin silently cursed the sheer wall of the house rising from him towards the high window.

He paused, caught by something deeper than thinking and looked once more over the upward route. Keen vision sent information to a mind that interpreted it in a new and confusing way. That straight, flat wall was not such a challenge, he found himself thinking. There was, after all, a rough surface and plenty of wood in its make up.

Trusting his senses, Benjamin stepped forward and placed a clawed hand to the surface of the dwelling's exterior. His fingertips brushed over rough plasterwork for a moment, testing its strength and texture. With the softest push, his nails bit easily into the wood and held. The grip was like iron, locked firmly onto the material. Benjamin reached up with his other hand and clawed into the wall as easily as before. Without conscious thought, he began to rise on arms that felt no strain in the effort. Adding his feet to the ascent, he felt the pads grip comfortably to propel him further. Hand over hand, foot after foot, he scaled to Jack's window as though he floated rather than climbed. The greater part of his mind brimmed with confidence in the ascent, though that pesky trace of mortal caution remained to keep him from looking down at the earth falling so far away.

Reaching at last to hook nails into the overhanging roof, Benjamin peered through the window of the darkened chamber. The simple attic room contained two beds and a low table on which a guttering candle sat by the brothers' night-time reading: a copy of the Bible. In their beds, the boys' slumbering forms were revealed through a steady rise and fall of blankets where they breathed in dreams. Cautiously, for fear of waking William, Benjamin rapped gently on the glass. 'Jack,' he whispered, willing his friend to hear. 'Jack.'

At first it seemed he was again unheard, but shortly there came the slightest movement from the bed nearest the chamber door. Encouraged by the sight,

Benjamin tapped his nails softly against the glass. He watched happily as Jack's tired head emerged from the sheets. The boy blinked in the gloom and looked about for a clue to what had drawn him from sleep.

'Here, Jack,' Benjamin whispered, with a single fingernail tap to draw the boy's attention.

Bewildered, sleepy Jack sat up and faced his friend, frowning at his presence outside his window. 'What...' he croaked through a dry throat, 'what are you doing, Benjamin?'

'Help me,' Benjamin implored. He watched Jack slip from his bed to step towards the glass. 'Please let me in.'

Jack yawned deeply and tried to divide sleeping from waking. 'Your night-shirt is torn,' he said, moving closer. 'Are you in trouble?'

'Yes,' Benjamin said. 'Please, Jack, let me in; I'll explain everything.'

Through a mind still clouded, Jack shrugged and reached wearily for the window catch.

The scream that filled the night pulled Jack violently from the glass. Shaken fully awake, he looked to William where the little boy sat bolt upright in his bed, his blankets hauled up in terror at what he saw.

'What are you doing?' he shrilled at his brother.

Jack turned back to the window, suddenly alert to danger, and Benjamin watched as the earlier look of confusion gave way to one of creeping fear.

'Wait,' he said, trying to calm the boy, 'you have to listen to me, Jack.'

'Come away from the window,' William shrieked, 'look at his eyes!'

'Please,' Benjamin begged, 'I need your help.'

'Why do your eyes shine so?' Jack demanded with his voice shaking. He took a faltering step back as the first sinister doubts crept into his mind. 'Look... at your teeth.'

'He's a demon, a blood-sucking demon, Jack!' William howled. His eyes flared to an awful under-standing. 'He was cursed by the witch's touch!' The boy sprang from his bed and scrambled for the Bible. Snatching it up, he hurled it towards the dread vision at the window. The book tumbled hard between the frames to smash a pane directly at Benjamin's face. Instinctively he whipped back his head and blinked against flying shards. 'See!' William stabbed a finger at the scene as his lips drew tight with fear. 'He's afraid of the Bible!'

Benjamin's gaze met with Jack's again and he searched in vain for a memory of the friendship they shared. As sounds of footsteps moved urgently towards the bedroom from deeper in the house, Benjamin found only revulsion and hate in the eyes looking back. He released his grip on the wood.

16

Benjamin tumbled into space.

Such was his agitation by events in the room, he was already well into his descent when he remembered how far from the ground he had climbed. Arms flapped in panic and he twisted in the air, aware at once and again of the new part of his brain attempting to overcome that which cried out desperately against the fall. Surrendering to instinct, he steadied thrashing limbs and pushed out, palms down, and tucked his legs in as the ground sped up. With perfect timing, his feet made contact in a mere puff of dust and his balance held precisely.

Shadows, an inner voice instructed, *find safety in shadows.* He obeyed at once and quickly, stepping without conscious thought into the lee of the house. There the shadows were inkiest and he was instantly lost to mortal sight.

'So, you see,' the voice said, hard by.

She stood, concealed in her cape and barely a step from his side.

'Jack thinks I'm a monster,' Benjamin said. He looked from her glimmering eyes towards the chamber window.

'He is mortal,' Juno replied with a shrug. 'He lacks understanding because of that.'

'He's my friend,' Benjamin argued, though it already felt hollow to say it.

'In that case, imagine how those who are not your friends will react.' The Roman cast a glance upwards, drawn to the flaring of a candle beyond the glass. She swept a wing of cloak protectively about Benjamin. 'We must get away from here.'

Lost for words, he allowed her to lead him away.

'We should move quickly,' she said with a last glance back to Ravenhill as they recrossed the cemetery. 'I fear your appearance will cause the entire village to wake.'

'Better I had died,' Benjamin muttered, still thinking of Jack's fear and the horror his eyes had offered.

'Oh, do you think so?' She stopped to regard him deeply.

'Yes. I've lost everything... my home, my friends. I am a vampire and what good is it to me? I'm an outcast from everything.'

'Yes, you are a vampire,' she agreed and passed an arm over the headstones. 'But would you prefer this? Show me the soul sleeping here who wouldn't swap places with you tonight if they had a voice to argue.'

In spite of his anger, Benjamin let his sight pass across the markers of the dead of Ravenhill. The cold truth of the Roman's words crept into his heart and he at last accepted them.

'I want to leave this place,' he said.

17

Back at the inn, Benjamin allowed Juno to lead him to a chair by the dying fire. He sat at her bidding, downcast, and avoided vampire gazes by peering instead to the last flickering coals until Varney came to stand over him with a bundle in his arms.

'I fetched you some clothes,' the holy boy said. 'It's hardly right to run around the countryside in your nightshirt.' He made his offering with a kind smile and stepped aside to reveal Brill waiting her turn.

She came with a card in her hand and a twinkle in her eye. A flick revealed a pair of drawn dogs, inclining to the sky with silent howls for a round yellow face staring back.

'The moon,' she said mysteriously, and then, with a swift motion of her free hand, produced Benjamin's gold coin from behind his ear. 'And a little of the sun for you to keep.'

Benjamin could not help but smile at her silly trick as he accepted the gold disc.

'This was with my other coins,' he told her.

Brill's smile did not falter as she surrendered his plundered purse from her tunic.

'As soon as you dress, we can get going,' Juno said.

'We're not going anywhere just yet,' Darach countered.

Juno looked with confusion to each of her friends. 'Why not? We can't stay here, not now.' She gestured to the body of Thomas, concealed beneath a blanket someone had thought to place over it.

'No,' Darach agreed, 'but nor can we leave. We'll not find a new hiding place beyond the village before the sun comes up.' He cast a sharp glance at Benjamin for wasted time.

'We have about thirty minutes,' Brill estimated to the turning of the Sun card from her deck.

'Just long enough to find somewhere else close by,' Darach suggested.

Varney mused. 'Then perhaps swift Brother Benjamin can help and be, as the psalms tell us, the guide to our desired haven.'

Benjamin felt the uncomfortable weight of stares on him again and he struggled to think.

'Is there another place?' Juno prompted. Her face brightened suddenly. 'The church, maybe. Is there a crypt underneath?'

But Benjamin shook his head.

'The schoolhouse,' Darach said. 'The war has seen them all shuttered.'

Brill made a revolted sound. 'Ugh, school.'

When Benjamin chuckled, everyone thought it was for Brill's reaction, but as he laughed on with a faraway look, they turned with quizzical frowns for his rising merriment.

'I know the perfect place,' he assured them.

* * *

The smugglers' store was revealed in the softest creak of hinges.

The vampires watched the sliding of the bench, leaned forward as one to peer into the unexpected space and together allowed delighted smiles to spread over sharpened teeth.

'No one in the village knows about it,' Benjamin offered as he ducked inside.

'Well, now,' Darach said, 'here is a worthy chamber indeed.' He led the rest to the cool interior where they examined boxes and barrels.

Brill knocked playfully on one of the crates. 'Hello? Anyone home?'

'Muskets,' Benjamin offered helpfully.

'No use against Adefina,' Juno said.

'But the refuge will do excellently well,' Varney

judged. He gestured to the wooden stores. 'When will the owners return for their goods?'

Benjamin sought to recall the words of Captain Hazzard. *Three crates for two nights.* 'Tonight,' he said, 'but long after dark.'

'We'll be miles gone by then,' Juno said.

'Then we have our lodgings for the day,' the satisfied Darach declared. 'Let's cover our tracks and get settled in.'

***

The morning came with a scream and the thump of a basket dropped.

The vampires listened in much confusion to a chaotic trundle of cheeses rolling across the floor above and a frantic clacking of shoes, as the wearer ran in hysterical circles shrieking of 'murder!'

'The widow Gibbons,' Benjamin told the others, and they listened on as the terrified woman ran about some more before finding her escape towards the village. The inevitable ruckus of humanity came a short time later; the cellar beams resounded to countless stomping feet and voices raised against the discovered horror of Thomas's body. Voices competed loudly in calling for the magistrate, for Reverend Harrington, for justice!

Peering up to the timbers, Benjamin attuned to it

all, discovering by slow degrees how his new hearing allowed him to cut through the din to individual voices, even when they whispered behind the greater clamour. Thus, he heard the weaver Armstrong quietly wonder how long he would be without his ale, and the reverend's hushed tone to a villager about knowing always Thomas Blake would come to a bad end, before offering up pious words over the body for all to hear. And Jack! Benjamin located him where he pressed into the yard doorway with a cluster of prattling boys, all eager to see the murdered man. 'I told you it wasn't a dream,' Jack told them earnestly. 'Benjamin's a ghost here now.'

'He is no ghost.'

Benjamin almost gasped aloud for the new voice that silenced all others. It came to a slow tread of boots on the boards where the speaker moved deliberately to the centre of Ravenhill's attention.

Benjamin whispered urgently to the others. 'The Witchfinder General.'

'The boy has become worse than a ghost,' Matthew Hopkins told the hushed assembly. 'Benjamin Blake has been carried off by the escaped witch, Adefina Corvus.'

Escaped! The word astounded those above and below.

'Yes! Escaped!' Hopkins roared above the storm

of alarm until villagers shushed each other sharply. 'Escaped last night, and not a man of her guard left alive! The scene I witnessed this morning would sicken the hardiest stomachs. You, boy, you spoke of a dream that was not a dream.'

'Yes, sir.' Jack's voice was quavering. 'I-I mean, we... we saw Benjamin at our window last night. He looked in at us and his eyes were aglow with burning silver.'

Ravenhill offered horrified gasps.

'The sure sign of a witch's familiar,' the witchfinder judged. Again, he raised his voice to be heard over the villagers' shrill chorus of fear. 'Good people, good people, steel yourselves. I am here. John Stearne is not far off and even now he seeks the witch's trail through your community. Together we will rid you of witches and boy demons and you will find it in yourselves to reward us. Go now; seal up this place made foul by the witch's actions. Offer prayers and stay close to your homes tonight.'

Thus instructed, the people hurried to obey. Feet scampered from the inn and paused for the movement of a smaller group which stepped directly above the cellar's hidden store. There came a heavy dragging on the wood and the group stepped more heavily away, bearing some burden along.

'Goodbye, Thomas,' Benjamin whispered.

After that, all sounds ebbed by degrees to a final

hard silence. The villagers departed in waves of guessing and gossip, and the end came with a slam and latching of the inn's door. Benjamin listened until the mice in the walls began to move again.

'Finally,' Darach muttered, 'now we can get some rest.'

'How can you rest?' Juno asked. 'She's loose.'

'And what can we do about that until sunset?' Darach pointed out. 'Who knows, perhaps Hopkins will see her recaptured by then, or chased off at least. Get some sleep.'

Sleep? While the rest appeared merely dubious, Benjamin was perplexed at the suggestion. How on earth was he expected to sleep after such a night and day?

How did vampires sleep, anyhow?

His mouth opened, closed and opened again, unable to give voice to questions so ridiculous. Looking to the others where they withdrew to nooks and corners, there to lose themselves in enfolding capes, he sought answers in their actions until Brill's soft laugh drew him.

Whatever about a vampire's need to slumber, the girl clearly had no intention of going to her rest just yet. Seated on a small barrel with a crate for a table, she turned card upon card, offering studious time to each and a little smile for their colours before reaching for the next one as she caught Benjamin's eye.

'Pick one if you like,' she said. She turned the deck

down as he slipped to join her.

'Witch cards,' Benjamin said. Reluctant to touch, he looked with distaste on the paper squares.

'Cards of divination,' Brill corrected him. 'They tell your fortune.' Her face shifted abruptly to a dream-like stare, and she cast up a hand for silence. 'They speak to me,' she breathed, 'oh, they speak to me now.'

'Brill,' Juno scolded from the shadows, 'don't tease.'

'But they do,' Brill insisted and her commanding hand floated to the deck. 'I see... yes, I see a storm, I see death, and a tower destroyed.' With a swift twist of a wrist, she presented the uppermost card for Benjamin's inspection.

The image was just as described. Benjamin looked to the illustration of a high tower struck to crumbling by a lightning bolt. He chilled at the sight of a woman, pictured in tumbling from an upper window to rocks below.

'Incredible,' Benjamin said for Brill and her ability.

'She's not incredible,' Juno sighed, 'she's a vampire. She memorised the order of the cards. It's an easy trick for us.'

'Spoilsport.' Brill poked her tongue in the Roman's direction.

'Even that's impressive,' Benjamin said, eyeing the stack of cards the girl had retained in her memory.

Brill snatched up her deck and shuffled quickly. 'An easy trick for a vampire. But just you wait till I get to a gaming table in Paris. I'll make a fortune.' With skilled hands she swept the deck to a broad fan and thrust it to him. 'Let's see what the cards have in store for you. Go on, choose one.'

Varney's prayerful voice came from the gloom.

'I know the plans I have for you, declares the Lord.'

'Go to sleep,' Brill snapped and held the deck again to Benjamin.

Watching for signs of trickery in her promise, Benjamin played fingers along the card edges and, with a slight retreat, slipped a square from the rest. He turned up the image of a robed man surrounded by flowers. One of the figure's arms extended high to present a rod, while his other rested close to a sword lying on a table.

'The Magician,' Brill said. She seemed impressed by his choice.

'What does it mean?'

'I have no idea,' she said with a titter. 'I picked these up while the others were grabbing Adefina's book. They looked pretty.'

The laughter they shared died at the sound of a snapping latch from the inn above.

All listened to the sound of a slowly turning door, the barrier driven by the hand of one wary of entering straight away. Only when it swung fully to bump the wall did the first light step sound on the boards.

The footfall was soft and testing but heavy enough to pull vampires urgently from their rest. Benjamin saw weapons drawn to flash in watchful orbs.

Cautiously now came the heeled shoes that entered, and the tread of a woman moved with cat-like stealth.

Silence then. The mystery visitor halted, directly overhead. Benjamin strained his senses to perceive the reason for her pause. Perhaps she considered her surroundings from the centre of the inn, perhaps looking upwards to the gallery and the rooms that ran about. But in a cold instant of knowing, deep from somewhere new and boldly instinctive, Benjamin knew for sure the eyes of the woman were trained down. With a fierce concentration, he could *feel* her gaze directed to the floorboards, and even through the wood to lock unknowingly with his own in peering up. Only after a moment's rising dread did he recall his uncle's body and the visible bloodstain it must have left on the boards.

The soft steps resumed. They approached the foot of the gallery stairs and Benjamin detected the slightest creak of pressure on the first step. But that was all. Something, something beyond mortal perception in the visitor, brought a fresh halt and next, a sharp rasp of turning. Heels clicked with predatory eagerness towards the bar.

The cellar erupted with a jarring sound: a squeal of hinges, the crash of a lid thrown back. A moment's pause, once more for traps, and afterwards again the slow tap, tap, tap of heels down to the stones below. The hidden listened again to a fresh rasping step, softer this time. Benjamin pictured her, out there, probing the gloom with a turn right, then left, and with a final slow turn to the workbench at the far end of the cellar.

With the first soft crunch of her approach across the flagstones, Benjamin turned too. Seeking knowledge in the faces of the familiars lined out to meet the advancing threat, his gaze found all faces save Brill's set in stern readiness. Only she offered anything more. Beneath moist eyes, her lip was trembling.

Again, a crushing silence fell. The bench was reached. The mystery woman was mere feet away and Benjamin wondered if a vampire's hearing was keen enough to detect the shift of her eyes examining the furniture. Before he could test the question, a new noise intruded on the hiding place. It was a rhythmic sound, repetitive, sending to Benjamin's mind the image of a horse galloping far off. But no.

Sharp nails were drumming on the bench.

She was confounded, Benjamin knew then, confounded by what she thought she sensed but could not locate. It was tickling at the corner of her mind: a pesky itch just beyond reach. When the drumming gave over to an angry slap on wood, he smiled and waited for the sound that would surely come next.

And there it was, the soft receding step marking her retreat from the cellar and quickening through the bar until silenced by the slam of the door behind.

'Was that who I think it was?' Benjamin whispered as swords grew heavy in relieved grips.

None dared reply and it fell to Brill to explain. As he watched, the girl lifted a card from the pack and turned it up.

Death looked at Benjamin with a skeleton smile.

18

'Where are you, brats?' Adefina quietly asked the dawning village.

From her eastern vantage point on a wooded hill overlooking Ravenhill, she kept her cat-like watch among the leaves. The hunter's trail had led the way, straight and true until the scent suddenly vanished, lost in the hours before sunrise, down there, among sleepy cottages and lanes between.

'Still here,' she whispered. Adefina played absently with the ring she wore, rolling its skeletal face over and back on her finger as though to gain magical sight across the village by the action. 'Where are you?'

The church? The schoolhouse? The inn standing closer to her place than the rest? Or perhaps some unvisited attic in one of the homesteads? At dawn's first light, while hunters slept and daytime life stirred, she had scanned the buildings again and again, iden-tifying countless hiding places in so small a place, hardly big enough to compete with a single neigh-bourhood in London.

If they should get that far...
'They won't,' she had snapped at her own shoulder.
They got this far...
'Lucky brats,' she scoffed.
The moon will shine brightly tonight...
Adefina was barely aware of her own sharp movements. Spinning through a fog of rage, her hand plunged of its own accord for her dagger, whipping it up to slash repeatedly against the voice she had long thought came only from her book. It had not come from behind either and her thrusts were in vain on the empty air. Blinking anger away, she looked breathlessly on the knife, so unexpectedly in her hand, and to the misshapen reflection of her face it offered.

The distant scream brought her striding back to the curtain of leaves. She was in time to see the flight of the woman from the inn, her basket of goods forgotten in a headlong race towards the village, and the concerned residents who stepped towards the cry.

That was the beginning.

Adefina had held her place through the passage of hours to witness the massing of people about the inn. Keenly she tracked the excited comings and goings, attempting to perceive what the villagers did in straining their necks through doors and windows, and all the more when *he* arrived.

'Matthew Hopkins.' Adefina uttered the name as a foul-tasting curse.

At last, in the hour to midday, there had come the removal of a covered form from the inn. Adefina curled her lip for reverent prayers drifting on the air as it was carried to be borne away on a wagon, bringing village interest with it.

Long after, she paid her own visit.

Carefully across the fields she had moved, halting at the final bank of trees to look for signs of life, a lingering guard at the building, perhaps. She listened for sounds to betray an occupant and found none, though her dagger was ready again when at last she moved to push the door open and slip inside.

The inn was a dead space. Nothing stirred in reply to her entrance, not from the bar or the gallery above. Thin beams of light filtered through unopened shutters to fall on empty tables and chairs, and revealed a large, dark stain on the floor between upended furniture. The sticky pool had seeped to the edges of the boards, there to drain into the cracks. Adefina knew enough of blood to identify the source.

She had dismissed it then, the violent event that had played out hours before her arrival, and she turned away to the stairs for a search of the upper floor. Her foot was raised and had already touched a step when she felt the first cold certainty she was watched.

It had turned her sharply to peer once more through the gloom for the origin of her discomfort and again down to that stain overlaying the floorboards. The discoloured pool was so unexpected a find, she had allowed it to distract her senses from the hunt, to make her forget this was an inn.

And inns have cellars.

She had flung up the hatch, ready to slash at thieves surging up in panic. But the cellar waited silent and dark below. Dark enough for sneaking vampires. But no brats skulked under barrels or in dark corners where she had searched. There was nothing.

And yet...

She had walked towards that nothing, drawn across the dusty stone floor towards its empty silence, until only a grubby work bench met her search. She looked blankly on nails and chisels, and with drumming fingers sought an answer she *knew* was just within reach.

You can't see what isn't there...

The slap she had offered the bench was vicious and it set tools rolling as pain flared in her hand, stinging hotly as she withdrew. It did little to curb her fury as she slammed the door and carried vows of torture back to her watching place.

***

Ilemauzar was waiting.

Lurking in the first cool shadow of dusk, the demon approached at her witch's signal, but slowly. She knew well to fear that burning look and to keep her own silver gaze lowered in creeping forward.

'Speak,' Adefina demanded.

'The way south is guarded,' Ilemauzar reported dutifully, 'no passing there. I held the eastern way, all quiet.'

'Where is Rok?'

Ilemauzar responded with a gesture to the heart of Ravenhill, where the first of night had sent inhabitants to the comfort of their homes. The streets around lay empty and quiet, but beneath lazy drifts of chimney smoke, and beyond the reach of weak candlelight, a single bulky form moved on the edge of dark. To an angry protest from a watchdog far off, it slipped noiselessly from house to house like a thief in the night.

'Your faithful servant entered from the west to search,' the demon explained, 'listening now at windows and doors.'

'The big Viking oaf. He won't find anything.'

'They have fled?' Ilemauzar gasped, fearing punishment more than loss.

'No, no, the brats are still here,' Adefina said, and as she spoke her gaze fell again on the darkly shuttered inn.

Something.

Rok's lumbering shadow reached another dwelling and lingered long in peering in at a window. Adefina heard an eager click of teeth from behind and read her slave so easily by the sound.

'What bothers you, Ilemauzar?' she teased without smiling. 'Are you afraid Rok will get to Brother Varney first?'

'Pah!' the demon snorted at the notion. 'That would be a short contest, and afterwards Varney would still be mine to beat.' She tapped the handle of her sword in desiring that showdown.

Adefina rolled her eyes. 'The endless battle of good and evil, so booooring.'

'I should have killed him at the very moment of his summoning,' Ilemauzar spat.

'It was more entertaining to make him to wreck churches,' Adefina chuckled.

The whinny of a horse broke the moment's amusement and seized Adefina's attention. It had come across the fields, from a black patch of trees running to the main road. And there was movement in the depths of the patch.

'A wagon,' Ilemauzar reported with keen vision, 'and men. Masked men.'

Adefina acted quickly. Facing Ravenhill, she sought quickly the gliding shadow of her distant hunter.

Spying his form where it rose to peek through another window, she extended a hand to it, crossing her middle finger over index as the magic required.

'Rok,' she whispered, 'Rok.' She watched the far off hunter stop, caught by the power of her whispered call. Pinpricks of reflected moonlight turned up with silvery attention to her watching place. 'Find the men who come. Watch them.' A swift passing to darkness was his obedient reply.

'One of them moves now,' Ilemauzar said with a finger stab to the trees.

Adefina joined in observing the man who slid from his horse to part from the rest, thinking himself so secretive in his creeping progress along the treeline to the road, thinking himself so swift in his dash between hedgerows to the edge of the inn. Rok was already there, his warrior axe poised to split shadow and skull should the command come. Thinking himself yet unseen, the sneaking man eased a pistol free and pressed on until swallowed by the black interior of the building. His vanishing was brief; his return made the more visible by a candle he flared in a gloved hand. The signal was raised, lowered, raised again, and answered by a crack of reins and rumbling wheels.

'Smugglers,' Adefina said. She looked on the empty wagon as it steered close to the building. 'Coming to reclaim their goods.' Her entwined fingers stretched out once again. 'Let them be.'

The inn became a scene of hasty activity. Racing the moon's steady ascent, masked men plunged inside as a third, in a dark cape, stood guard. Unaware of observers near and far, the men reappeared with the first of their load and heaved up the long crate to slide it aboard their vehicle. The grind of wood on wood brought a curse from the driver for hush. The workers ignored him to duck inside again, repeating their trip twice more until the last heavy box was set atop the previous two. Without a word, the men leapt back into their saddles while the guard scrambled for the wagon, even as its driver urged the horses into a galloping turn northwards.

The returning silence became almost absolute save for a single rhythmic tapping. Adefina's fingers played a frustrated beat on the handle of her dagger and Ilemauzar shifted uneasily at the sight. The demon moved to step back but her retreat was blocked by the arrival of Rok, huge and hairy, where the Viking pressed between branches to block starlight. He looked on the others with eyes made permanently dour by a thick sloping brow.

'Where are those little brats?' Adefina demanded of her slaves, of the village, of the trees and of the risen moon. The sight of its pale glimmer inflamed her anger. 'We are running out of time.'

Ilemauzar and Rok exchanged a confused glance for their witch's words and she refocused them with a dagger pulled gleaming to their faces.

'They are still here!' she fumed. 'Down there, somewhere, playing hidey games with us.' Her blade switched from throat to gulping throat. 'I want my book. I want those thieves. I want their...'

Blood.

Adefina wheeled from her slaves with a gasp. The turn to the full truth made her light-headed and her advance was a stumble towards the edge of the trees. She slashed at leaves to open her view of the inn and sent her mind racing ahead of her feet as they plunged down the hill.

You can't see what isn't there...

'There was no blood on the cellar floor.'

Her slaves raced to catch up, to protect her, to understand their mistress in her blind charge on the inn. They flanked her to the road, to the door and inside, to gaze in bafflement on her motions across the floor to a stain on the boards. Then they came on as she raced behind the bar and demanded light for her descent to the cellar space, there to turn about and about with eyes and lantern raised before rounding on a bench set to the far wall.

'Move that!' she cried to unleash Rok's talent, and stepped aside to watch his axe sunder the bench to sticks.

Light flooded to the corners of the hiding place, pushed deeper by Adefina where she led her armed vampires. She looked about the empty place and up to the stained rafters, finding at last the betraying stain, but nothing more. Her confusion was brief and crushed by a new and terrible understanding.

'Find those smugglers.'

19

'Clever,' Darach whispered from the top crate, 'but not comfortable.'

'You have more comfort than the rest of us,' Brill hissed from her rumbling confinement. She looked into Varney's face close to her own, serene despite the crush. 'Your sword is sticking into my hip,' she grumbled.

Pressed to Juno, Benjamin tried to suppress his amused smile.

'It was clever,' she congratulated him.

'Thank you.'

'We should have drawn lots for travelling companions,' Brill moaned, her voice made shaky by the wagon's bucking drive.

'Stop complaining, *Brilliana*,' Darach said, made daring by the wooden barriers between them...

'Call me that again and I'll come up there; you just see if I don't!'

'*For you are my hiding place*,' Varney recited softly,

*'The Lord says, I will guide you along the best pathways,
I will watch over you.'*

'Aw no, he's praying,' Brill whisper-wailed.

Benjamin chuckled with the rest.

Juno looked on him with surprise. 'I think that's the first time you've smiled since we met,' she said, and her own smile brought dapples of silver fire to her eyes.

'I've not had much reason till now,' he said.

'Your father,' she said, 'I'm sorry for what happened to him.'

He eyed her quizzically a moment before understanding. 'You mean my uncle. I never knew my father.'

'I didn't know my father either,' Brill chimed in, 'or my mother. Not for long.'

'You're lucky,' Darach whispered absently from above.

'I knew my mother,' Benjamin said, and something in his words drove the shine from Juno's gaze.

'Varney thinks his parents were angels,' Brill tittered. 'Ow!'

A harsh signal for quiet came through the wood from Darach and the vampires stilled to listen. Close by, the wagon driver's voice raised in calling for halt and the vehicle slowed amid protesting snorts and slackening hoof beats.

'What do you see, Darach?' Varney prompted.

The warrior reported his vision between the slats. 'We're in a forest clearing. The horsemen have dismounted.' He shifted for more than his narrow space allowed as the wagon creaked with the departure of driver and passenger.

'Maybe they've stopped to rest,' Juno said.

'Firewood,' Darach reported. 'One just ordered men to fetch firewood.' 'They're making camp,' Varney sighed, relieved.

'Or a signal for their customers,' Benjamin cautioned.

'Don't say that,' Brill gasped at the idea. 'What if they open the crates?'

Darach muttered a curse above. 'We'll know about that in a moment. Benjamin is right. There's someone coming.'

Vampire ears filled with sounds of tramping feet and clattering metal.

'Swords,' Varney said. 'Soldiers?'

'Six, no, eight soldiers,' Darach confirmed. He watched a line of uniformed men emerge from the night, leading horses as they slowly entered the clearing. Hands stayed close to weapons, even as the smugglers' leader raised a hand in greeting.

'Now what do we do?' Benjamin asked of his partner.

'We'll slip away as they do business at the fire,' Juno said. 'The flames will dull their vision and help us.'

'We shouldn't wait,' Brill said.

'Not long,' Darach assured her, 'the kindling is already aflame.'

'Not the twigs?' Brill asked, her tone increasingly nervous.

Darach was as confused as the others by the question. 'What?' he asked. 'No, not the twigs.'

Brill's voice was thin and frail. 'Then why do I hear twigs snapping?'

Darach's movements above became urgent as he scanned the clearing and the shadows pressing so black on all sides.

'I hear it too,' Benjamin said. He felt Juno grip his arm.

'The men are tense,' Darach said. 'They've drawn weapons and... the fire is making shadow and... there's something moving in the trees.'

'Oh, no,' Brill whimpered, 'I warned you.'

The night forest howled and burst asunder. From the edge of the clearing, a gigantic figure reared up to bound forward on thundering paws. Razored claws smashed branches aside as green eyes sought hungrily, first for terrified men and next, the wagon and its stacked crates. The hellhound scented its prey and howled once more.

'Move!' Darach bellowed, already surging from his hiding place.

Lids and sides gave up to splinters as vampires emerged. Benjamin felt himself hauled up through the storm by Juno as the hound's bristling head snapped towards the disturbance. Benjamin froze at the sight of massive teeth bared to a dripping anticipation. The jaws turned upside-down as Juno's fierce push at his shoulder sent both of them toppling from the wagon.

Mortal cries of alarm filled the night and horses shied in terror. A pistol exploded from the gathering of men and the shot found its mark, punching a wound of sickly yellow blood at the werewolf's shoulder. The beast snarled bitterly and sought the attacker where he stood, suddenly isolated from the retreating others and fumbling desperately for his sword. Claws were quicker and more punishing than steel. The cries from soldiers and smugglers grew louder as the hound fell and feasted.

Brill sprinted to Benjamin and Juno. 'This way,' she urged and raced between the leaves.

In the midst of slaughter, the werewolf sensed the escape. Between running men and kicking hooves, it spied vampires preparing to flee. Fighting off the delirious taste of blood, the creature remembered its mission and lunged forward. The gathering of mortals became a flailing of bodies on the air as the creature smashed through.

Benjamin ducked as a stricken form whirled by. A man, sent flailing by a werewolf paw, slammed to the trunk of an oak and rolled helplessly to earth, his hat and mask torn away by the impact. Halted by his plight, Benjamin stepped to help, even as the smuggler sat upright with a pained cry and drew up a cocked pistol to aim blindly at him.

Captain Hazzard looked with unmasked wonder at Benjamin, and looking back, Benjamin hesitated in perceiving for the first time the man's full face of blue eyes and black hair.

The night shook on a charging roar and Hazzard shifted his aim.

'Run, Benjamin,' he cried and fired.

Benjamin vanished behind pistol smoke.

20

ranches lashed vampire faces in their racing through the forest.

Driven by fear, the five sprinted a broad track to the limits of their speed. Clouds of mist swirled as they vaulted over fallen trunks to scatter leaves in their wake.

With no sense of direction to the onward rush, Benjamin scanned desperately ahead for his companions for fear of getting lost in the escape. His new vision cut the gloom and he was heartened to spy them not so far off and making good headway towards a break in the trees. He angled to join their speeding line, but no sooner had he done so than each of the running figures vanished, seeming to fall into holes in the earth. Benjamin slid to a halt and cast his senses wide, probing for movement ahead while listening for sounds of monstrous pursuit behind.

He was seized. A speeding form caught and pushed him from his path to press him to a tree. Juno held him fast and cast a finger to her lips.

'Move quickly but quietly,' she instructed. She took his hand and showed the way.

Weaving between trees, Benjamin followed Juno in ducking low to sink beneath concealing ferns, there to crawl forward to the place where the others waited.

'We have met an obstacle,' Darach whispered to him. He directed Benjamin's attention through the stems.

The vegetation serving as the vampires' hiding place marked the border between the forest and a road running beside a burbling stream. And on that road, the feet of innumerable soldiers marched. To the right, the army snaked endlessly on, while to the left, Benjamin saw troops progressing over a stone bridge, rank after rank between cavalry formations. The army line approaching from the little span showed no break in its cutting across the vampires' intended route.

'Perhaps we should move north beyond the bridge and cross the river there,' Varney suggested.

Darach shook his head. 'Somewhere there lies this army's encampment,' he guessed. 'We would struggle to pass undetected.'

'Whatever you decide,' Brill said, 'do it quickly, please.' She looked back into the depths of the forest from where distant sounds of movement reached them all.

'The beast is trying to find our scent,' Varney said.

'We should cross now,' Brill insisted. 'Let the soldiers see us, who cares? We can fight through.'

'I'm not fighting an army and a werewolf together,' Juno said.

'We should turn and face the hound,' Darach declared with a firm hand to his sword.

'We should wait.'

All eyes fell on Benjamin where he peered, not back but on, towards the bridge and the army.

'Wait?' Brill exclaimed. 'I don't like that plan at all.'

'We should wait,' Benjamin insisted again. With sparkling vision he watched the march, soldiers and cavalry, cavalry and soldiers, as Juno crawled to his side. 'They already sense it,' he told her.

Juno looked but did not see. 'What do you mean?'

'Look at the horses.'

The others joined in observing the unending march. Another body of armed men walked in time across the bridge, stomping to keep up with those ahead. Behind, a cavalry rank clopped forward but at the middle of the crossing place, horses bucked and became unruly, advancing reluctantly and only to the hard spurring of their riders.

'The hound smells us, but the horses smell the hound,' Benjamin whispered.

Darach understood. 'Be ready to move,' he commanded.

The sounds of rummaging within the trees grew louder, ever closer. Branches made visible against the starry sky whipped at some gigantic passing. A form hulked swiftly through the trees, offering no more than a fleeting glimpse where it broke cover and vanished again. Yet brief though it was, the movement was enough to offer a flash of twin green sparks.

'There,' Brill whispered, pointing to an empty space where low branches shifted in evidence of a rapid passing.

The night wood fell to complete silence.

A horse shrieked on the bridge and reared. Its rider, taken by surprise, tumbled from his saddle amid stomping hooves as panic quickly spread. Mounts kicked and broke ranks, terrified by what they sensed now so close on the air. Soldiers fought to calm them but the struggle was in vain. The advance stalled and the army split.

'Now is our chance,' Juno said. She plunged for the road and drew the others on.

Putting the creeping menace behind, the vampires crawled to the edge of cover, watching as the severed tail of the column worked its way past and disappeared into the gloom. As one, the friends moved down the short embankment to the road and on to the water, there to wade into the slow-flowing stream towards the far bank and the covering trees beyond. Only the squinting moon tracked their progress and the continuing disturbance on the bridge distracted all mortal attention from efforts on the open water.

Behind his companions, Benjamin cleared the stream just ahead of Brill and he clambered up the bank to wait for her at the first of the trees. A mere instant later she arrived, turning to look with undisguised terror back across the water. Following her gaze, Benjamin saw their terrible hunter.

It moved behind the veil of shadows created by the foliage, indistinct still but huge and sinister, and cunning enough to avoiding betraying itself to the vision of the mortal men struggling nearby. In the dark it halted, turning to the vampires who paused. Two baleful eyes of shimmering green regarded them from the blackness, filled with all the hate a witch had placed in its heart.

Transfixed, Benjamin and Brill watched the monster's orbs flare brighter, and the fearful, hairy body they were part of began to paw its way down the embankment.

'Time to flee,' Brill cried and together they ran.

The wood flung obstacles in their speeding path. Benjamin leapt over a fallen trunk that sent brittle fingers to snag at his flying legs. He lost Brill where she refused the jump, preferring to weave into the cover of thick foliage. Startled birds flapped up from the ground to impede his vision further, and he almost collided with the vampires where they had again halted. Benjamin saw weapons drawn and bodies tensed for the fight.

'Get behind,' Juno ordered.

Brill arrived in a burst of branches.

'It's right behind me.'

Weapons sang on the air and the vampires spread out to face the threat.

'I need a weapon,' Benjamin said desperately.

Only Brill acknowledged his plea. 'You need to stay back and be ready to run,' she snapped as she joined the others.

Benjamin made to argue but his senses abruptly demanded silence as he felt the press of eerie quiet that had again descended. Through the natural world pausing in expectation of a dreadful storm, he gave over fully to his instincts, barely aware of his own feet turning from the others to a black space nearby. From that inky place, a smell at odds with the lush ferns rose to offer an essence of rot mixed with a stench familiar to Benjamin from the living world. Mortal memory lit to the smell of wet fur even as green orbs flared.

'Behind you!'

The undergrowth surged up and the hellhound was revealed. With a deafening howl that rolled across slavering teeth, the werewolf loomed over its prey and sought the scent of fear. A fisted paw swept out and Benjamin was struck. The world turned end over end to offer a muddy ditch as vampires closed on the nightmare beast.

Rising on hind legs to meet the assault, the hound flexed claws and snarled a dripping malevolence at the group. Spurred by the promise of carnage, lips pulled back from a maw of blackened teeth to the imitation of a smile.

Darach was quickest to the fight. He lunged forward, sword sweeping from side to side, but the creature was ready and cast him away with a smashing back-handed blow.

As Darach was hit, Juno and Brill struck together. Brill's rapier whipped the werewolf's flank, drawing a pained yelp, and Juno thrust her sword tip for the creature's middle. But the werewolf was not distracted by the first cut and recovered quickly to drive the attackers back with slashing claws. The creature brought its glimmering focus to bear on the solitary, waiting Varney. Locked on to this new target, the hound slicked its lips and roared into a charge.

Stock still and peering along the length of his moonstruck blade, Varney heard Brill utter a terrified cry but held his place in the very path of the thundering hound. '*The Lord is my light and my salvation,*' he intoned softly from his warrior stance.

Claws reached set to rip; teeth opened to pierce

and rend asunder. But in the final moment, as the beast's deadly embrace threatened to bring him to certain destruction, the holy boy moved, spinning a half circle outside the werewolf's reach. His blade flashed bright and cut deep, and the hound clawed with an anguished howl for the ugly wound that spread along its back.

Benjamin clambered to watch helplessly as the vampires gathered themselves in the moment Varney had gained for them. They rushed to the monk's side and lined out for the next furious onslaught. Benjamin scrambled to join them, driven by a desperate sense to be of some use in the battle. Drawing close, his movements attracted Varney's attention and the boy spun briefly from the fight, just long enough to pull the grimoire satchel free and toss it to him.

'We protect you; you protect this,' he said.

The monk's very act seemed to attract the hellhound's attention. Its great head swung to Benjamin and the beast hungrily sniffed the air, appearing to sense that which it sought. It shifted heavily for an attack in the boy's direction.

Even as the beast prepared to spring, Juno made a fresh lunge, ducking under the monster's sweeping arms to pierce its side. Infuriated, the wounded beast was forced to disregard boy and book while it dealt with the converging vampires.

Brill was again punched away, and Varney was forced to avoid snapping teeth. Juno dived from the path of the beast but here Darach took the initiative, smashing his weapon against a hairy limb. The blade bit cruelly and bubbling yellow blood oozed from the cut to soak the warrior's sword. Dazed and frustrated, the snarling beast fell back from its attackers and roared defiantly to mask the first traces of distress.

Circling the line on all fours, the werewolf divided attention between its opponents and the prize: the satchel Benjamin held so tightly. It kept a safe distance from dangerous blades and paused in its movements, appraising the situation ahead of another charge. With lethal speed, one claw flashed out, but not towards the vampires. It pierced the undergrowth to a fallen branch and sent it spinning into the air. Vampires were batted aside and the werewolf seized its chance.

The creature plunged for Benjamin, rearing upright until it filled his vision. Benjamin could do nothing but pull the book tighter and scramble back from the terrible advance. Kicking away, his back struck hard against a fallen trunk, the blow hard enough to daze momentarily. The satchel tumbled to earth from its wrapping and all hope of escape was gone. Benjamin saw teeth.

Juno came from above. Dropping like a stone, she passed into the diminishing space between beast and boy. Her sword cut the air as she faced the oncoming attack, unwavering. Lips parted to reveal savage teeth to the hound.

And she roared.

The deafening sound Juno issued was one no mortal could offer. It was a lion's roar, a thundering bellow of supernatural rage in the night, exploding on the air to shake the deepest reaches of the forest.

The werewolf tried to match the girl's ferocity but the attempt was a weak imitation and the creature's charge faltered in a moment of doubt. Juno saw a chance and swept her full might behind her weapon, targeting one outstretched claw. She contacted perfectly with giant fingers, and hairy digits tumbled free in a yellow spray.

With piteous shrieks, the werewolf staggered back, grasping frantically at the awful wound. Blinded by pain, the mewling hound threw itself from Juno's advance and her dripping sword, where it raised for another blow. The beast collided heavily with a tree in agonised confusion and was spun by the impact to find the other vampires closing round through cascading leaves. With eyes of bottomless hate, the werewolf read its losing situation and fled, crashing away through the forest.

In the first peace left behind, Benjamin gazed, astonished, at Juno. Stunned by the power of the war cry she had released, he remained fixed on her angry face until she detected his fixed stare and softened her features with an awkward shrug.

'What?' she said.

'Nothing,' he said, when in truth he meant *everything*.

'Are you wounded?' She hurried to examine him for signs of injury.

'No.' Benjamin looked to the spot where the werewolf had disappeared through the trees. 'Thank you.'

She responded with a smile. 'We have to get away from here quickly. That thing must be Adefina's own creation: her personal hunting dog.'

'You hurt it,' Benjamin said, 'it won't come again so quickly.'

'No, but it will set the witch onto our trail for sure.'

Brill piped in. 'Hello? Hello? I hate to say, "I told you so".' She pointed her rapier after the beast and made sure all eyes were on her. 'Werewolf,' she added before gesturing to herself. 'I'm not just a pretty face, you know.'

'We must listen better to Sister Brill in future,' Varney indulged his friend. 'Don't you agree, Darach?'

The warrior boy offered no response. On the edge of the group, he knelt in close examination of the ground and the great paw prints left by the hound. As his companions closed round, he scanned the werewolf's escape route back to the site of battle, his features filled with remembering as he came to some deep understanding from the clues he uncovered. Like a keen hunter, he silently replayed every move that had taken place in the last few minutes.

'What is on your mind?' Brill asked.

When he at last spoke, Darach appeared to answer not his friend's query, but questions posed mentally to himself. 'The beast was weaker on its hind legs, slower,' he reflected. With a satisfied nod for his conclusion, he addressed the others. 'That's important, something to remember.'

'We can discuss that on the move,' Juno said, 'but we should move now.'

Benjamin prepared to travel, brushing leaves and clay from his clothing. He silently wished he could as easily sweep away the indignity of being useless in battle as the dirt from his hands.

His empty hands.

In a surge of panic, he searched around for the fallen satchel, fearing the worst. The moment of concern faded on a sigh of relief when he spotted a shimmering beneath the trunk he had struck. There the book lay, almost lost from sight in a dark hollow but for a curious glow surrounding it. One portion of the infernal volume lay exposed from shadow and was changed somehow by the weak light. Tiny points of reflection drew him and he gazed intently at the gentle shine as he reached to ease the book up. There was an immediate increase in the strength of illumination as the volume emerged and Benjamin stood amazed at what he witnessed. The previously mute decoration across the grimoire's cover yielded two glittering circles, one within another, and between them a flow of symbols that shone brightly, clear as moon-glow.

Awe-struck, Benjamin pondered this new magic. Instinctively he placed tentative fingers to the glowing script. Falling beneath the shadow of his hand, they faded at once, only to glow brightly again as he exposed them to the light of the moon.

Was that it, he mused, the key to the book's secrets? Could this be the reason why witches celebrated their unholy sabbaths by the light of the moon? Eager to learn more, Benjamin teased open the grimoire.

The book erupted.

An explosion of power and light surged to crash over and through him... strange and dazzling shapes... ...in a storm of symbols blasting all sight... ⟨symbols⟩ ...burning into his brain in seconds. Without turning pages, his mind detected yet more symbols... ⟨symbols⟩ ...and more... ⟨symbols⟩ ...until his brain seemed filled to bursting with codes to boundless knowledge. The book hurled long and short groups of symbols together, and lines and paragraphs that flew through the imagination like burning spears. He was overcome, dazzled by visions of power and magic, helpless to react to the storm raging within.

⟨symbols⟩

Struggling to regain control of arms and hands, willing them to move, Benjamin fought to close the book against the power bursting from it. But the very pages seemed to defy his efforts, becoming heavy as lead in his grip. Only through summoning every reserve of strength did he turn the fight, and the book covers slammed together with a crashing that echoed through him as a melding of rolling thunder and all the fury of a scream.

With his head spinning, Benjamin looked towards his companions for some explanation, only to find them standing together in full debate, oblivious to all he had just experienced. The dazzling event had been his alone; its magic offered only to him. He tried to speak, to call out urgently and reveal to the others the bizarre event. But his tongue slipped over a mash of words and shapes and brought nothing but a croak to his lips. Overcome by confusion, he peered on the book weighing on his hands. The tome remained indifferent to his puzzlement, though the magic circle shone cryptically.

With the greatest of effort, he flexed his jaw and struggled for words.

'Look at this!' he forced himself to whisper drunkenly. 'Look at this!' But the vampires continued their arguing and paid no mind. Grouped together, they locked in heated debate on a new strategy in light of the monster's attack.

'We were stupid to think we could outrun Adefina,' Brill said, gesturing after the creature. 'She can't be far behind that *thing*.'

'Are you saying we give up?' Juno challenged.

'I didn't say that!'

'Do not despair, Brill,' Varney soothed. 'We beat her attack dog. There is hope yet.'

'But the beast is a sure sign that Adefina follows us,' Darach said. 'And she has power yet, or how else could she make a beast like that?'

'If she gains on us, all is lost,' Brill exclaimed.

'If she gains on us, we will deal with her too,' Juno said.

'How?' Darach demanded.

In the silence that came in answer, Benjamin tried once more to announce his amazing discovery, only to be drowned out by all voices raised again at once in fresh arguing. Turning amongst themselves, none saw him at the edge of the gathering with the glowing grimoire or heard his appeals for their attention. At last, bursting with frustration, he elbowed between and thrust the opened book above his head for all to see. 'Look!' he shouted.

All conversation stopped as the gleaming book rendered tongues dumbfounded. Benjamin switched slowly between the vampires, allowing the light to play on their bewildered faces as he answered the question shining in each one.

'The book gives up its symbols to the moonlight.'

'Well done,' Juno said, stepping forward to reach for the exposed ring of text.

'The witch's circles,' Varney said thoughtfully and with displeasure. 'Ever her protection and strength.'

Juno was eagerly flanked by the others as she opened the book, and all gasped aloud as the grimoire's pages flared to the moon's caress.

'What does it say?' Darach asked with a glance to Benjamin.

'That is still a mystery,' he admitted.

'Can we decode it, then?' the warrior asked next of Brill.

'Perhaps,' the girl offered, unsure as she looked across the pages. 'Eventually, I would say, yes.'

'Eventually,' Darach repeated. 'Does that mean before or after Adefina arrives?'

When Brill merely shrugged in reply, Juno spoke. 'Very well, Brill, you have skill with codes. Sit with Benjamin; see what you can come up with. Darach, Varney, we need to plan.'

In silent agreement the smaller groups divided to pursue their tasks.

'Now,' Brill said as she settled on a stump, 'let's see what else the book might surrender to us.'

'What skill do you have in codes?' Benjamin enquired as they pored closely over the volume of mysterious script.

'In my daylight life I was employed by Queen Elizabeth,' Brill said casually. 'The work had use of coded messages.'

'You were a spy.'

'The youngest in the service of the crown. Who thinks of a young girl as an intelligencer? But making codes and breaking codes are different skills and, I'm sorry, but this book has me befuddled.'

'But there are clues to help us,' Benjamin said. He offered a random page. 'Look here. Each page is divided in two with text to the left lining up to a shorter line of symbols on the right. Do you see? Are these instructions and ingredients maybe?'

Brill was intrigued but dubious. 'They could be. But they could just as easily be incantations and days of the week, or months of the year. How can we tell?'

'This might help,' Benjamin said, pointing to a distinct line of symbols. 'Each right-hand block contains the same group over and over, a pair of words repeating on each page.' He drew a finger over a line of symbols: ◈❖◊❖T◊ and ◊◈. 'All but one of these symbols appear on the cover too.' He swept quickly back to the title page and pointed out common symbols among the fourteen there: ◈❖◊❖ and ◊.

'Could it be as simple as one symbol per letter?' Brill mused. 'What do you think?'

Benjamin shook his head. 'There are twenty-three symbols used in the book, but there are twenty-six letters in the alphabet.'

'You counted the symbols already?' Brill said, impressed and bewildered in equal measure.

Benjamin paused under Brill's gaze, gripped by his own confusion. 'No,' he said absently, his mind working to reason how and when he came to the knowledge. He had not tallied the symbols employed in the grimoire, yet when prompted, had immediately known, and certain sure, that the total number of individual symbols was twenty-three. Neither had he counted the grimoire's pages but now, in pondering, he knew the volume contained fully sixty-eight pages. Benjamin blinked for his uncanny store of learning.

'How bizarre,' Brill said with raised brows, 'a book

of magic that does not need to be read to be known. I hope it gives up more to you just as easily.'

Bemused still, Benjamin turned his attention back to that strange circle of shapes introducing the witch's book:

Here, surely, was the key to the mystery. But while he now viewed symbols with ready familiarity for the letters making up his everyday alphabet, their new language defied his efforts towards understanding. Unconsciously, and despite his revulsion for the feel of the grimoire, Benjamin placed a finger upon the coded circuit and traced it fully around it as he considered the vile book.

Fourteen symbols sat within the rings. Was there something in that, some diabolic meaning to the number itself? He peered hard at the strange etchings and followed again their shapes and sequence with a brushing finger. Fourteen? Why a number so seemingly random?

Why random? The voice, an unrecognised trespasser in the dark recesses of his mind, rose to meet his questions.

What?

The number. It's not so random, is it? Why, the answer is at your fingertips even now, young vampire, young apprentice. Look.

The voice drifted like smoke, and Benjamin was afraid even as he was lulled by it.

Turn over those fingers, young novice. How can you fail to see? Fourteen is the perfect number: perfect for magic, perfect for symbols and numbers. The perfect key to everything.

What?

'Benjamin.'

'What?' he asked, startled by the one voice, and by another. 'What?'

He came with a gasp from the deep reverie he had been drawn into, pulled back by Brill's voice. Yet still he looked down with deep attention, but not on the grimoire's pages. Now he peered on the single hand he could not recall turning up at the behest of the voice in his head. His eyes travelled a landscape of lines and creases in his palm, across the joints to the pads of fingers: two at each thumb and three at each digit. Fourteen there were in all.

'What is it, Benjamin?' Brill prompted softly.

Benjamin flexed his fist as though to seize the truth. 'Nothing,' he said. The grimoire was not ready to give up all its secrets and Benjamin was suddenly glad of that.

Further study was interrupted by Juno's return.

'Have you uncovered anything more?' she asked.

'A little,' Benjamin offered, 'but not enough to free any magic yet. I need time as well as moonlight.'

'We have lots of one and none of the other,' Juno sighed.

'One thing *I* know,' Brill said. 'Benjamin has some strange link to the book since he opened it. Whatever happens, he must not be separated from the grimoire. The answer lies somewhere between the two; I'm sure of it.'

Juno looked on Benjamin in search of some meaning, but he could only shrug in return. 'Very well,' she said. 'We move on and we move quickly.'

21

The vampires sank into the black embrace of the forest.

Though the streaming moon sought them, it could not find the band of friends as they moved ever more cautiously from shadow to shadow. Darach and Brill, watching for ambush at every step, led the way, avoiding misty hollows and obvious paths in favour of overgrown tracks. Protection to the rear was offered by Varney, who kept soft prayers on his lips and a hand to his swords. Between, Juno walked at Benjamin's side in silence, reluctant to interrupt his search, page after page, for the secrets of the grimoire. More than once he stopped, held abruptly by some momentary inspiration and she listened to his muttered reasoning until, and with a disgruntled 'that can't be it', he started forward again.

A cloud drifted to snag on the moon and Benjamin cursed quietly as witch symbols faded for want of fuel.

'Anything more?' Juno dared now to ask.

'Nothing,' he grumbled, 'less than before, even.' He slammed the book's foul covers. 'Pointless.'

'Perhaps you should let it be, just for a time.'

'But I want to be useful,' he admitted awkwardly. 'I wasn't much good in the fight back there.'

'Ah,' she understood. 'The new vampire wants to run before he can crawl.'

'You know I can run,' he shot back.

'You know my meaning,' she said. 'Besides, who was it that found the grimoire's moonlight secret? You're not so useless. Rest your burning brain for a while. Find more secrets when the moon returns.'

Her gesture to the cloudy crescent drew Benjamin's attention from symbols to the beauty of the night world. She watched his mood lighten at the sight and found, in addition to her amusement for his wide-eyed tripping, an unexpected pleasure in seeing him smile again.

'Is it always like this?' he asked, looking up to diamond sparks of moon-glow and down on gleaming night plants.

'It is. Landscapes change and seasons turn, but wherever you go in the world, night is the same.'

'Wherever you go,' Benjamin repeated as a vital question occurred to him for the first time. 'Where *are* we going?'

'That depends on the traveller,' she said. 'For the longest time, we've held to our own dreams of freedom.

Varney longs to see Jerusalem. Brill wants wild parties in Paris. Darach speaks endlessly of the New World. "Lots of adventure, but no witches," he says.'

'And you?' Benjamin pressed. 'Let me guess, Rome.'

'No,' she said a little too quickly. 'But we must cross deep water if we hope to shake Adefina.'

'Across the sea?' Benjamin gasped at the prospect of seeing the ocean, that vast expanse he could only ever envision stretching beyond the Blackwater.

She nodded sombrely. 'When we couldn't find a way to destroy the grimoire, it was agreed our only choice was to let the sea have it. I don't believe a witch's magic is strong enough to touch the bottom of the ocean. But, if I'm wrong...' She shrugged rather than give voice to a terrible possibility. 'Either way, we'll board the first available ship when we reach London.'

London! Benjamin could not even give voice to his amazement. They were bound for London!

Juno caught his look of wonder. 'Have you never been to the city?'

'Never,' he was at last able to say. 'What's it like?'

'Oh, I haven't been there for many years. It was a swamp when last I visited. I hope the natives have improved their manners since then.'

Benjamin was on the cusp of asking more when Varney was abruptly with them, slipping from the gloom with a finger at his lips for urgent silence. The same finger moved to send them peering between trees to a rise overlooking the forest.

On the distant hill, and betrayed by the sinking moon, two dark riders paused and surveyed the land.

'More of Adefina's hunters?' Juno whispered as the vampires sought concealment shadow.

'Mortal men,' Varney judged in staring hard towards the twin sentinels.

Benjamin peeked between leaves to the far hilltop. With eyes that saw more than darkness could now keep from him, he studied the ominous horsemen. Across the distance, the night surrendered details to vampire vision of saddles he had placed on those horses, and broad hats and capes he had looked on before. He searched further by the weakest rays of light to confirm his suspicions and spied sword handles and pistol grips.

'Hopkins and Stearne,' he told the others.

Juno cursed under her breath. 'Does that mean Adefina is close?'

'It would be safest to believe that,' Varney suggested.

'What are you all looking at?'

The female voice behind was unexpected and close, and the vampires spun in fright to present weapons to it, startling Brill where she had arrived unobserved. Looking warily on sharpened swords, she cast a thumb behind to the east.

'We are out of time,' she reported. 'Dawn approaches.'

'How long?' Juno asked.

'No more than an hour. Darach is scouting a place nearby.'

'Very good. Let's leave the witchfinders to blunder about in the dark.'

Moving after Brill to step from the track and push through undergrowth, they arrived at a place where the woodland surrendered to cultivated fields rolling to a curious spectacle.

Amid the farmland, on a low rise where a church stretched to touch the sinking moon, a mass of people walked in procession by the light of flaming torches. Slowly they moved to encircle the building before raising and lowering their lights in ritualistic fashion. All the while chanting words the travellers could not hear from their concealed place.

As the vampires continued their watch, Darach slipped across the fields to rejoin them. Keeping to the shadows, he zigzagged quickly to the cover of the trees.

'We have our beds for the day,' he announced, gesturing to the activity over his shoulder, 'just as soon as they depart. There is a roomy crypt to the left of the church.'

'Well done,' Juno said as she scanned the land.

'What is going on over there?' Brill asked, eyeing the torch-lit crowd.

Darach shook his head. 'I know not. They arrived during my scouting of the churchyard.'

'They are *clipping*,' Benjamin said, pleased to offer knowledge the others did not have. 'I've seen the folk in Ravenhill do the same. It's a ceremony to protect the church from evil forces.'

Juno grinned. 'In that case, they won't be expecting us.'

'Let us pray the Christians finish soon,' Varney said with a glance to the brightening horizon.

They moved forward in silence, stealing quickly over the churchyard's boundary wall like wisps to disappear among the headstones. Even as they advanced, the mortals about the church ended their ceremony and began to make for home, away from approaching vampires.

Benjamin crept from headstone to headstone, staying low and leaving the cover of each only when he was assured that no one in the mortal procession was looking in his direction. Finally, he approached the last grave plots flanking a stone structure, the tomb Darach had found. Moonlight played against its stout metal door and brought into sharp relief the image of a skull and crossbones etched there. Benjamin's trace mortality sent a shiver to his skin as he eased past a headstone, and in his moment of distraction, he almost tripped over an old man sitting there.

They met in an instant of shared astonishment across a lighted taper the man held to his pipe. Its glow caught the trembling lips of one and the glimmering eyes of the other and showed pointed teeth when Benjamin opened his mouth to plead for silence. Recoiling against the headstone he had chosen for a pillow, the old man tensed and prepared to scream.

Juno rose up. Seemingly from nowhere, she appeared and pressed her face close to the mortal man's, setting her fiercest gaze to transfix him, stilling his cry before it could issue forth.

'Sleep,' she commanded sternly. 'Sleep and dream.'

The insistent words wrought a strange and instant transformation to the old man's features. Benjamin watched mortal fear and physical tension ebb away to quiet calm, and quickly after came a fluttering of eyelids as the man surrendered to deep sleep. The unlit pipe fell from slack lips and, as the old man's hand relaxed, Juno nimbly plucked the burning taper from his fingers and snuffed it out.

'A fairly easy trick,' she informed Benjamin with a wink. 'I'll teach you later. Let's go.'

They hastened to catch up with the others where they gathered about the crypt's door.

Benjamin watched them huddle together and strained to see through the darkest dark, thinking to see one picking the lock. But as he peered on, the shadows shifted to trick his vision. Where an instant ago he thought he detected Varney, Brill and Darach against the black of the door, he found only Brill and Varney. He cast about in search of the warrior boy but found no trace. And now, when he looked again, he discovered that Brill likewise had disappeared. Varney stood alone in the shadow of the crypt and faced him with a smile.

'Fear not, Benjamin,' the monk assured, 'it's not difficult.'

Benjamin opened his mouth to ask, only to be stilled in watching Varney retreat into enveloping darkness, allowing himself to be swallowed by it, becoming one with the shadow until only twin pinpricks of light remained. A moment later they too vanished.

'Go,' Juno ordered as she scanned the churchyard.

'Go?' Benjamin asked, exasperated. 'How do I "go"?'

'Like the others, between the door and the frame.'

'But...' The word betrayed the mortal doubt still so strong within. Benjamin wrestled with indecision as he looked on the iron barrier, unable to shake its hold despite all he had seen and learned. It forced a daytime understanding of the world on him yet, but so loudly it covered Juno's approach until the moment her lips were at his ear.

'You are a vampire,' was her dreamlike whisper, and its power was such to drown the last of mortal doubt forever.

Supernatural instinct flooded into the space left by the receding tide of life and he opened himself to it, accepting its flow. Willing himself forward, he faced the challenge she had set, trusting her and the abilities she had gifted. The way was wide and clear and Benjamin plunged through and down.

Down to join the dead.

22

Adefina plucked at her skirts and stepped nimbly through the clearing.

The werewolf had been fierce and she did not care to get blood on her shoes.

The flames of the campfire leapt high to illuminate the path she followed in searching through the devastation.

'Smuggler,' she guessed dismissively in stepping around a sodden mass of clothing. 'Soldier,' she deduced of another shredded pile, this time with the first measure of frustration. Hoping for recognisable victims, she angled towards the wagon still in its place, the dead horses still in their bridles. At the tailgate, she looked on the wreckage of crates and read a tale of violent escape in the splinters.

'This is becoming ridiculous,' she said without turning, and her words drew Ilemauzar simpering into the firelight. And then she did turn, to fix her slave with a piercing gaze as she howled her poisonous judgement. 'Unacceptable!'

The demon wilted and clicked her teeth to a weak, defensive smile.

'Well?' the witch demanded, unimpressed. 'I'm waiting.'

Ilemauzar's reaction was unthinking. She offered a reckless motion instead of good news; she shrugged.

With a scream, Adefina lashed out. Her clawed hand snatched the air and closed fiercely.

'Exprimo.'

Ilemauzar gagged as the magic closed her throat. Instinctively she reached to relieve the pressure, only to feel it increase in time to Adefina's twisting fingers. She sought appeasing words but the violent constriction prevented all but the weakest croak from reaching her lips. Bulging eyes pleaded for release and grew wider as the answer to her pleas became a dragging progress towards the fire.

'No book and no brats,' Adefina taunted, 'just smiles and shrugs.' With a sharp thrust she sent the demon closer to burning. She saw tears in rolling eyes and they pleased her, and she pushed a little more.

A lumbering movement into the clearing cut through Adefina's fatal rage and she looked to the limping approach of her werewolf. The magic held a moment longer, until Adefina saw in the creature's wounded limb the possibility of news, and she ended her spell with a flick. As Ilemauzar collapsed gasping to the earth, she stooped low to offer her demon a harsh whisper. 'Serve me better or I will return you to the flames where I found you.'

The hound shrank low before its mistress, and lower, as she drew near. It whined softly to the hand she offered, accepting warily her gentlest touch.

Adefina felt the truth beneath her fingers.

'You found them,' she said dreamily, 'all running and running, so frightened. But they were a match for you and have my book still.'

Adefina's fingers began to close and the werewolf hung its head with a whimper.

Rok's noisy arrival interrupted all. Returned from the hunt, he shoved bodily through the undergrowth and dragged a helpless form with him. Weakened by injury, Captain Hazzard winced against the pain in slashed legs and cried aloud when the Viking dumped him against a wagon wheel at Adefina's feet.

'A survivor,' Rok offered with a bow. 'I found him crawling away.'

'Well, this is something,' Adefina said with a pointed stare for the others. 'Who are you?'

Breathing hard in his anguish, the prisoner offered nothing in reply but a defiant glare.

'Speak,' Rok barked. He launched a kick at the prisoner.

With a hand held sharply against further punishment, Adefina knelt by the captive to offer her best attempt at a kindly smile.

'Does it hurt?' she whispered. 'Are you in too much pain to speak with me? Would it help if I cut your legs off?'

'No,' Hazzard wheezed, 'but you might cut your own throat and give me peace.'

Ilemauzar gasped at the insult and a dagger whistled free.

Adefina merely smiled the more. 'My servant likes to cut, don't you, Ilemauzar? But we have no need of that.' Her drifting touch came tenderly to Hazzard's face. 'I can spare you all pain. Just tell me of runaways; whisper to me of sneaky plans.' Fingers caressed the prisoner's ear for her words, and up to stroke full black hair. Her grip closed to a clamping of nails.

Magic came as lightning, flaring beneath her fingers. Hazzard bucked against the fiery anguish she brought and howled his agony to the sky. The witch's hound darted back at the sound, while Rok's gaze flared in relishing the torture. Ilemauzar held her dagger as a guard against dangerous magic. Through the crackle and smoke of conjuring, Adefina held fast until knowing came to her in a blast.

She released, ending the sorcery with a pained cry, and fell back to clutch her hand and to stare at the palm in confusion and fury.

'What boy?' she demanded. 'What boy?'

The question reached Hazzard's heart through the waves of torment. 'Benjamin,' he whispered absently.

Adefina found the rest in the smoke rising from her hand.

'Benjamin Blake.'

She absorbed the name, familiar to her tongue, and the remembering of it burned behind her eyes. She looked once again between cage bars to a face she had touched.

You will sleep with the dead, Benjamin Blake.

She lunged for Hazzard, cupping his face violently to bring him back from the edge of unconsciousness.

'Tell me of Benjamin Blake. You know him. Tell me!'

Hazzard let slip a weak but sneering smile.

'You learned his name with a touch,' he breathed in her grip, 'I am impressed. But I learned something too. You are afraid.'

Releasing an enraged shriek, she finished him with a cracking twist of neck bones.

The slaves watched nervously as their mistress walked her anger to the edge of the clearing, there to brood over her gained knowledge and watch the day's first light pursue the sinking moon. At Rok's nervous and silent urging, Ilemauzar slipped close to her.

'Who *is* Benjamin Blake, my lady?'

Adefina uttered a dread certainty. 'The boy who opened my book,' she said, looking for him through the trees, out there somewhere, between the dusk and the dawn.

23

Moonlight in his mind.

In a quiet corner of the tomb, behind closed eyes, Benjamin saw the symbols again.

By a memory of lunar gleam, he pored over the shapes, tracing them once more. With mental agility, he plucked each one for meditative consideration before setting it back in place among lines of endless swirling. Over and over he sought understanding in the forms and their mysterious patterns, probing tirelessly the lettered ranks that closed as a cage around him but kept hidden the doorway to magic.

He looked again and worked to see with different eyes. What did Adefina perceive when she looked on the symbols, he wondered. Could she even see the pattern in her mind this way? Perhaps, but who could know the mind of a witch? No, in the same instant he discounted the idea. She was a mortal seeking power with a mortal mind and was limited by that. Why else the chase to regain her book?

It's not her book. You opened it. You own its magic now.

He sagged under the weight of fresh mysteries and opened his eyes to coffins and cobwebs. Three, no, four hours at least had passed since entering the crypt, and he was no closer to knowledge. His fingers tapped an impatient rhythm as he sought the vampires in their places.

Across the musty room he spied Brill and Darach, seated either side of a casket. As before, the girl used the wooden surface as a gaming table for her cards while the boy reclined in some approximation of sleep. Likewise Varney, in his place, appeared to slumber. He had settled to kneeling before a wall of memorial stones, with his eyes closed in an aspect of prayer, though Benjamin noted how the boy's hands did not stray from the ornate swords at his waistband.

How they fascinated Benjamin, those strange weapons. He let his vision rove over their matching snow-white handles to marvel at the intricate dragon carvings whose mouths opened to needle-sharp fangs, as scaled bodies curled beneath flowing manes from the sheathed blades. These mythical beasts, ever awake and watching over their master, peered at Benjamin through the gloom, filling him with curiosity. Where had such fine and beautiful weapons as these come from, he wondered.

Hypnotised by the pale serpents, he felt himself drawn from his place by an eagerness to examine them more closely. Hardly aware of his movements, he glided slowly and quietly across the stone floor to the slumbering Varney and within touching distance of the swords. He gazed directly into the jewelled eyes of the serpents, into the hearts of those tiny precious stones that gave them a living sparkle. Lost in their gleaming beauty, his hand reached out unconsciously to touch.

Varney's response was dizzyingly swift and was a blending of actions as he moved. Surging up from sleep, he rose swiftly to one knee while his hand snapped to the handle of the shorter sword. He drew in a flash to create a whispering arc of silver that ended with a sharpened blade touching Benjamin's neck.

Brill sniggered. 'Never creep up on a sleeping vampire.' She played her Ace of Swords.

The determined look that flared in Varney's features softened to a smile, and Benjamin was reassured he was not about to lose his head.

'Nice try, little brother,' the monk said, 'but you still move like a bull calf.' He brought his weapon away from the boy's pale neck to raise it between them. 'Here,' he offered, 'hold it.'

Benjamin gladly accepted, slipping fingers about the dragon-grip and testing the sword's heft. It weighed no more than a feather in his hand and cut through the air with incredible ease. 'It's beautiful,' he said, perceiving for the first time a fine system of patterns swimming across the surface of the blade, like smoke on water. 'Where did you get them?'

Varney drew the larger of his swords and found memory in the reflecting metal. 'These came to me when I was a missionary in the Orient. They were the gift of a mighty king who summoned me to explain my presence in his land. His Majesty Nobunaga declared me fierce in faith. But he said even a warrior of God should have weapons. Thus, the mighty katana...' He swept his sword in the air to chime on Benjamin's, 'and little brother, wakizashi, forged together as protection against evil in front and behind. I confess, Nobunaga was right; they have served me well.'

'Could you defeat Adefina with these?' Benjamin asked.

'Not Adefina,' Varney admitted. 'Besides, I doubt she would get close enough for me to try. But I would strike down those creatures who reject goodness to serve her.' He jabbed his weapon at imagined enemies.

'Rok and Ilemauzar,' Benjamin recalled.

Varney nodded. 'Ilemauzar,' he repeated the name darkly. 'Rok is a lumbering fool. I could defeat him with a broken stick while wearing a blindfold; may the Lord forgive my lack of humility. But Ilemauzar, that demon, she will be a worthy prize for my blade, and her removal from this world an act worthy of Heaven.'

Benjamin held the wakizashi to Varney. 'Will you teach me?' he asked, aware that he alone did not possess a weapon against the dreaded forms of Ilemauzar, Rok and Adefina Corvus.

Removing the weapon gently from Benjamin's grasp, Varney considered the request over the sword's edge. 'Perhaps,' he said finally, 'in time. When you have mastered those skills you possess naturally as a vampire, we might investigate the way of the warrior.' He snapped the wakizashi into its scabbard.

'I'll teach you.'

Juno's voice came hollow from the deep dark and Benjamin found her by a twinkling of eyes in the stairwell. She sat, engaged in dreamy consideration of a shaft of daylight falling on an upper step. As he stepped to take a place facing her, Benjamin felt a soft prickle of heat on his cheeks and brow.

'Be careful,' she said, 'not too close. Remember, you're new to this.'

Challenged by her warning, Benjamin eased a hand forward until it touched the surface of the step. The stone was cool to his palm but the exposed skin felt an increase in heat. Closer, and the sensation increased uncomfortably, forcing a short retreat. Undaunted, he extended his reach again and to the same stinging discomfort as before. Allowing his hand to linger, he watched wisps of smoke coil upwards to join the dancing daylight. With a hiss, he snatched back and Juno reached to take his hand protectively in her own.

Brill scoffed nearby. 'You goose.'

Benjamin and Juno smiled together.

'How does it feel?' she asked, tending the wound.

'Better now.'

'That was from a single sunbeam. Imagine yourself caught outside.'

Benjamin shuddered at the thought. 'Have you ever seen such a thing?'

'Thankfully, no. It was Adefina's constant threat, but we never gave her a reason to carry it out.'

'Until now,' he said. He felt her grip tighten against dark fears. 'Do you miss the light?'

Juno pondered. 'I miss things I used to do in the light. I had a balcony in Rome, and I would sit like this and enjoy the sunrise with the taste of fresh fruit until it was time for my lessons. I didn't enjoy them so much, except riding lessons; I loved those. In the full heat of the day I would saddle my favourite white Labros, and race my father to the hills. We would take shade there to let the horses rest, and he would test me to point out the senate and Caesar's palace and the forum. He would remind me every time how I was a citizen of the greatest city in the world, gleaming below in the sun. I could have stayed there all day, every day. But the cool afternoon was perfect for sword practice and dreams of following his army away.'

'Why did you want to go away?'

She ignored him wilfully. 'Where do you want to go?

'I didn't *want* to go, remember? Besides, between magic books and falling on my face, I've had no time to think about my destination. I suppose I'll find out when I get there.'

'We could find out together.' She eased back to concealing shadow but didn't let go.

'If I stop falling on my face and learn to be a proper vampire.'

'We have forever for that,' she said, and their laughter blended in the stairwell.

Watching in her seat and idly turning her colourful deck, Brill spied Darach's sidelong observation of the laughing pair and she flicked a card to tease him.

The Lovers.

He covered it with an angry slap. 'You're not funny, Brill.'

24

Something akin to sleep eventually overtook Benjamin. As the daylight hours wore on towards a new dusk, and the vampires reclined in their version of slumber, he slipped unawares into a state of rest where dreamed memories flickered uninvited through his mind.

Here again, Macbeth's witches worked their stage magic over a bubbling cauldron. Here once more, the witchfinder Hopkins, conjuring hellfire and smoke from the fireplace at the Straw Hall; smoke that broiled and pulsated to erupt in a pistol blast illuminating Benjamin's death.

He jerked awake, though whether by need to flee the nightmare or to some outside disturbance, he could not tell. Quickly recognising the cold walls of the tomb, he sought his companions in those places where they had made their rest only to find each spot vacant. Sounds of some distant clamour beyond the tomb door reached his ears, and he turned to find the others gathered in the stairwell. Together they listened intently to the noises without.

'What's the matter?' Benjamin whispered.

'The villagers have returned,' Darach said, 'and they are much vexed.'

Moving quickly to join the vampires, Benjamin listened carefully to the outside disturbance, immediately detecting many voices making up the one of an angry mob.

'It sounds like they're heading for the church,' Juno said, tipping her ear closer to the door.

'Do we wait?' Brill asked.

'What if they remain through the night as before?' Varney warned.

'All right, we go,' Darach said and looked for agreement among his friends. 'Use the tomb as cover as we leave.'

Juno laid a hand to Benjamin's shoulder. 'Stay close to me,' she said.

Darach led the way, merging as before with the shadows between door and frame. Brill quickly followed with Varney close behind. A moment later, Juno moved after.

All too aware that he was suddenly alone in the dank burial chamber with the mouldy dead, Benjamin did not hesitate. He jumped to follow.

Passing through the inky black, he emerged into the night-time world with ease and crouched low where the others had taken cover behind headstones. From this vantage point they watched the unfolding scene at the church.

The villagers swarmed noisily about the door of the building and pounded on the barrier for response. Faces animated to anger were revealed by blazing torchlight as voices raised in urgent calls for their priest, justice and revenge. Summoned at last by the great protest, the clergyman appeared before his people, alarmed by their cries and much confused by their unified action.

'What means this riot?' the vampires heard the holy man demand when he had hushed the clamour.

'The witch!' the crowd wailed. 'We have the witch at last!'

At this, the multitude parted to reveal a terrified young woman held between strong villagers, her arms secured against evil trickery.

'Bess Hardy,' the priest said, and he nodded sagely. 'I might have known.'

A round woman of middle years stepped forward to speak for the group. 'We seized her in the preparation of spells,' she proclaimed, and the crowd cheered for more. Spurred on by the cries, the woman plucked from her garments a pouch which she tore open to reveal flowers and herbs. 'Elements of a wicked potion,' she charged. She flung the pouch and contents dramatically to the ground at the priest's feet. 'Ingredients to make more of our animals sick, I'll wager.'

'Or our children,' came another shrill voice in the crowd, and the villagers cried louder.

'No! No!' the girl protested. 'Those herbs are to help my father. You know he is ill. My mother taught me long ago what herbs are best to ease a fever.'

'A witch teaching a witch!' the accusing woman shot back, and the crowd agreed riotously. 'Where is old Tom Oliver? Let him be heard.'

The one named Tom Oliver was hustled quickly to the front of the gathering and Benjamin recognised at once the elderly figure he had stumbled across among the headstones. The man came to stand before the priest, where he shuffled uncomfortably under the eyes of the crowd.

'Well?' the priest said. 'What have you witnessed?'

Encouraged by a sharp jab to his arm from the woman, Tom Oliver cleared his throat to address the gathering.

'Last night,' he began awkwardly, 'in this very place, I was met by a demon child summoned from the grave.' The crowd hissed fearfully at this information and swept torches in a dread search for the demon's reappearance.

'That was me,' Benjamin said, his voice chilled to a whisper.

'A witch-summoned demon!' the round woman added hysterically. 'While we prayed to protect our church, a witch was at work. And who was the only one missing from our ceremony last night? Bess Hardy!'

'I was nursing my father!' Bess tried to explain, but her voice was swallowed up by the villagers as they shrieked for final judgement from the clergyman.

The priest considered deeply the words just heard, cupping his chin profoundly with a hand while he judged both Bess and the mood of the crowd. At last, he nodded, his conclusion reached. 'Bring her along.'

The villagers issued cries of tumultuous joy and raced to follow the priest the way he led. From the church they progressed, torches swarming towards a towering oak at the farthest end of the churchyard. Jostled and pulled along, Bess Hardy screamed for release, crying innocence, but her protests were lost in the storm of bellowing.

'Now is the time,' Darach said. He moved away and followed a path amid the shadows, motioning for the rest to come quickly.

'But it was me the old man saw,' Benjamin said again, turning from vampire to vampire. 'The girl didn't summon anyone from the grave.'

Looking to Varney, he saw in his features a deep brooding, the first stirrings of a plan spied also by the others.

'What are you about, Varney?' Juno asked, made wary by a look she knew well.

Ignoring her, Varney addressed Benjamin. 'Your purse of money, Benjamin' he said, 'give it to me.'

Benjamin obeyed immediately, passing the witch-finder's coin and its partners from his tunic.

'It's not sensible to meddle in mortal affairs,' Brill cautioned nervously as she watched.

'Why?' Varney challenged. 'Because it might go worse for the girl?' In the blink of an eye, he was gone from them.

Searching urgently about for the vanished monk, the vampires at last saw him where he reappeared from the shadow of the church. He moved forward cautiously from cover to reach the spot where Bess Hardy's pouch of herbs still lay discarded on the path. He bent for a moment's examination, what he found causing him to stiffen and stand upright, anger and burning determination evident in his demeanour. Without a word, he marched purposefully towards the great crowd gathered at the oak tree.

'Oh no,' Brill breathed in dread.

Darach reappeared and looked in confusion at his friends. 'What is going on?' he asked impatiently before catching sight of the departing monk. 'What in the world is he doing?'

Juno sighed wearily. 'Varney is going among the mortals.'

25

They raced after Varney.

At the path, and just as the monk had, the vampires paused to allow for Brill's examination of the discarded pouch.

'Common herbs,' she explained with a sniff of petals crushed between fingers, 'combined as a remedy for minor ailments, nothing more.'

'No witch has need of flowers and weeds,' Juno added.

Darach interrupted the examination. 'If we are to stop Brother Varney,' he pointed out, 'we must act at once.' He gestured to the striding monk who had almost reached the edge of the chanting crowd. From its centre, the vampires saw the sudden ascent of a rope thrown over a branch in the oak tree. The time for a hanging had come.

'What do we do?' Brill gasped for Varney's safety.

'We watch,' the Roman answered quietly. She stared as the rope drew tight to the testing of a volunteer hangman. 'If Varney needs us, we move in.'

'I count twenty-five men in the crowd,' Darach said with a casual wave. 'He won't need us.'

The vampires settled into the shadows to watch.

Drawing near the jostling villagers, Varney also made use of shadow. At the first turned backs, he pulled his hood to shield his features and began to elbow his way through. He emerged on the edge of a circle formed about the terrified Bess Hardy and the priest who held the hangman's noose.

'Bind her,' the clergyman ordered dourly. He watched the girl cry out in pain as her captors worked with relish to secure her hands. When the task was completed, he stepped forward to offer the rope for her terrified consideration. 'Will you, young Bess, admit to being a witch and save your immortal soul from all the fires of damnation?'

'I am no witch,' the tearful girl protested, unable to pull her eyes from the terrible cord.

'If it be true, the good Lord will know it and have mercy on your soul,' the priest declared and swept the noose about her neck.

'What is this nonsense?' Varney barked.

A shocked silence washed over the crowd, and all turned with their priest to seek the cause of interruption.

'Who speaks there?' the clergyman demanded of the hooded figure.

'A humble travelling monk,' Varney replied, 'stumbling, it seems, upon murder.'

'No murder,' the priest corrected him firmly. 'We deal with witchcraft here.'

At this, the crowd took up its clamouring again, while a group of burly men moved closer to Varney. They studied him grimly as they flexed their fists.

'What evidence do you have for a charge of black magic against this frightened girl?' Varney demanded, ignoring the glares that burned into him.

The priest rounded angrily to face the hooded boy. 'We have all the evidence we need to deal with this matter, Brother Monk,' he snapped, 'and enough to ignore questions from a boy not of this village.'

The crowd cheered its loud assent and the men about Varney stepped dangerously close.

'The girl is innocent,' Varney declared, 'and you damn yourself by this action.'

The villagers issued a collective gasp for the words and the priest fumed at the blatant challenge to his authority. 'And you damn yourself by your defence of a sorceress. Remove the witch's defender!'

The men pressed forward and reached for the boy monk. The nearest, approaching Varney from behind, dropped a great hand on his shoulder. Varney responded at the first touch, thrusting a hand across his body to seize the invasive fingers. A cruel snapping of bones accompanied the twisting motion that loosened the villager's grip, and the man screeched in pain as Varney pulled him forward. Spinning on one foot, the monk's other kicked to propel his anguished attacker into a line of advancing menfolk, and the gang collapsed to a mass of cursing, twisted limbs.

A second group moved swiftly to take up the fight. Emerging from the ranks of women, the men raced towards Varney. The lead figure bore down with a blazing torch, raising high for a strike at the lone boy. Varney's response was so subtle as to be missed by all. With the slightest motion, he shifted a thumb to the outside of one fist and calmly watched the lumbering advance. At the last moment, just as the burning club reached his head, he ducked under the strike and thrust his thumb forward and up to the very centre of his opponent's chest. With a great wheeze of air forced from puffed lips, the attacker passed by and collapsed in agony.

Individual attack was now set aside in favour of a charge by assailants towards Varney. But he blocked, punched, sidestepped and kicked in a dazzling array of techniques, blasting each challenger aside. At last, encircled only by collapsed men, he whirled to stare down the priest.

'Release the girl,' Varney demanded, 'and I will spare you the same treatment.'

As monk and priest glared at each other, the stunned crowd directly behind Varney parted quietly to admit two more men, this pair more heavily armed for the fight than their neighbours had been. The hands of one brought up a gleaming dagger while the other aimed a musket. The soft clicking of the weapon timed perfectly with the victorious smile of the priest.

Varney read the signals oh so easily.

The gleaming katana flashed, its blade sweeping through the night air on a whisper. The monk cut down to a shower of sparks as metal struck metal and the barrel of the musket was cut cleanly in half. Its lead ball tumbled from the shorn remains and thumped harmlessly to the earth. The startled gunman was cast backwards by the monk's fist into the ranked villagers as Varney rounded on the second man. The singing katana arced to slap aside the opposing blade and passed on to meet the attacker's neck, there to rest coldly on unbroken skin.

The outmatched attacker faced Varney in speechless wonder. He stared into the monk's set features, frozen by the dangerous ability in one so young. Quickly and wisely, he dropped his weapon and offered hands of surrender.

'Release the girl,' Varney commanded again, his patience at an end. He swept his katana round to point menacingly at the priest.

'What monk goes so armed?' the priest demanded, though his voice cracked. 'What servant of God does such harm to others? I condemn you, monk. I condemn you.'

With a deafening battle cry, Varney swept his weapon behind and advanced on the priest. Villagers screamed as the man tumbled fearfully from the attack and fell at Bess Hardy's feet. Squealing, he threw up his hands as though to push Varney away even as the monk pressed on and struck out in rage. The blow severed the hangman's rope and swept on to cut the girl's restraints. As the priest took the opportunity to scurry towards his panicking congregation, Varney addressed the frightened girl.

'Leave this place at once,' he whispered amid the confusion. He pressed the coin purse into her hands. 'Take your father and go with God's blessing.'

Before the girl could form words of reply, Varney left her. He advanced boldly with sword and ferocious gaze on the retreating villagers, spurring them to shrieking flight. Injured men hobbled before him or were dragged to safety from further attack, all led by the panic-stricken priest, who ran faster than the rest. Varney passed unhindered through the sea of chaos to the shadow of the church where his companions waited, smiling and much impressed. His sword whistled back into its sheath and he offered his friends a satisfied nod.

'Shall we go, brothers and sisters?'

26

At the rising of the moon, Ilemauzar brought Adefina the items she required.

With Rok and the hound looking on, the demon served as assistant to the magic. First, she presented the bag discovered in the smuggler's wagon. Next, the necessary dagger was slipped into the witch's opened hand. Ilemauzar backed away, bowing low, though fear of what was to come loosened her lips as she retreated.

'Have a care, my lady.'

'Are you afraid?' Adefina asked.

'Only for you. You do not have your book for this.'

'I created the hellhound well enough without it, didn't I?'

'A thing of despicable beauty,' the demon cooed agreeably. 'But *this*.' She would not utter the spell's title. 'This is a dangerous spell.'

'This is an opportunity,' Adefina insisted, 'look around you. Besides, what else would you have me do? My book slips farther off with every sunset. We need more hunters.'

'We need but a scent to follow,' Ilemauzar declared. She sought support from the Viking with a jab.

'We came close already,' Rok offered. He gestured to the dead men of the clearing.

Ilemauzar nodded eagerly. 'We will not fail again. Perhaps one more night is all.'

'Perhaps, perhaps,' Adefina spat. 'The book has been opened! I felt it like it was cut from me. I cannot wait.'

Ignoring her servant's clicking teeth, Adefina prepared. With the slightest stroke, the bag was pierced and she began tracing with the powdery stream of flour that came.

Twice around the clearing she progressed, moving with precise steps until she stood finally within twin white circles holding bizarre symbols between. More than twice she checked for breaks in the magic lines, and more often again, she checked the twenty-three shapes as she consulted her fading memory for their accuracy.

For it is fading. Don't deny it.

There was no denying. Last night she had doubted the first inkling of loss, a sensation of ebbing behind her eyes. She was weary from her escape after all and the strain of pursuing wayward slaves. Rest would restore. But at the dawning of this day, waking alone with the dead of the clearing, her mind found no refuge from the truth. Her magic was slipping from her, passing off as mist in the morning sun, steadily draining like blood from a deep cut.

She was being bled by a vampire.

Adefina flung doubts aside with the bag and held the dagger forth on trembling fingers.

The slightest error, oh my, and what dread outcome will you face?

What choice did she have?

'Incipe,' the witch recited, and the first word passed from the circles to fall on the dead ears of soldiers her slaves had assembled.

The summoning began.

27

'Maybe it's a double bluff.'

Brill's whisper made Benjamin start in the quiet of hiding.

They had moved quickly after Varney's encounter at the little church, racing to create distance from the fuss that must surely spread from the villagers to others and, inevitably, to Adefina and her hunters. Despite their haste, the vampires kept to the cover of hedgerows and overgrown tracks where Juno led and Darach followed. Here now was their first pause since then. A sharp signal from Juno had sent them to crouching in the shadow of a tree, there to wait the Roman girl's return.

'What is?' Benjamin asked. He turned to Brill who peeked back from behind the vigilant Varney.

'The grimoire,' she explained. 'Maybe the code is in English, after all.'

'How could that be? Twenty-three letters, remember.'

'Exactly.' She shifted forward to offer her theory. 'A reader's first thought with twenty-three letters is, "Oh, it can't be in English," and we stop thinking about it. But what if it's part of some devilish trick? You just have to leave out X, Y and Z to do it. When you think, very few words begin with those letters.'

'Ah,' Benjamin countered, 'but how would the witch know to use lizards in a spell, or practise devilry, or make things explode?'

'I've seen Adefina do that,' Brill conceded on the last point. She sighed at the toppling of yet another theory and grumbled quietly.

'Who is to say what language the Devil uses in speaking to witches?' Varney said.

'In that case, I'm lost,' Brill said. 'Besides English, I have a little French, enough to know the language also uses twenty-six letters. Blasted book!'

'That's bad language,' Varney observed wryly.

'The witch's book is almost as annoying as that Bible you carry,' Brill muttered.

Varney adopted a look of mock indignation. 'Its truth lies ready for those with the eyes to see and the heart to accept,' he offered with gentle certainty.

Brill nudged Benjamin. 'Brother Varney is forever trying to convert me.' In a flash, she drew out one of her tarot cards.

The Fool.

'Oh, but we have *forever*,' the monk laughed, 'so who is the fool?'

They shared the joke, a chuckling trio to confound the gaze of a passing owl. Benjamin tracked the bird on its gliding way until it settled to a ghostly silhouette among the branches above.

'The moon is up,' he said. 'Why don't we use the time for another try at decoding?'

Brill sat close as he drew the grimoire from the satchel and angled its cover to the lunar wash.

'*By your magic all nations are led astray,*' Varney prayed as he looked with distaste on the text.

'Twenty-one signs,' Brill calculated quickly, 'is there something in that, perhaps? Something about numbers and not words at all.'

'Not twenty-one,' Benjamin corrected and pointed to repeating symbols within the circles, 'fourteen.'

The perfect number, perfect for magic: the key to everything.

Brill felt his shudder. 'What is it, Benjamin?'

Varney's hand plunged abruptly to draw his waki-zashi. 'Someone comes,' he warned.

Juno emerged noiselessly from the gloom, the grimoire's shimmer reflecting in her eyes.

'Solved?' she asked, but she read downcast faces quicker than text.

'Not even close,' Benjamin admitted.

'Then study later,' she instructed, 'we have another challenge.' She cast a thumb over her shoulder. 'The forest ends just ahead. Past that is a wide plain with no cover until we reach farming land beyond. Even with our great speed, we will be exposed under the moon for a time.'

Silver eyes exchanged nervous glances until Varney sheathed his weapon with a snap.

'Then let us begin,' he declared.

'Wise words, Brother Varney.'

It was Darach who spoke. Arriving from the receding track, he squatted with the others and probed the trees with a deep uncertainty.

'Hunters?' Juno asked.

The warrior struggled with his senses. 'I cannot be certain. But we should not tarry here.'

The friends slipped through undergrowth.

Very soon, the forest thinned to a treeline at the head a long slope descending to open countryside. A thickening moon betrayed its featureless landscape stretching far and wide, where even night animals did not wander for lack of cover. Hedgerows lining tilled fields past the borderland were of a distance to challenge even supernatural vision.

'Not good,' Brill said.

'Only if we slacken,' Darach said. 'Let's go.'

He led the way down and they let the slope take them to a final gathering at its base, there for a moment of reassuring glances. Juno added a wink for Benjamin.

'Don't fall,' she joked and disappeared.

Benjamin took but a moment. 'Remember you are a vampire,' he echoed.

And he ran.

The world was swept to a river of vision. Light streamed in ribbons towards encircling night and Benjamin plunged through the tunnel at its heart. So slight were his footfalls, it seemed the earth was passing away beneath him, or else he was falling over the surface of the spinning world. Tufts of growth brushing his feet served to assure he was grounded and not flying up towards the comet-filled heavens. Only the moon held, sitting back to watch, though its horns rippled like pale banners.

A shape rose ahead: an obstacle in silhouette to be avoided. Benjamin easily altered his stride, putting the object to his left and spying it as he flashed by. It was Darach, halted in his ready stance and with his sword drawn.

Benjamin dug his heels in. He slid upright across wet grass and stayed up even as he turned to look back to where one form became two. Varney had also stopped to join the warrior, his katana flashing, and Benjamin dashed to them.

'What do you see?' he asked, scanning the empty field.

'Nothing,' said Darach said, 'but I smell something.'

Benjamin tested the air. He grimaced against a sickly scent travelling on the air just as Brill appeared and wrinkled her nose.

'That's foul,' she said.

Darach grunted in agreement. 'I have smelled such an odour before.'

'The smell of the battlefield,' Juno said as she stepped to his shoulder, 'when dead men have spilled blood.'

'There!' Varney pointed.

From the inkiest space between trees, the riders came.

Benjamin counted ten horsemen progressing at a steady pace to the bottom of the slope, there to assemble in a single rank as the advance continued.

'They look like soldiers,' he said as moonlight reflected against breastplates and helmets.

'They ride like the damned,' Brill whispered.

Closer the troop approached, and in gaining on the vampires, they sent ahead a stench of corruption that grew more cloying with every measured hoof-step. Moon-glow flared now on new sources of metal as the troop drew swords to an unspoken command. And the same light fell for the first time on the faces of the riders, revealing slack and discoloured features with eyes as dead as those of their rotting horses.

'Cursed witch!' Darach spat.

The vampires lined out in the open and braced for battle against the army of the dead.

Juno swung to Benjamin.

'Go, head south like the wind,' she ordered. 'If we come through, I will find you.'

'You'll find me right here,' Benjamin replied with a boldness of heart he did not feel in his legs.

Juno made to argue further but a swift move by Darach cut her short. With a flick of his wrist, the boy cast towards Benjamin, sending a dagger to shine in his hand.

'Add that to speed and cunning,' he instructed.

The dead riders charged. Towards the little line they sped, their attack unyielding as vampires raised blades in reply. Broadsword, rapier, Roman sword and katana gleamed to the fight amid thundering hooves that shook the open ground.

Battle was joined in a clamour of steel. Horses shrieked and reared in the melee. Benjamin saw all as massed confusion, his companions plunging through a hail of strikes to meet blow with blow. Separated from the others, Brill tumbled and was set upon by a group of undead opponents, only to spring up nimbly once more, slashing and thrusting to claim the first victim with deft use of her silvered blade.

Varney swept his twin weapons on the air and drew soldiers from their saddles in pursuit. He adopted his stance quickly and commenced the fight against four enemy swords at once, spinning and cutting to claim two more opponents. Retreating fast, the monk sought Brill with his back and they partnered against closing enemies.

A shot! From an undead rider, a pistol erupted in fire and smoke. Darach was struck in the chest. Hurled backwards, the Celt was thrown to earth with shattering force. But no sooner had the vampire landed than he launched to his feet again. With a defiant vampire roar, he brought his weapon to bear on those descending upon him. Soldiers were blasted to the four winds by the swinging of his broadsword.

Juno charged to enemy thrusts and Benjamin gasped as she was struck once and twice, the swords cutting deeply into her body. Undaunted, she surged against the assaults and struck dead limbs with her short blade, then with its butt, and next her fist to destroy a snarling, discoloured face. Soldiers fell in rapid succession to her roaring ferocity.

Brill took a sword thrust directly to her stomach, the blade passing cleanly through to emerge at her back. She managed a smile in the moment and seized the opportunity to drive her rapier into the assailant's heart and finish him.

Slowly the battle turned. The vampires received blows but struck back doubly hard and with lethal cuts of silver each time. The ground at their feet filled with the corrupted dead.

Again, the foul smell of rot washed to Benjamin, and he pulled his face back from the intensity of it. But the very act made the stench worse and he realised with a chill that the source of the odour did not issue from those fallen before him. He turned in all directions, seeking the ambush that had been set.

Metallic flashes revealed two soldiers shambling forward from the cover of night, assassins held in reserve until the distraction of battle. Mottled hands brought sabres to bear as the undead closed on Benjamin.

He tested the weight of the dagger, suddenly so small but terribly heavy in his grip, and he prepared himself for the coming attack. Nightmare eyes in sagging features transfixed, and the first enemy sword strike arced towards him.

Mortal thought had no place in what followed.

Benjamin lowered his body and tightened his legs in a single motion. He primed for the sweeping of the first blade, tracking its arc towards him until contact seemed inevitable. He sprang upwards and over to clear the whispering sword. The world of attacking soldiers hung upside down for an instant and he watched their passing, trusting completely to his leap behind them. Astonished at his feat of dexterity, he laughed aloud as his feet touched down until a jabbing sword reminded him of his perilous situation.

Benjamin retreated with twin attackers in pursuit. He looked into dull, watery eyes regarding him above blackened lips that dribbled hungrily. What manner of vampires were these monstrosities? A sword cut towards him. He slapped it down inexpertly with his short blade. The violent clash sent shudders along his arm and he came dangerously close to dropping the weapon.

Add that to speed and cunning.

Varney's words echoed through another hacking assault and Benjamin listened from a place beyond rising fear. Speed he had in abundance but what of cunning? What did he know of tactics or swordplay?

The answer came with the next attack, launched by both soldiers together. Swords swept overhead on either side, and in instant of clarity, Benjamin saw his chance. At the midpoint of strikes, when the dreadful undead were fully committed to their assault, he plunged between, spinning as he went. His weaponed arm extended and slashed a wide circle through rotting garments. Coming to rest on one knee behind his attackers, Benjamin heard their swords chime against each other and sing away to silence.

The result of his actions became slowly evident. The confounded soldiers shuffled about to face him down, their weapons once again drawing up. But with the first step, one of the shambling corpses issued a confused and gurgling sound. A hand reached to find a great tear in the creature's side, precisely behind its armour, and touched there the seeping black wound drawn by Benjamin's blade. The stricken soldier issued an inhuman cry of alarm and collapsed, fully and finally dead.

Benjamin's sense of triumph was short-lived, for all at once he came under the hateful glare of the remaining soldier. Slavering lips peeled back to a sneer of fury and the creature drew its sword higher. Light glancing from the blade offered a measure of life to blackened eyes and a new attack began. The soldier lumbered forward, pressing the charge with a groan of aggression. Benjamin rose to meet the challenge and, with his vision filled with that grotesque face, he paused as the vampire in him perceived all.

Events played out in his mind a split second before

occurring in time and space. He read the soldier's immediate weakness in pushing his full weight into the attack and saw the arc of the blade in the motion of his shoulders. Benjamin saw too his own response, how he would meet the weapon with his for the briefest strike as he swung past the soldier's unprotected flank, and just how the dagger would follow in a rising circle to present its tip to an exposed back. Benjamin shifted on his toes in preparation.

All turned to a blur of speeding motion. Sparks flew where metal clashed. Benjamin whirled to travel behind flaring light. He pulled the dagger's hilt close to his hip and, from there, drove the silver blade hard up. The strike found the soldier's leathery back and drove through to an airless moan. With a shudder, the force that has sustained the soldier passed off and the witch's servant fell dead beside its comrade.

Still possessed of his supernatural faculties, Benjamin sensed a form rising from the shadows to his right and struck at once and without thinking. His blade was on target and was only prevented from cleaving Juno's neck by the speed of her own response. Through crossed blades, she peered in wonder at the ferocity gleaming in Benjamin's eyes.

'That is the one strike I could not have survived,' she said with a nod to his silver weapon. She cast off the attack and sheathed her sword with a smile.

'We won?' Benjamin asked, stunned to see the girl unhurt.

'We won,' she confirmed.

Benjamin looked across the field of conflict at the devastation wrought by the vampires. Bodies lay strewn all about the victorious warriors.

'I didn't think we had a chance,' he admitted. He sucked a harsh breath on watching Brill pull a long dagger from her stomach and cast it aside with a casual shrug and a sigh for her torn shirt.

'Our advantage was in their mortal weapons,' Juno said. 'There was not a trace of silver among them.'

'They still hurt, though,' Darach said. Through his garments, he plucked the musket ball that had struck so fiercely. After a cursory inspection, he dropped it to the earth where the hot projectile hissed on dewy grass.

'What were these... men?' Benjamin asked. He gazed in wonder on the corpses.

'Vampires,' Juno said, 'but not like us; not so well formed.'

'Adefina used the summoning spell,' Brill said. 'She keeps her power yet.'

'Read the signs around you,' Varney cautioned the girl. 'As Juno said, these creatures are not like us. They were not summoned with the same force, nor were they equipped with the necessary weapons to face us. There is desperation here, and more, a fading magic.'

'What did Adefina hope to gain through such madness?' Darach asked.

'Time,' Varney replied. 'She is trying to buy time in slowing us down for the one who follows these soldiers.' He closely scanned the trees. 'There is another scent on the air.'

Benjamin joined the others in urgently probing the night, but to no avail.

'What are you about?' Darach demanded of the monk.

'Adefina is close,' Varney said, 'but Ilemauzar is closer. I sense the demon. That means she senses me and we can use that.'

Juno eyed her friend dubiously. 'Use how?'

'I will steal back the time we need. I will create a false trail for Ilemauzar to follow and mislead the witch.'

'No!' Brill's horrified cry came of itself, unthinking to pierce the night.

'We are stronger together,' Juno said.

'This far we have been,' Varney agreed, 'but can we remain so long enough for Adefina to fail? This gives us a better chance.'

Benjamin stepped forward. 'You're forgetting the book. I can decode it. I *can*. We'll turn the tables on Adefina with it.'

Varney smiled. 'I believe you, Brother Benjamin, but we are back to the question of time. *When* can we hope to turn the tables?'

'You can't do this,' the exasperated Brill cried abruptly. 'Darach, tell him.'

The warrior returned from his own deep thoughts to face them all.

'The plan has merit.'

'What?' Brill was horrified. She searched Darach's face for madness. 'You can't be serious.' She wheeled and advanced on Varney. 'I won't let you do this. I won't.'

Juno caught her in an embrace so tight only her tears escaped.

'What is your plan?' Darach asked his holy friend.

Varney pointed the way.

'I continue south and lay my trail. You others go west or east for tonight. Don't tell me which. That way I have nothing to reveal if I fall into Adefina's hands. We meet in London tomorrow or the night after at the latest.'

'In the shadow of the city's tower,' Darach said. He offered his hand to his friend. 'You don't have to do this.'

Varney smiled as the appropriate passage came to mind.

'*Greater love hath no one than this, to lay down his life for his friends.* Though I pray it won't come to that.'

Brill's fury gave her strength enough to shed Juno's hold and she strode to face the monk. Her eyes were liquid fire as she sought words of her own.

'No greater love? No greater love?' She bristled with hands flexing as though in search of him but not daring to touch. 'You will come back; do you hear me? You will... you will...' Exasperated, she wheeled from him and paced away, muttering through her tears about boys and pig-headed idiots.

Benjamin and Varney watched her go, the one confounded by her outburst, the other enlightened by it.

'Can you decode the grimoire, truly?' Varney asked.

'Yes. I think it wants me to.'

'Then make good use of the time we gain. But be careful with dark magic, Benjamin Blake.'

'You be careful, too.'

Varney's smile vanished as he darted from Benjamin and sped south between his standing friends, with just a moment for an unseen touch of Brill's hand as he went.

28

est to chase the moon.

Between farmland and meadow they kept their new course, faster than ever to outpace the night, but soft past sleeping cottages. The vampires' glide was as the smoke rising from homestead chimneys, and let sleeping dogs lie.

At Juno's prompting, the friends turned south again after some hours, adding an extra layer to Varney's plan, and setting them on a parallel path to his towards London. Brill looked time and again as though to see the boy on their left, while the others spied a long pale strip rolling with the landscape on their right. Each recognised the London road and mirrored its course as the moon offered its smile from the nearing horizon.

And all the while ⬨𝍫⚿𝍫𝗧𝕌 and 𝕌⬨. The patterns played behind Benjamin's eyes even as he watched closely the guidance of Darach ahead, and for signs of alarm from Brill behind. ⬨𝍫⚿𝍫𝗧𝕌 he saw in the twisting of branches. 𝕌⬨ in constellations of the sky.

There was even a moment, when Juno looked to him, that he saw the shapes tumbling in her hair.

'⏃⏁⏃⌰ ⍜⍜⏁ ⏃⍜⍜ ⏁⍜⍜⏁⍜' she asked.

He must have jerked from her unnatural words, for she grew concerned and reached as though to steady him. But his reflexes were quicker and he snatched her hand on the air, and turned it over, unthinking, to look at the pads of her palm.

The fourteen pads. Permutations endless. Try one.

'What permutations?' Juno asked and he realised he must have spoken aloud. 'Benjamin, are you all right?'

He looked blankly at her, unable to offer any kind of answer. Something in the twisting confusion of his face prompted her to reach with a comforting hand, and he felt his own ball to a fist under her touch.

⏁⍜⌊⍜⌰⍜⏁⌊⍜

The symbols burst up, flaming in his unprepared mind. With a cry, he reeled from them, from Juno, from the burning. He heard her voice as he staggered and felt her protective grip tighten on his own.

⏃⌊⍜⍜⏁⍜

Thunder roared to deafening with the rising of the text. Benjamin's teeth clamped against a wash of agony as the symbols ripped his brain and took him to the brink of collapse. He felt a blow at his back, harsh enough to crush symbols. Through the storm he was dimly aware Juno had shoved him backwards against a tree.

'⸎⸎⸎ ⸎⸎ ⸎⸎,' she said, and forcefully again, 'look at me!'

The storm abated slowly, rolling off to distant lightning in her eyes.

'It's the book,' he tried to explain, shaking feverishly.

'Forget the book,' she ordered gently. She tightened her hold to keep his attention. 'Just see me.'

He did as she instructed, blinking against nightmare shapes to give himself over fully to her face. Framed within tresses undone in the struggle, her cheeks, pale and cool as the moon, angled to a gleam of tipped incisors in parted lips, and to eyes shining for his prolonged gaze.

'I see you,' he said.

'Can you stand if I let go?'

'Yes, but I don't want you to.'

'Be careful, Benjamin Blake. The last time we were this close, I bit you.'

'I don't think you will this time.' And he was right. Night offered a veil of shadows for the vampires' kiss.

'Oh.'

Brill was suddenly, awkwardly there. She moved through nervous turns in seeking to be somewhere, anywhere else, provoking amusement in her friends.

'We should get moving,' Benjamin said at last. 'Stay close.' With a squeeze for her hand, he slipped Juno's grip and pushed on.

'Is he a good kisser?'
'Brill, I can hear you.'
'Oh.'

29

A defina followed the scent of death to her fallen army.

With silent curses for the moon and stars, and every wayward vampire, she read the battle in the prone soldiers, wishing for time enough to summon them again, for punishment.

'No time,' she told herself bitterly.

And no spell. It's gone, isn't it? Another one that's fled from your mind back to the book.

She bit her lip forcefully against reply and cast up instead to the moon, measuring the portion of night left to her in its sleepy descent to treetops.

'No time,' she insisted as though to make the dead believe. Fingers moved unconsciously together and played on the skull ring as she pondered. 'What now?' she whispered, questioning the brats' next move while trying to predict her own response from a dwindling store of options. Unsettled by that, she looked east in hope of clarity. Somewhere out there, she knew, Rok probed expertly, seeking a trail, some clue to betray a desperate change of plan by the vampires, a flight of panic after the battle with the undead. Perhaps a changed course, from London towards a harbour, any harbour. Panic would be a good sign.

Better yet would be the return of Ilemauzar from the dark horizon in the south. She might bring positive news or the grimoire itself, torn from the hands of a slain pretender to magic.

Too much to hope for.

This time she reacted and brought up a vile curse to hurl at the chuckling inner voice. But the oath died suddenly on her lips, lost to the sound of a pistol's dry click and the cold hardness of metal against the back of her head.

'Stand fast, witch,' John Stearne commanded.

Adefina's motions were slow but her witch's mind was quick. She offered hands, empty and submissive, as her eyes roved the ground and the weapons at her feet.

'Please, good sir,' she said softly, 'I am no witch. You see but a poor woman in search of coins from the dead. These are cruel times.'

'As cruel as you are, Adefina Corvus.'

She turned to her name and shed all pretence with a fiendish smile.

'John Stearne,' she intoned and added hatred to her smile.

'I told you not to move,' he growled. He filled her vision with his pistol.

'All alone,' she said with a scan of the surrounding dark, and in the dark her fingers moved.

'Matthew Hopkins is not far off,' he warned. 'He comes even now.'

'Really?' she replied. 'I don't see him.' What she saw instead was the momentary shift in John Stearne's eye, a mere flicker betray the doubt arriving there from his heart. She seized eagerly on it. 'Did you divert him? Did you send him looking in the wrong places so you could claim for yourself the glory of my capture?'

'Enough!' he barked.

'A reward,' she guessed with a wink. 'Enough for two, but more than enough for one.'

'Hopkins will put you to the test and prove you are a witch,' Stearne insisted.

'Why bother?' Adefina scoffed. 'I can prove it myself.'

Her whispered conjuration was a gentle breath, soft as a dagger's flight from dead hands.

The witchfinder howled as the blade she sent spinning cleaved skin and bone at his wrist. He looked on, wide-eyed, as the weapon turned under invisible control to slash knuckles open and drive scorching anguish to his brain. Flinching by terrified reflex from further harm, he tightened on the pistol's bloodied trigger.

Through the blast of flame and smoke from Stearne's wild shot, Adefina whispered again. A sword leapt obediently to her direction this time and spun to bury itself in the witchfinder's unguarded leg. The man staggered, his disbelieving cry brimming with fear for weapons sailing from all sides. One after another they found their mark, driving into his back, his shoulder, and deeply into his stomach to send him to his knees with a grunt of shock.

'Matthew!' he tried mindlessly, though the shout was made a weak imitation by the sight of her face rising to pour its maddened fury down on his.

'You would test me?' Adefina shrilled. 'You would dare, with nothing but tricks and deceits. You think I am a shrinking woman to test and send to the fire?'

He saw it then, the clear intention of her words in her shifting features, in her slow retreat from him as she conjured again, and he begged to be mistaken. 'No,' he pleaded through tears and bloodied lips.

'Have your fire,' she snarled.

John Stearne burst into flames. At her command, he plumed to become a thrashing bonfire, an uncontrolled beacon rolling and filling the night with tormented howls. His pleas for a witch's mercy became shrieks for release, for Matthew's rescue, and again for Matthew, until all hope was burned up, and John Stearne tumbled to smoulder among the ranks of the dead.

30

'Over here.'

Darach's whisper from deepest gloom drew the rest on between trees, there to find him in an area of thick undergrowth. He waited eagerly to show what he had found.

At the treeline where they gathered, the vampires looked across a cultivated lawn to the facade of a grand manor house rising against the sky. Shuttered and dark, the building frowned with angled roofs as it stretched broadly beneath a crown of chimneys. A forbidding doorway set in a stone portico suggested the fanged snout of a beast ever hungry for trespassers.

'No dog barks; no candle flickers,' Juno noted.

'It is abandoned,' Darach said, 'I have already scouted. Beyond, the estate drops to a wide lake we must travel around to continue south. Once there, we will find little cover.'

Brill consulted the stars. 'Two hours till dawn.'

'Then we should not tarry,' Darach said as he made to rise.

'Wait!' Benjamin's warning came with his sharp turning back towards the trees. 'Did you hear that?'

They blended with the dark to listen to the forest. The wooded land was a brooding abyss of criss-crossing stems. Not a creature stirred; no wind rose to play on leafy branches. The night fell so still as to make vibrant the twinkling of stars through the canopy, and so quiet that when wood snapped under a careless tread, it reached the friends like a musket shot.

'That was very close,' Juno said.

'And getting closer,' Benjamin added, now catching a careless brush of leaves, the snort of a horse. He spun to Darach in hopes of a strategy.

'The lake route would be suicide,' the boy said.

'The house,' they said together, and moved.

In a blinking, the four crossed the lawn to reach the grim portal, their arrival marked by a frightened gasp from Brill. With a finger-stab she indicated the door panels and the red cross daubed there.

'A plague house,' she exclaimed.

'The least of our worries,' Juno countered quickly as she shoved her friend between door and frame.

The house breathed a hollow gasp for the vampires' intrusion. Cobwebs shifted, fluttering as though disturbed by ghosts fleeing through them, across the entrance hall and up the staircase, there to creak the boards of the gallery and scurry behind dark panelled walls.

Stepping across polished tiles, Benjamin sent clipping echoes to farthest reaches as he surveyed rapidly the interior. Beneath glaring portrait faces, the others followed him through shafts of moonlight that came to pierce long gloomy corridors leading from the hall.

'Which way?' he asked, and the house asked again in his voice.

There was no time for answer. All heard together the grinding turn of the door handle behind.

Vampires fled in all directions.

The barrier moaned slowly on its hinges, driven by one who did not immediately follow but held back a moment to the safety of the portico. Only slowly, and behind a readied pistol, did the figure advance. From his hiding place, Benjamin watched Matthew Hopkins step between patches of moonlight, as gingerly as his riding boots would allow.

The witchfinder's weapon tracked his narrowed gaze fully around the hall and upwards to the gallery in search of lurking evil. There came a sudden harsh scraping, emanating from the hall's broad fireplace. Hopkins whirled to it and took aim at its cold depths. A rat scurried noisily over the hearth, untroubled by the man's presence in this domain of night creatures.

With a muttered curse, Hopkins returned to his search. He approached the gallery staircase, adding his jewelled dagger to the readied pistol as he mounted the steps to advance on silent corridors.

The vampires travelled as phantoms after him.

Through dim halls they flitted, shadow to shadow, their movements lost to mortal sight beyond the witchfinder's vision.

Like his friends, Benjamin tracked with an assured stealth that came more easily to him tonight. He was at one with the gloom and made it a cape of protection when he drew daringly close to the hunting man. When Hopkins gazed suddenly backwards, Benjamin spied the motion even as the witchfinder shifted and was gone before the action was complete, hiding as swiftly and effortlessly as the rest.

Stairs brought them to new heights where mortal and vampires roved through abandoned rooms and galleries. In one, a wall of books waited, ranks of untouched knowledge, and Benjamin saw how the volumes glittered in pale imitation of the grimoire, as moonlight played on their gold-touched spines.

A doorway from the library offered access to another chamber, and here Hopkins paused carefully once more before stepping through. But the room caused him at once to forget his wary hesitation. Lowering his weapons, he stepped along the aisle of a little chapel and to the simple altar at its head where a tiny item there drew his gaze. With a final step to the platform, he looked down on a solitary tarot card lying on the altar top.

The Fool.

Brill bit her lip against laughter and shrugged off scolding silver eyes.

The witchfinder's previous caution returned and he pressed on to an attic of stored ghosts, tall and short and broad in their dust covers, each barely shifting to the passing of familiars. Then down to a cellar of coffin-like trunks Hopkins roamed, until his hunt took him back to the entrance hall. There, suspicion was replaced by frustration. With a last look for wicked-ness in the dark, he retreated, his departure marked by a great booming of the door through the house.

'He's turned back towards the woods,' Darach reported, at a peeking place between shutters. 'North.'

'We must watch out for him when we reach London,' Juno cautioned.

Brill scoffed. 'He's out of his depth. I could have stabbed him you-know-where a dozen times. Silly mortal.'

'Adefina is mortal,' Juno shot back. She watched Benjamin turn to leave them. 'Where are you going?'

'Hopkins is still hunting for Adefina, and Adefina still hunts for us,' he said. He gestured to moon glow angling through the shutters. 'I'm going to study while there's still time.'

31

Study.

It wasn't study. It was pointless peering, a blank staring in hope of some unexpected inspiration to allow study to begin.

And it was becoming hopeless.

Spread open under a beam of moonlight falling on the library floor, the grimoire stubbornly resisted him yet. It dared him through mute goading to try and try harder, and all the while with the promise it would make no difference.

Benjamin ground his teeth against solid circles and unbreakable codes and tried again. He glared on pages, willing the answer to reveal itself. He caressed patterns as though to tease up their meaning but perceived nothing besides a slow decrease in light from the sinking moon.

'Tell me!' He slapped the grimoire with strength enough to crack the floorboards beneath. But its text glowed indifferently and even a tad brighter perhaps, just to mock his anger.

Benjamin bitterly withdrew his hand and turned it up from the sickly feeling of skin-pages. He mirrored its flexing fingers with his other until the witch's book was glimpsed within the cage of digits he formed.

Permutations endless within fourteen.

'Not this again,' he despaired. He pushed up from sitting with an exasperated cry and stalked about the moonlit grimoire, offering it the fury of his face. A sudden urge to kick the book across the room overtook him and he turned for the blast.

'It's not going well, I see.'

The voice in the depths held him and he looked for Darach on all sides. But the boy warrior was expert, concealed until he chose not to be through a momentary wink of silver at the bookshelf.

'Not going well?' Benjamin groaned. 'It's not going anywhere.'

'Perhaps the magic was never meant for you, after all,' Darach suggested.

'Then why is it in my head?' Benjamin exclaimed. 'Why all the whispered clues driving me senseless? It's so annoying!'

'You lack something. A vital key, maybe.'

'Like what?'

Darach moved through darkness again. Benjamin sensed his swift motion behind the veil, though not the destination.

'Are you wicked, Benjamin Blake, cruel in your heart?' The boy's challenge came from a place by the shuttered windows, where pale light and dark combined to shield him from all sight.

'If I need to be, I'll never understand the book,' Benjamin replied, squinting into the gloom.

'Why do you want to understand it?'

'I don't *want* to. I didn't ask for this.'

Darach's soft chuckle drifted through the library. 'I wish Varney was here for this.'

'Is this a test?' Benjamin demanded. He perceived the warrior's onward flight.

'Varney shared concerns with me, Benjamin.'

He turned to the voice. 'About me?'

'Not so much. He sees the light of goodness in you. But this dark magic... can your light survive this dabbling with darkness?'

'Light holds back the dark,' Benjamin said.

'That's a good answer,' Darach's soft laughter was everywhere and nowhere.

'What about Juno?' Benjamin pressed, searching.

'You care what she thinks?'

'Yes. Very much.'

Darach's sigh was a sad draught from the doorway.

'Juno doesn't care for magic. She dreams of the light.'

Darach passed as a whisper but now Benjamin was keenly tracking.

'What about you?' he challenged the warrior. 'Do you dream of having the magic for yourself, Darach?'

'Not the magic, Benjamin.'

Even the dark could not hide Darach's truth.

'You dream of the light too?'

'These nights past I've dreamt of nothing else.'

He fled from his own words to plunge for a new hiding place, but this time Benjamin was ready. In a blinking, he moved to reach for the speeding wisp and the warrior passed into his enfolding arms. Benjamin drew Darach's startled face to revealing beams of moon glow.

'Perhaps when you have your magic, you can make dreams come true,' Darach said, 'or perhaps I'm mad for thinking that.' With a forced smile, he nodded to the shutters and the filtering shafts they allowed. 'I have heard it said a vampire who stares too long at the moon goes mad in the end. But some only have the moon.'

He wrestled abruptly and forcefully free of Benjamin's arms and stepped backwards, seemingly angry, to find inky depths again, until only the embers of his eyes remained.

'You could come with me to the New World, Benjamin.'

The moon flickered to its end and Darach vanished.

32

ome to me.

The voice came drifting, smoky soft in a morning dream. Or maybe the voice *was* the dream. He couldn't tell yet.

Rise up.

Had he fallen asleep? When had that happened?

Benjamin lifted his eyelids and the effort was a weight of mortal straining, sluggish and heavy. Squinting against beams of dawn now falling on the boards, his focus came swimming to find the grimoire there. Its wicked text lay unyielding to the sunlight, despising it. Benjamin reached for the exposed pages, thinking dimly to answer its call, and his fingers seemed to stretch miles away for the touch, pushing through wearying space.

Forget the grimoire. I am waiting.

He drew up, his legs already responding to the command to bring him to standing. Whose voice *was* that?

Night is coming on. Come with it.

No, wait, was it? The sun seemed barely risen. He could tell by the shallow angle of its rays and...

I want to see you.

Juno's voice? No, it wasn't her. Not the book, not Juno, definitely not her; he could see that as he stepped from the library. She was there, rising from the couch she had made her bed, rather, *trying* to rise, hauling up from her own reverie of deep fog to look on him with bleary eyes. And when she spoke his name, he could only read it on her lips as her voice was lost to the coming again of the other.

Pass by and reach me.

'Benjamin?' Juno said again. She frowned on his dreamy motion and his passing to leave her behind and she swung her feet from the couch, intending to follow. The action was a labour to set her mind spinning and she could only look as Benjamin disappeared through the doorway. She could only gasp as a shimmering figure replaced him there, framed with hair like her own and with a face shaped as hers, but with a simmering bitterness in eyes she had last gazed into countless centuries ago.

'Mother?'

Benjamin neither saw nor heard. The corridor was a misshapen tunnel distorting sound and vision. Its walls shifted to catch his shoulders where he stumbled along towards the gallery, so many, many miles away. He staggered by an open doorway, almost falling off his course and towards Darach who was clawing up from disturbed rest, his sword held as a crutch against tumbling back to the depths of some nightmare.

'Mother,' Juno cried again, and she tried to rise with proper respect.

'You still call me that?' the shimmering figure spat.

Tears, heavier than all else, brimmed in Juno's eyes.

'You are always my mother.'

'How so when I no longer call you daughter?'

Darach reached for Benjamin in the doorway on a trembling step. But his sword cleaved through boards and sent him back to his knees, as his friend looked on in cloudy confusion and left him. The doorway hung empty a moment, then filled to a caped, black shape bringing its own ready sword. Darach's voice became toneless with fearful recognition.

'Father.'

'Wretch,' the hazy form cursed. 'You dare yet carry the sword of a warrior.'

'You gave it to me,' the boy protested.

'I ought to have taken it back when I banished you.'

Benjamin toppled into the gallery. Only his crashing against the rail saved him from plummeting to the hall below, where Brill's tiny form stumbled and pawed blindly in her trance.

Nearly there, Benjamin. So nearly with me. Come.

Benjamin spun from the voice at his ear, in his ear. And now he did fall. A heel slipped beyond a step and he followed, arms flailing through addled vampire senses. The upended stairs received him tumbling and offered its long hard path to the floor below.

Brill heard the wooden thunder and turned dizzily to it. The name of the boy on the steps slipped her mind in all efforts to remain standing. The entire hall swung around; that must be why he... B... the boy, was finding it so difficult to rise. But why, then, could the shawled woman behind him stand so steadily, and stare so keenly back with her familiar eyes?

'Brill, my darling, I've found you.'

Benjamin regained his feet and pushed through aching heaviness. Brill looked scared, wide-eyed where she stood, but he paid no heed. There was no pain worse than fighting the voice.

The door. Come to the door.

Juno used the couch for support and dashed tears from her face. 'I am my father's daughter, too,' she argued under her mother's withering gaze.

'You are a parents' disgrace! You are a girl, not a boy. Your place was at home, with me.'

Hurry now, night is coming. Come to the door.

Darach hauled his sword free for his father's vision. 'I brought you honour in battle, so many times.'

'A king must bring sons who will be kings after him. What could you bring in your sin but an end to everything?'

'Brill, my baby girl, I've searched for you so long.'

Benjamin faced the door handle. One simple twist and he would be there, with the voice, without barriers. And yet, far off, another voice was urging him back. It whispered of... danger. No, it screamed it, but from so very far away and deep down beneath the other voice.

Don't wait.

'Wait,' Brill mumbled and with a blinking, 'you... my mother never called me Brill.'

Juno's gasp was an ice dagger for phantoms. 'Benjamin.'

'Benjamin,' Darach cried, a battle cry against witch-conjured demons.

Benjamin's arm rose to the handle and his fingers drummed the air like a clattering on boards. They contacted, and the metal seemed to call his name. And he pulled on hinges that screamed against the motion, turning with it to find Juno running towards him.

The light came howling.

It burst through the portal, a wall of daylight fire sweeping in to fill the hall with its hurricane power. Benjamin felt it scorch his arms, his hair, his face, and he threw up defensive hands only to feel pinpricks of fire through skin and nails. He curled away and through the sun's white heat saw the storm reach Juno. Then he was falling, caught by the body blast of a vampire tackle. Helpless, his eyes stayed on Juno's terrified face as he was torn away from her, and he watched the vision of her vanish beneath a caped form descending from the gallery.

The door slammed with a crash against hellfire, kicked with all the force Brill could summon in her passing with Benjamin. As the light died, they slid entwined across the floor to strike the hearth and smouldered there in restored shadows.

'Are you all right?' she asked through a shroud of smoke. She looked down on him in an urgent search of injury.

'It's nothing,' he assured her. Somehow the burning he felt was little to the voiceless ache in his head. Abruptly, a renewed fear came rushing through the pain. 'Juno.'

He carried Brill up to race for the centre of the hall and the smoking heap lying there. He had paces left when Darach flung off his burning cape with a gasp and revealed Juno, safe in his arms. Uncovered, she met the relief in Benjamin's eyes with a pained smile.

'Cursed witch,' Darach groaned to the ceiling as he fell back, though he smiled with the others.

33

None dared walk alone after the witch's attack.

At Darach's suggestion, pairings were agreed until dusk: one to watch the other in close vigilance against further diabolical tricks.

And no sleeping allowed.

So it was, in the little chapel through the burning hours, Brill played with her tarot deck as she sat her guard for the warrior, smiling wistfully for his sword practice against unseen enemies as he watched over her.

Benjamin left them to drift through the corridors of the plague house. Regardless of Darach's stern command, he held no thoughts of sleeping. How could he while Adefina stalked the daylight world? So instead, he sought a quiet space in which to give free rein to a head filled with symbols and their constant shine.

But, keeping to the warrior's advice, he did not walk alone.

Though he looked back more than once, Benjamin caught no outward sign of Juno, on his trail, room after room through the day. She played expertly with shadows and dust to thwart his senses, veiling herself behind sunbeams at each backward glance. But she was there. He felt her.

The truth of it caught him by surprise. The sense of *presence* that had been so vague just nights ago had become sharp as his teeth and nails. It was so acute he could tell with certainty, without even needing to see, the posture she held in the gloom while looking at him. He could *tell* she was looking, though she deadened her silver gaze against his.

Was this a test? Was she using his own distracted thoughts against him, stalking through the shadows the grimoire placed in his mind, to make him the vampire she promised she would?

At a chamber door, and catching sight of what stood within, he hid from her the smile that rose with an impish thought for tricks. He slipped inside.

By the time she followed, Benjamin was gone.

Too old and wary for novice vampire tricks, Juno flitted only so far and held long at the doorframe. Her keen senses probed within, coursing along panelled walls and into dusky patches before sweeping up to scan the ceiling where tricksters often hid. Only afterwards did she turn attention to the most obvious hiding place: the curtained four-poster bed at the heart of the room.

He wouldn't be so clumsy, she decided at once, and just as quickly doubted. Would he be? Deliberately?

Was this a test, she speculated wildly then? Was he using her own thoughts against her? Why, the cheeky...

With a hand to her sword, she flowed invisibly into the bed chamber.

Circling purposefully far from the bed, she scanned it on all sides, not forgetting underneath. She smirked for the sight of a chamberpot lurking there. She pressed to a wall, waiting yet for a surprise assault from elsewhere in the gloomy room. The shutters here were more secure and allowed no betraying shafts to cut through the space, though weak embers of sunlight glowed in the chimney grate. No place for a prowling vampire there, then.

Abrupt and determined, Juno plunged for the bed. She clutched material and flung the curtains wide on rattling rings to find crimson bed covers and snowy pillows, unrumpled and awaiting occupancy.

Benjamin's rapid advance was a sharp breath in the dark. A hand swept to hers, and teeth growled at her neck.

'Impressed?'

'Where were you hiding?' she demanded.

Teeth gave over to a toying smile. 'Did you look in the chamberpot?'

Juno laughed, but even then she used laughter to divert. She moved swiftly through the shuddering waves to send her opposing hand for the sword. She drew in turning, her motion a silver chime as she brought the weapon to bear on Benjamin's throat. The action merely deepened his smile as he pressed a concealed dagger tip to her heart.

'Now I am impressed,' she admitted.

He withdrew his weapon with a grin but then frowned on the blade she held fast to him.

'No more tricks,' he assured her, yet the sword lingered. He found her features knowing but playful in silver light.

'Never trust a boy in a bedroom,' she said, and let slip her defence.

* * *

They returned to the little chapel under Darach's watchful gaze and to Brill's coy smile.

The girl had taken a pew close to the altar and was engaged in some idle activity, with her blade on the seat as Benjamin leaned to see. She swept a hand to drive peelings of wood aside from her carved love token.

'I wish Varney was here,' she admitted with a sigh.

'You'll see him tonight,' Benjamin promised as he admired her work.

'I hope so,' she whispered, more in hope than certainty.

'He will smite his foes,' Benjamin vowed mockingly in a deep voice, and he watched her chuckle for his silly theatrics. 'His mighty right hand will sweep before him the enemies of truth,' he added with a comic earnestness, and she laughed into her hand. 'Lo, he will... he will...'

Words failed as his eyes fell again on the cutting in the wood. He stood, dimly confounded by it at first, doubting the vision it prompted even as the turning cage of symbols in his head began to slow. Then, with a first tentative experiment, Adefina. He gasped at the possibility, and again for the truth of Corvus, and he grew weak. The hand he stretched for the carving was forced to steady him instead on the seat back.

'Benjamin?' Brill's voice, filled with concern, came from miles off. 'Benjamin, are you all right?'

He sensed Darach and Juno closing on him, drawn by the edge to Brill's tone. Hands reached to hold him, though he could not tell whether his or hers, and he could not look to see, could not turn from the image in wood that clicked like a sprung lock in his head.

Brill had placed their names together within a circle, the letters traced to follow its edge from one to the other in a way to make it impossible to tell where one began and the other ended. Through her romantic gesture, letters were meaningless in their flow without the key of knowing who Brill and Varney were, of knowing how much they shared beyond a common letter 'R' in their names, despite the....

Vowels.

The eruption of truth in Benjamin's head sent him reeling back into a pew. He landed heavily enough to drive the seat back with a squeal over the tiled floor.

He saw into the circle and through it in the same instant, and the undeniable truth sent a resounding gasp to the rafters.

'Benjamin, what is it?' someone, Juno, asked.

He sought through a language of symbols for words they would all understand.

'I can decode the book.'

34

'Easy, easy,' Juno tried, 'tell it slowly.'

Benjamin's excited attempts to explain all had become little more than a series of manic gestures. The race to produce and open the grimoire had done nothing to calm his frenzy and he babbled and pointed to the mute pages as another bout of insensible ranting flowed from him.

'Shall I knock him down?' Darach offered.

'It's something about letters,' Brill guessed.

With determined will, Benjamin seized control of his tongue and fought to ease his movements, though his brain still rebelled, demanding its flood of contents be communicated totally and all at once. He walked back and forth through the room to dispel the storm within and find an order to the lesson he needed to impart.

'Where do I begin?' he asked of himself and again, 'Where do I begin?'

'I'm going to knock him down,' Darach determined, and he squared his shoulders.

'All right,' Benjamin said at last as thoughts cleared. 'The book gave us symbols. Then the moon lit symbols within symbols. These are coded words in mysterious sentences, yes?' He waited for Juno's nodding assent. 'But we haven't been able to say what symbol stands for what letter in those words and sentences.'

'No decoder,' Brill said.

'No decoder. That's right. No pointer to symbol and letter. But now I have fourteen.'

Vampire mouths dropped open. The speechless group looked from each other to the book, and to him in search of an explanation to his claim.

'Fourteen?' Darach said.

'Fourteen.' He looked to Brill. 'Your token of love on the wood, the letters in a circle.' He pointed to the grimoire's cover. 'What if ownership of the grimoire is simply the same here?' His finger traced by memory the dull circle.

'But where does it begin or end?' Darach frowned for the flowing circumference of text.

'Where it all began,' Benjamin said, 'with Adefina. Look here.' He confined a portion of the circle between fingers. ⊠◈Ŀ?↑ℕ⊠ 'Seven letters, starting and ending with the same symbol.'

'Adefina,' Brill whispered. She threw a hand to her mouth as though to catch the truth.

'And here,' Benjamin continued, 'here are two symbols from her name that appear elsewhere.' His fingers jabbed to the forms of ↑ and ·Ŀ.

'Let me,' Darach cut in. His mind worked fast to a sharp breath of understanding. 'The letters I and E.'

Benjamin nodded and traced another arc of text, ⬧丂↑÷◎↑丂·Ŀ. 'Grimoire,' he suggested. His finger moved again, this time to focus on the symbol ◎. 'The O of Grimoire. Repeated here in the last line of six symbols.' He framed the arc.

'Corvus,' Juno breathed her astonishment.

'Grimoire Adefina Corvus,' Benjamin decoded.

Juno reached out, pressing fingers to the book as though to convince her mind through touch. 'We expected it to be so difficult,' she said, 'could it be as obvious as that?'

'I think it is,' Benjamin said. 'If I'm right, the most important pieces of the puzzle so far are the vowels, all right here in front of us: A, E, I, O and U.' He smiled broadly. 'Show me a word that does not contain at least one vowel.'

Darach slapped a hand to his forehead and stumbled back, dizzied by the flood of information. Juno gave in to a smile of joy and rushed to Benjamin.

'You did it!' she exclaimed, embracing him, 'you did it!'

'Let's see if I did,' he said. He opened the grimoire at a random page of mute text. 'See, when the moon shines, these two words are exposed over and over.' He guided her to the recurring group of symbols: ⟡⟐⟒⟙⟛ and ⟛⟡. He worked rapidly to assign letters to symbols. 'Oh,' he said, deflated by his finding.

'Oh?' Darach echoed him suspiciously. 'What 'oh'?'

'I-I really thought I had it,' Benjamin stammered with a frown for the nonsense thrown up by his decoding. 'But it makes no sense.'

'What makes no sense?' Juno asked, her smile faltering. 'Tell me.'

Benjamin shrugged awkwardly. 'The two words that repeat over an over through the book decode as 'digi-a ad', with just one symbol left unknown. But that can't be right. No matter what letter you put in the space, the words make no sense.' He offered the book to her. 'I was wrong. I forgot the true language of the book. It's one made up of just twenty-three letters. I can't understand the language.'

He turned from Juno's look of furrowed confusion, not wanting to see the disappointment that must surely follow in her features. But instead, he heard her chuckle and turned back to see her smile, and a moment later she was laughing, the sound increasing to a shoulder-shaking delight. Made helpless by it, she jabbed a finger to the page, striving to make him understand.

'Benjamin,' she choked, 'you're a genius.'

Benjamin looked to the others, to Brill who was nodding happily, her understanding complete, and to Darach, scratching his head through an enduring confusion.

'What?' Benjamin demanded. 'Tell me.'

Through chuckling hiccups, Juno touched the unknown symbol of the group, ⊤. 'This,' she said, 'must be the letter "t". The complete word is "digita" and the phrase is "digita ad". That's Latin.'

'Latin!' Benjamin cried. 'I can't read Latin.'

Juno first, then Brill and Darach, after an instant of clarity, surrendered to helpless laughter. They shared their raucous joy with backslaps, and kept one another from tumbling to the floor as Benjamin looked on, bemused. Juno staggered towards him in her merriment and held his face.

'Veni, vidi, vici,' she said. 'I came, I saw, I conquered. Benjamin, I am Roman...'

'*You* read Latin!'

Their laughter raised to fill the house.

35

Through the sunbeam shift of burning day, Benjamin studied hard, learned fast.

'Digitus.'

'Finger,' Juno replied, turning to hold up her index finger.

'I see. Digita ad.'

'Fingers, plural. To, or towards,' she revealed, pointing here and there by way of demonstration.

With each passing hour, symbols became words, words became instructions, and all tumbled to understanding through Benjamin's feverish decoding and Juno's translation.

'Pollex?'

'Thumb,' she jabbed into the air. 'Tell me,' she asked, 'did we perhaps steal a book on anatomy instead of spells?'

Benjamin grinned and tried to concentrate. 'Palma.'

'Palm,' she offered with a bored tone, holding flat her hand.

'Condylus.'

'Knuckle,' she groaned, visibly sagging.

'Incendium.'

'Ah,' she said with more interest. Easing from her chair, she slipped across the library floor to Benjamin's side. 'That is not a body part. Incendium means fire.'

'Interesting,' he said, angling the grimoire for her. 'See here, all the previous words, standing for the parts of the hand, appear to the right side of the page. It's a list that appears on almost every page. But "incendium" comes from the coded words to the left. It appears the use of the hands and their parts, the fingers, thumbs, even the knuckles, are vital parts in conjuring the spells, for fire, for...' He rapidly decoded another symbol group to the left of a page, 'Sterno.'

'Sterno,' Juno repeated and punched at the air. 'I knock down.'

'Very good.' Benjamin quickly examined and deciphered the corresponding right-side text. In a moment the instruction was clear: fist, thumb on first finger. He formed the shape and held his hand up for Juno's consideration. 'Sterno.'

The change of space between them was instantaneous and violent. An invisible force, like a sudden expansion of the air, erupted with strength enough to cast Juno backwards. Like a straw in a blasting wind, she careened across the polished floor and crashed against a bookcase.

Dodging falling volumes, she pulled herself up and cast a disapproving glance his way.

'At least we know it works,' he offered sheepishly.

'More studying; less conjuring,' she instructed, but with a smile she could not suppress.

Chastened, Benjamin returned to the pages of the grimoire.

With mental agility beyond mortal limits, he pored over the surrendering text, his brain working ravenously in multiple directions at once. From symbol to text to instruction to movement, he arrived at conjuration; the correct alignment of finger and digit with the keyword to activate individual spells. His fingers touched to an uttering of 'levitas' and the grimoire in his eyeline rose from the floor to drift like a strange bird before his startled face. 'Incendium', spoken oh so carefully, caused flames to leap at candlewicks.

Permutations endless.

Reading tirelessly on, Benjamin learned combinations innumerable, made possible with two thumbs, two palms, eight fingers, ten knuckles, ten fingertips and the fourteen digits they contained. He flexed and recited, whispering the Latin phrases into his memory, storing them like weapons in a precisely arranged armoury for his use alone.

Knowledge became the greatest weapon of all.

36

Touched by the last of the sun, the waterfall became a torrent of molten gold. Reflected fire roared in defiance of night, pressing between trecs and tumbling from it, preferring the rocks below to a dusk coming to steal all colour from the forest.

Varney, in his hiding place, watched the display and gave silent thanks for God's beauteous creation. Then, with shadows deepening to stain the fall, he eased up from cover, shaking off leaves and twigs. He kept his eyes to the trees about as he shifted weapons for greater comfort, and even when he stepped towards running waters to wash his hands of the clay that had been his bed. Caution was required now more than ever.

As intended, he had been heavy-footed to betray his travels, but not so recklessly as to speak of a planned deceit to hunters. His trail of bent branches was subtle in offering its false story of haste and panic.

The first evening star winked on darkening waters and Varney rose to prepare for his onward flight. Despite all danger, he took a moment's pause to offer a soft prayer for the journey, for continued safety on his way.

'I will not be afraid, because you are with me. Your rod and shepherd's staff comfort me.'

The reply that came was a throated hiss.

'Vaaarney.'

It issued from behind trees on the river's opposing bank, a poisoned breath that seeped from one of the black patches of night growing there. It sent prayerful fingers slipping to find dragon handles.

'Vaaarney.'

The distraction was clumsy, a voice-throwing act to scare little children, and Varney, who recognised it of old, was not fooled. As he drew his katana, he was already turning to his attacker's charge from behind.

Metal sparked on metal at the edge of the boy's defensive circle. A form made almost invisible by its speeding advance was deflected towards the river, and on to an explosion of water mid-stream.

Varney took up his ready posture, the weapon in his hands lightly suspended in expectation of another onslaught by land or water. The river ran through a night forest held perfectly still and he watched the water's surface keenly until, at last, it broke to the rising of Ilemauzar's glaring face. Rivulets of liquid did nothing to wash her features free of the hate she held for him.

'Consider yourself baptised,' he taunted.

With a shriek, she tore at him through a spray of parted water. Blades chimed once more as Varney side-stepped and knocked his opponent's weapon aside in a fluid motion. But Ilemauzar followed her sword and powered instantly for a counterattack, aiming to slice across Varney's stomach. The holy boy expertly read the angle of thrust and jabbed his katana downwards to meet the blow. Stopped in mid-flight, and with no follow-up plan, Ilemauzar stared with dumb rage at Varney and offered a breath of grave rot. The monk merely smiled and punched her back into the river.

Ilemauzar thrashed in a watery storm of screaming petulance. In place of Varney, she slapped the river, slashed its waves, and stabbed its depths to a cascade of foul utterances for him. Only her bitter desire for his end was strong enough to force an end to the tantrum.

'My lady will have her book,' she vowed as she regained the bank, safely wide of Varney's blade.

'I carry but one book,' Varney snapped in return, 'and you could not read it. Its pages would burn your sinful fingers and its truth your wicked heart.'

Ilemauzar's chuckle was a death rattle of sly amusement.

'I know *you* don't have it,' she scoffed. 'Why do you think only I followed your tracks?' The demon winked and raised her blade to the look of doubt she saw in him. 'My lady will have her book.'

The attack began as the truth clutched Varney's heart with fingers of ice. He swept against it where the demon drew her weapon high but failed to see the trick lying behind. She grabbed his wrist and held it, and licked his face to startle him more, as they spun into a fierce struggle. Through the distraction, she plunged to draw Varney's own wakizashi blade and drove it for his heart. His ancient training was instinctive and swift, and sent a diverting hand against hers, even as the blade passed into him.

The agony of silver came. It flowed from the wound, an immortal share of torture to blast supernatural strength from muscle and bone. Varney gasped to a scorching of ice fire. It raced through him with power enough to draw sparkling tears and to a crashing in his mind that was the sound of Ilemauzar's exultant howl. With eyes dimming, suddenly in search of Brill, he found only the face of evil and used it as fuel for a last defiant cry.

'My God brings me to living water, and washes away every tear.'

He pushed hard, driving forward with a last reserve of failing strength, and Ilemauzar's cry was transformed to one of cold terror.

They fell together, across the edge of the roaring world.

37

Juno came running for the others at sunset.

'You need to see this,' she gushed and fell back, drawing Darach and Brill with impatient gestures.

Abandoning their preparations for departure, they ran after the girl, expecting some fresh crisis where she led, pounding through the gallery to the library, there to halt in the doorway with gasps for what they saw.

Everything was floating.

Throughout the room, every item previously set in neat order drifted above the floor, rolling in a smooth, uncanny motion. Bound volumes followed one another in circles horizontal, perpendicular and inclined, while the most powerful of books, the grimoire, traced its own spinning path high above all others. Chairs tumbled lazily after candlesticks pursuing a stepladder, each rising and falling as though juggled by invisible hands. Nearer the floor, a chess board rotated on its diamond axis, with pieces black and white wheeling through intersecting circuits about. A ball of fire crackled past startled vampire faces: a slow-moving comet in this universe, orbiting its creator.

Benjamin sat at the heart of it all, cross-legged and apparently lost behind closed eyes. Motionless, save for a rhythmic tapping of fingers on his knees, he controlled all with an effortless grace, a dreamy indifference, even.

'He's doing all this?' Darach said in wide wonder.

Juno was giddy. 'Yes.'

Drawn forward by fascination, Brill eased into the room ahead of the others, seeking to experience more of the unfolding phenomenon. She reached, but did not dare touch, a streaming line of books. A tiny object they had all missed from the doorway floated before her, and she giggled at the sight of a mouse free-falling about its own tail. Following the rodent's helpless progress, she stepped forward.

A ball of fire roared up. In the face of the girl's advance, it sped to intercept her path, increasing in size with moulding tongues of flame to the dimensions of a closed door. Stopped by the inferno, Brill stood rigid in fright, unable to retreat until a hand pressed gently on her shoulder.

'Let me,' Juno said. She eased Brill back to the waiting hands of Darach and faced the fiery door. 'Benjamin,' she said softly, 'it's me.'

The blaze churned, taking on a new shape as though

to her voice. The door spread from its edges to become a raging disc, and the flames at its centre peeled back to a flickering ring for Juno to step through.

Passing into the heart of magical space, Juno struggled at first to find a path to Benjamin through the chaos of tumbling items. Finally, she went to her hands and knees and crawled beneath until she drew close to his dreaming face.

'Benjamin,' she whispered again, 'Benjamin, it's time to go.'

From somewhere deep within his dreaming universe, Benjamin offered a wistful smile.

With a smile of her own, Juno tried again.

'It's nightfall. We have to go.' But his creation remained unaltered and his eyes held firmly closed. Her words were no match for his magic and something stronger was required.

She pressed forward into a lingering kiss.

Benjamin's universe collapsed. Darach and Brill ran from it, the storm of furniture and books raining down. The fire was blown to smoke as candlesticks chimed like tuneless bells on the floorboards. Chess pieces fell as clattering hail to present an obstacle course for the mouse in its race to a hole in the wall.

Benjamin returned smiling to her.

'That's powerful magic,' he said with a gleam.

She tried her hardest to be stern. 'We have to go.'

The others assailed him with questions as they returned to the hall.

'What else can you do?' Brill asked eagerly and raced ahead of him on the stairs. 'Do you have the whole book in your head now? How does it feel? Can you fly?'

Darach stepped to block his path with a more important query. 'Do you have enough to face Adefina?'

Benjamin stopped for the question, pondering deeply over pages flicking rapidly within him. His friends deserved an answer, though he chose his words carefully when it came.

'I have almost every spell from her book,' he said, 'but nowhere near her years of practice.'

'But back there in the library,' Darach said, 'what you did...'

'Took me hours to get right,' Benjamin revealed. He felt the weight of hopeful gazes. 'I don't know how best to explain it. It's as though I've been handed a sword but it's new and it's heavy. Some moves come quickly; others take longer to perform.'

'Two nights ago, Benjamin could not do what he can now,' Juno reminded them. 'Imagine what he'll be able to do two nights from now.'

'So we keep running,' the warrior concluded.

'Very soon I'll turn hours to a split second,' Benjamin promised him. 'Then we can stop running.'

'Until then, let's get moving,' Juno suggested impatiently. She swept her hand towards the door to urge them on. With the same hand, she pulled on the grinding barrier and cried out against the form revealed in the portico.

Adefina wore a smile so false it could not reach her eyes.

'Hello, children,' she said.

38

Falling backwards, Juno slammed the door and tumbled into Benjamin. Vampires drew weapons and began to retreat.

The door exploded to smoke and fire. Sundered by a devastating force without, wood shards and metal bolts rained across the hall in a clattering tempest. The vampires drew back from it, shielding themselves against the chaos and the one who came after.

'Finally,' Adefina said, stepping into the hall with an air of satisfaction, 'here we all are, together again.'

A sound behind brought gazes about to find Rok entering from the rear of the hall, blocking escape routes there with his lumbering frame.

Only Benjamin did not turn.

Watch her fingers. Permutations endless.

Over the shrill demands of his own fear to '*Run! Hide!*' Benjamin heard and obeyed the voice of his instincts, so insistent it held all other emotions in check and left room for just one other soft voice close to his ear.

'Stairs,' was Juno's whisper.

'You.' Adefina's finger lashed out to find Benjamin. She smiled for his flinching reaction. 'Benjamin Blake, I said you would sleep with the dead.' The finger circled the air as her smile withered to a thin slip of hostility.

She's testing you.

'Go!' Juno dragged Benjamin back and the race for the stairs began.

The vampires hit the first steps, blurring to vision in their flight towards the gallery. But Adefina was already conjuring, fingers flicking as fast as slave feet could run.

'Incendium.'

The upper steps erupted to flame, the varnished wood igniting in an instant to a wall of fire across the breadth of the staircase. The route was instantly blocked by falling timber. The vampires turned as Rok placed himself at the foot of the stairs, with his axe and a sluggish smile.

'Give me what is mine,' Adefina called over the inferno's roar. She reached with insistent hands, her ultimatum clear: the book or more magic.

Benjamin sought desperately through his store of knowledge amid the jostling of his friends. Spells and combinations lay scattered by fear, the order he had known in the library's quiet disrupted by the witch's glaring face. Symbols rolled and danced as so many tongues of fire out of control, his control, fire and symbols.

His to control!

'Arripio!'

Pulling from Adefina's hypnotic glare, he shot a hand forward, fingers clawing together in a fist to seize the weapon he sought. The space between shuddered on a wave of power and under it the fire obeyed, its riotous dance collapsing to a churning ball of light needing only the fuel offered by Benjamin's magic. It held on the air at his command, until he turned again, and with a sweep he flung the ball from the escape route to explode on the bottom steps.

'Go!' he ordered and made to dash after his friends, pausing just long enough to see Adefina's enraged face beyond leaping flames.

The gallery was blasted by a shrieked command, her magic seeking through splinters and flames for those sprinting for the upper corridors. Fire raced across walls and ceilings, feeding on portraits and frames, blackening roof beams and doors. The floor ahead burst to a jagged hole, leaving Benjamin and the rest but one avenue of escape, back along the gallery. They plunged towards it.

Rok leapt roaring through the flames. His axe was already in motion as he landed, sweeping for Darach who was barely in time to protect against the blow with his sword. The boy was driven to his knees by the collision, and the Viking drew up for another strike.

'Sterno!'

Benjamin's memory accelerated the spellbinding. Faster than sight could follow, his fist struck out to offer the required form. Encircling fire swept back on the wave of power he sent towards Rok. It collected the Viking and took him off his feet to a tumbling flight from the gallery. In mid-air he slashed ridiculously at the spell carrying him and howled aloud as the hall's fireplace received him with a great belch of bricks and soot.

Benjamin splayed his fingers. 'Pulvis.'

The shattering magic attacked the chimney above Rok. Supporting stones exploded and the Viking could only watch as the tower of bricks ripped free, driving down through the mantle in a deafening cascade to bury him.

Adefina screamed her fury through a tumult of flame and collapse. Driven from the hall's destruction to the deeper reaches of the manor house, she struck out on all sides in search of her slaves, hurling bolts of sundering magic to ceiling beams and walls, tearing down the building in her wake as she howled the name of her prey over and over.

'BENJAMIN BLAKE!'

There, through a hole in the ceiling, she spied him suddenly, leaping the gap after the other brats. She launched daggers of fire through the space and sought targets. But even in seeking, she was forced to dive for cover as he sent back a salvo of floor nails to pin her skirts. She cursed bitterly against her confinement, enraged at his use of *her* power. Material ripped and Adefina stepped on, now to witness the unbelievable, as a flock of books came flapping towards her. She fell beneath whipping pages and swatted the volumes away. Infuriated, she rose again and attacked the air with both hands, flexing under the heaviest magic.

'Rima!'

The world crashed upwards and vampires tumbled. Lifted on floorboards punched asunder, they flailed amid collapsing walls and dragged for twisting doorways. Darach clasped a frame and reached back to pull Juno through, her grip on Benjamin's hand fierce where she hauled him along. He strained in turn, his fingers reaching for Brill's.

The room collapsed, its form lost to a plunging chaos. Brill sprang forward over parting timbers, her arms extended for the hand seeking her from the doorway. She fell short, collided with the upending floor and clawed at it even as the wood tumbled through the heart of the house. There came a burst of colourful cards and her scream travelled down to raging fire.

Benjamin and Darach fought to prevent Juno's return and dragged her on, still wailing Brill's name.

The last room was gained. Smoke from the fire was already seeping between creaking boards as Darach drove forward to hurl a side table through leaded panes. Vampires leapt into the night.

They fled the dying manor house towards the lake, Darach leading the charge down to orange-tinted waters, and west towards the promise of cover among distant trees. The fire bloomed behind, surging up to offer a human-like bellow to the moon from the collapsing heart of the manor house.

Benjamin weaved through thickening vegetation, vaulting deadfalls and slapping aside jutting branches in his flight. He plunged through a veil of leaves into a clearing and pulled up before the tumbledown ruin of a cottage. Scanning about quickly in search of ambush, he used the space to seek his friends. The night pressed about and offered nothing to vision, but slowly his ears detected a racing pursuit. He faced the approaching sound and backed towards a stone wall with shifting fingers.

Juno burst into view with Darach hard behind. The girl angled to Benjamin, her tears a mixture of relief and sorrow as she reached to hold him.

'Brill,' she said, but there could be no good answer.

'We must not stop now,' Darach warned, his sword levelled to the path behind.

But the threat was not there. It rose instead with its wet scent on the angled wall of the cottage, climbing high despite its injured paw to perch there with baleful eyes and a slavering of anticipation for the fight.

Benjamin stepped towards the hellhound, hands poised. 'Run,' he told Juno.

'You both run,' Darach barked as he pushed by his friend. 'This is meant to delay us more. Adefina is coming, get gone.' He sensed the rising of Benjamin's objection and spun to hold him, fierce and close. 'No greater love, Benjamin, remember?'

'You can't alone,' Benjamin protested.

Darach's smile was weighed with sadness. 'I always have,' he said. 'Ah, Benjamin, if you were the face of the moon, I'd happily go mad. Get gone!'

Benjamin felt the pull of Darach's eyes, and Juno's hands at his back.

The warrior watched them dart away and turned to fill a heavy heart with fire as he faced the hellhound's slow descent to the clearing. Twin spots of green luminescence flared in the shade of the ruin as the beast edged grimly forward. Claws raked the earth and fangs bared to the semblance of a smile at finding Darach alone.

The warrior returned the smile and took up his bold stance with a whisper.

'Father, see what I do, not what I am.'

The werewolf roared and sprang forward.

Darach offered his war-cry and charged.

The night filled to a clamour of steel and claws, and abruptly, silence.

The forest shook to the werewolf's howl.

39

Benjamin and Juno raced hard, due south, all notions of diversion and deception gone.

They sprinted to the limits of vampire ability, running to make the manor fire a speck on the distant horizon, and on until its smoke became a mere tendril against the sky. Only when many miles were passed did Juno stop sharply by a derelict boundary wall. Fearing a trap, Benjamin slid to a halt and probed deeply beyond fallen stones and among crosses that marked the way to a towering ruin. Finding nothing, he looked to the girl for some clue to her pause.

She stood with her back to him, head lowered as though drawn by something at her feet, though Benjamin could perceive nothing but dead leaves.

'What is it?' he whispered.

'I'm tired,' was her soft reply.

Confused by the statement, Benjamin stepped to her. 'How can you be tired?'

She rounded on him then, and with a look of such anguished fury, it caused him to reverse his step. Her fists bunched as tears streamed to lips pulled danger-ously back.

'I'm tired of running,' she hurled at him, and her voice rolled hollow between graves. 'I'm tired of it, and everything to do with Adefina, and her book, and your magic.' She struggled through her rage for more, searching for the words but found only one, so heavy it broke her, 'Brill.'

He was there to catch her as she stumbled, and he held without a word while she gave in to her grief with hitching sobs.

'We have no time for this,' she argued weakly from the folds of his shirt and made to pull away. But his vampire strength bound her to him.

'We have time,' he assured and offered whispered comfort to her ear.

> *'Close thine eyes and sleep secure,*
> *Thy soul is safe, thy body sure.*
> *He that guards thee, he that keeps,*
> *Never slumbers, never sleeps.'*

She believed him.

'I'm stronger than this,' she told them both, 'I'm stronger than this.'

'Stronger than a Roman army,' he agreed and felt her hiccup of laughter before telling the rest. 'That's why you ran away from home, isn't it? You knew back then how strong you were. When your father marched from Rome with his army, you didn't just watch. You followed. You saddled your favourite horse in secret and went off to be a warrior. That's why you're here.'

'He was furious,' she remembered, 'mostly with himself for training me as a son. Daughters of Rome were not meant for fighting. I was supposed to be a "good girl" and eventually the wife of some perfumed senator. My mother had one picked out for me before I turned twelve.'

'Did he even know you?'

'Not as well as you do.'

Her kiss was salty with tears.

'Ready to go?' he asked gently afterwards.

Letting go slowly, he led on through the cemetery, weaving towards the ruin that was a collapsed church. Like shadows they slipped along the building's sole remaining wall, a jagged pyramid whose blank round window looked down on them. Benjamin angled to bypass the structure's gaping doorway when Juno's soft touch came at his shoulder.

'This way,' she said, and led him in.

Through rolling mist, she guided him over memorial stones and along an aisle of shattered columns which ran to ring the altar space. There she held him among the rubble and prompted him to look beyond, into the exposed night to what lay there.

From their position on a high outcrop, the land swept down and away to the far horizon where a vast shadow rose to hulk in waiting.

'London,' Benjamin heard his own awed voice declare it.

The city snaked across his line of vision, its huge shape in the dark appearing as a single great construction placed on the land by giants rather than the hands of mortal men. Across its broad sweep, innumerable flickering lights traced the contours of the cityscape, burning from the lowliest dwelling to the highest tower, and along the high wall that hemmed the constructions as a fortress.

'There,' Juno said, pulling him from his overwhelmed regarding of the city. She pointed their way. 'Our entry point is there, between the gates. Do you see?'

Benjamin fixed on a dark length of battlements stretching between two mammoth sets of gates. 'Yes,' he agreed, though in his examination he could not fail to notice the armed men who guarded those gates and patrolled the high wall.

Reading his concerns, Juno stepped close. 'Remember what you are,' she reminded him once more. 'They will not see you unless you wish it. The night is ours. Do you understand?'

'I do.'

'Ready?'

'Yes.'

They blended to the black.

Moving swiftly, Benjamin trusted his skills and kept close to her in advancing through shadows along the way. But after a short distance, and for the first time, he sensed a part of himself no longer merely following. Drawn to the feeling, he caught a spark of that deeper instinct plotting his course and predicting each move seconds ahead of Juno making it. This keen impulse, he understood readily, needed no guidance in tracking the surest way, and he listened closely to it as he advanced. And in moving, no, *gliding* on, he felt the new truth of things. Just as instinct drove him to the safest pools of shadow, he noted how his actions within the darkness responded, becoming a series of effortless motions. He was thinking as a vampire, and in thinking so he easily found his own way to pass swiftly and in total silence through the night, as though born to it. Trusting his skills, he attuned every faculty towards his goal.

The base of the wall soon loomed, and the raft of new feelings gave way to a not-so-new experience. As in Ravenhill, when he had climbed to Jack's window, Benjamin reached out to hook his fingernails effortlessly into the stonework. Without hesitation this time, he scaled weightlessly, hand over hand towards the stars. Beside him, Juno matched his pace, her frame gliding impossibly forward with every stretch of her clawed hands.

Benjamin had climbed to within reach of the top when vampire senses pulled him abruptly to stop. He did so at once and unquestioningly, in perfect time with Juno who obeyed her own internal warning.

They were not alone.

Hanging together in space, they cast upwards to the edge of the wall just as a hand appeared on the stone and the full face of a mortal man drew slowly into view. A guard on his rounds had stopped directly above to search the night for enemies and intruders. Little did he realise a mere glance down would present him with his catch for the night. But he gained not a hint of vampires at one with the dark, and after another sweep of the horizon, he issued a bored sigh and stepped away.

Benjamin and Juno held fast, giving the wandering sentry a safe passage of time to move on. To the fading of footsteps, they continued their ascent, slipping quickly over the battlements to seek the protective shadows staining the walkway.

Yards off, the guard's silhouetted form walked his route, oblivious to those behind. But all at once, and as though gripped by keen senses of his own, he halted. He looked initially from left to right for an explanation to growing suspicions and afterwards peered back along his route. So slow were his mortal movements, however, that by the time his turn was complete, vampires who had moved so very close to him were already gone, down the wall and into the draping night.

* * *

Adefina stalked the burning skeleton of the manor house. Through acrid curtains of smoke, she navigated a new landscape of ruptured walls and smouldering timbers, halting briefly when an avalanche of roof tiles came in a deafening clatter to strike blackened floorboards. The collapse reverberated through remaining corridors and rooms, its echo rolling back to trigger another collapse in the hall. She watched as a mountain of chimney bricks began a dusty slide and uncovered the battered Rok. The Viking clawed free of the mound and swatted soot from his beard as he frowned at a movement through the shattered main door.

Adefina followed his gaze to the arrival of Ilemauzar. Wearied, and for some reason soaking wet, the demon hung in the doorway to offer a wan smile and a nod for her task completed.

Ignoring idiot servants, Adefina paced on, knowing what she sought but not precisely where it lay. She passed through a still burning door frame, and by its wavering light, traversed a room overflowing with rubble. Chairs, curtains, boards and bedding lay in chaotic piles between walls rising to open sky. She smiled for the destruction she had wrought and more as she spied a vital clue curling in the heat by a mound of ragged blankets. She stooped nimbly to save it from burning. With a hand, she shook the paper free of licking flame and with her other, snatched a blanket aside to gaze on smeared features looking fearfully back.

'Brilliana,' she said with soft delight.

Adefina turned the smoking tarot card up for the girl's terrified consideration.

Judgement.

40

London peered on vampires with grim suspicion. Rising to glower down on all sides, white-washed dwellings loomed ghostly and tall; windows and doorways gaped at the new arrivals. Their midnight brooding offered silent disapproval for the nocturnal intrusion and reared from it to a jagged rank against the sky.

Just as forbidding to Benjamin's first close gaze on the city were the muddy routes, which somehow squeezed between cramped terraces to form ominous tunnels. The winding pathways glistened like snake bellies and meandered to the promise of some dreadful fate in the crushing darkness beyond.

'Which way?' he asked, barely daring to raise his voice.

'This one,' Juno decided, pointing to a street which plunged off to their left. 'Towards the river.'

They passed like smoke through shadows.

The chosen street, like all others, ran silent and free of mortal citizens. War pamphlets peeling from walls ordered all to their shuttered homes during the hours of night. Nevertheless, more than once, Benjamin and Juno were forced to seek cover as armed patrols on the hunt for curfew-breakers and spies tramped the maze of routes.

It was in hiding from yet another clattering band of armed men that Juno suggested a safer route. Tapping Benjamin's shoulder, she pointed upwards. 'We'll take to the rooftops,' she said.

Swiftly they climbed to move amid chimney pots and over a cityscape of pitched roofs. They skirted the very edge of dwellings, confident as hawks in leaping the chasms of winding streets below. Pausing on high to take in the breadth of London, Benjamin spied the landmarks he had imagined so many times. To his right, the hulking form of St. Paul's Cathedral towered amid buildings that were mere doll houses in comparison. Directly ahead, and thrusting over the river's black waters, an uneven line of houses lined the span of London Bridge. And on his left, on the river's edge, the majestic Tower of London rose, its white stone walls gleaming between the masts of ships at anchor hard by. Benjamin caught Juno also taking in the vision, her vampire teeth glinting to a smile.

'Freedom,' Benjamin said.

She nodded. 'Let's go.'

Another short period of roof-hopping brought them at last to the line of buildings flanking the tower.

Here the dwellings maintained a respectful distance from the structure and surrounded a broad open area, which sloped gently to the castle walls and the river beyond.

'This is good,' Juno judged. 'A place to watch for Varney.' She propped her back against a puffing chimney and gazed across London as she settled down to wait.

Benjamin eased to a place by her and shared the girl's view of the slumbering city.

'Memories,' he guessed by her face.

She looked for them in dark water.

'Just two,' she admitted. 'One is the morning of my last battle, out there on the foreshore. Our enemies charged through mist from the river, howling like wild animals. I didn't run. I stood with my father and remembered my training. Even when he fell, I didn't run. The sword in my hand put three barbarians down. Then the sky turned black to a storm of arrows and there was no shelter from the rain. I closed my eyes and looked for my father in Elysium.'

She stayed long in her reverie before Benjamin's gaze pulled her back.

'The other is a witch's nightmare. It was waking alone and afraid in the dark, crawling up through the earth and into the night rain to find Adefina standing over me in her painted circle. I remember how the lightning seemed to come from her and not the sky.'

She shook off wicked visions. 'I wonder if my third visit will be any luckier.'

Benjamin tapped a hand to the grimoire. 'This time you're here with more than swords and arrows.'

Juno laughed. 'Then let London beware!'

***

The weary hours of the watch dragged on the gate guards.

The fire at their post crackled dreamily through a silence that had long since replaced conversation, its warmth lulling the two soldiers into a losing battle with sleep. Eyelids grew heavy and pulled on weary heads, and the men gently faded where they propped themselves on weapons or against the rough stonework of the gateway.

A sharp noise from the darkness along the northern road brought them back to snorting wakefulness. Clutching at weapons, they exchanged urgent glances and squinted into the gloom beyond the flames for the source of the brief disturbance. The veil of night betrayed nothing to sight, but slowly, and on the very edge of hearing, there came the sound of footsteps approaching their position.

'Halt there!' the taller of the pair commanded with the jabbing tip of his long pike.

'Identify yourself or be shot,' his white-haired comrade added as he cocked his musket.

The traveller walked slowly into the area of firelight, drawing back the hood of her red-lined cape to a pretty smile. 'Please, gentlemen,' she soothed, 'I am not worth a musket shot.'

Presented with the pleasing vision, the soldiers lowered their arms but kept a firm eye on the new arrival. Women could be spies as easily as men, they knew.

'If you seek entry, you'll have to wait till first light,' Tall Soldier informed her.

'Oh, what a pity' the woman sighed, passing her gaze along the high battlements. 'I do so long to move through mighty London.' She used the words to hide her movement around the guards to further consider the city gates, and her graceful steps drew the men's attention along.

'What is your business?' White-Hair asked.

'I wish simply to visit my family,' the woman replied, 'my poor uncle has been ill these past days and I am most concerned.'

'Even so,' White-Hair said, 'we cannot allow entry until dawn. These are dangerous times. There are desperate men everywhere since the defeat of the king.'

'But I am hardly a man,' the woman chuckled, and her blushes showed beneath playful eyes in the firelight.

'True,' Tall Soldier agreed, appreciating the lovely

form that smiled at him, 'but there is talk of much worse abroad. There are witches.'

'Witches?' the woman gasped. She cast frightened glances about in dramatic fashion.

'Aye,' Tall Soldier confirmed gravely. 'All sorts of tales have come from the north these months past. Devilish stuff.'

'Are you a witch?' White-Hair joked with a playful wink and laughed with his partner at the very notion.

The woman laughed the louder and placed a discreet hand to her mouth, revealing the silver skull ring she wore. 'How did you guess?'

Adefina's vampires rose from the dark and plunged on the distracted guards. Rok flung a mighty arm about White-Hair's neck and snapped it like a twig in an instant, but Ilemauzar took longer. Baring her fangs, she sank into Tall Soldier's throat with wet-eyed relish. Puncturing the flesh, she clung gleefully to the man's death struggle as he tumbled to earth.

Adefina watched it all with a cold disinterest.

'Get this gate open,' she commanded once the grisly work was complete.

Her slaves moved to obey, crawling rapidly up the wall to take care of any obstacles, human or otherwise, that might be waiting. In a minute the barriers rumbled aside and the witch entered to scour the city.

'Pick up the scent,' she ordered.

41

'Incipe.'

'Begin,' Juno translated idly from her watch. With sudden realisation that Benjamin was studying the grimoire again, she shot a warning glance. 'Please don't perform any unknown spells,' she said. 'I don't want you turning me into a frog.'

'That seems unlikely with this spell,' he said. 'It's longer than the others, and there are no hand or finger movements with it.' He frowned over a page containing a detailed illustration, allowing his finger to trace a pair of circles, one within the other. In the space between the rings, bizarre signs had been inserted at regular intervals around the circuit. He considered their weird angles closely, turning the book over and back to follow the arcs.

'Decode some more,' Juno suggested.

Benjamin scanned cryptic words, 'Vox mea audite.'

For a moment Juno hesitated, as though memory for her own language eluded her. When finally she did speak, the words came seemingly from miles away, whispered in dread. 'Hear my voice.'

'Solis candor...' Benjamin began the next sequence.

'Stop!' the Roman barked furiously. 'Stop reading!' She moved through a blur of speed to slam the book closed in his hands. 'Never recite that spell.'

'Why not?' he asked and felt a shiver in her arms. 'What is it?'

'The summoning spell,' she barely dared to say, 'the very one Adefina used to create us. It's an obscenity, the farthest step a witch – anyone – can take from goodness. It is useless to us.'

The summoning spell! The magic to create a witch's band of slaves! Benjamin felt the possibilities grow between fingers to fire in his mind.

'But-but it's not useless,' he argued. 'With this spell we can turn the tables on Adefina. We could raise others to fight her, a whole army.'

'No!' Juno said in horror. 'Don't you remember those awful soldiers? Do not even think it. This is not the weapon we need against Adefina.' She pulled from him and from the unsettling feel of the book, until the chimney was again at her back. 'Let the dead lie,' she commanded.

He peered on the closed grimoire, this weapon of spells at his command, and struggled for an argument that would make her reconsider. But looking at the revulsion she offered the book, he thought it wiser to say nothing. Instead, he reached for the satchel, resolving to study no more for now.

'Isn't the city beautiful by moonlight?'

'Yes,' he agreed.

'What?' said Juno.

'You're right,' he said, 'London is beautiful under the moon.'

'I didn't say anything.'

Adefina chuckled in his head.

'I know you can hear me, Benjamin Blake.'

Through numbing fear, he recognised and sought the spell. Middle finger over index and, after a wary pause, the whispered conjuration.

'Loqui.'

'Clever little brat.'

'It's one of the easier spells, Adefina,' he dared reply. He watched Juno make to cry out and hushed her with a hand.

Adefina's sigh was a winter's wind through his mind. 'Don't the ships look pretty too, with their masts so high? I know you can see them. In the shadow of the tower. That was the agreed meeting place, wasn't it?'

In the shadow of the tower. Uttered by Darach, told to Varney, heard by Brill. Benjamin signalled urgently for Juno to be vigilant.

'Part of the diversion we planned,' he said.

'Oh, no lies, Benjamin,' the witch clucked, 'you're not a good liar. But you are a good boy. And good boys shouldn't play with magic.'

He heard the words but also the edge to her voice when she uttered them, and he read impatience and growing anger in it.

'But I'm good at magic,' he teased with affected innocence and now the silence she offered told more than her voice. Benjamin joined Juno in closely watching and prepared her with a touch. 'Besides,' he went on, 'who better to have the book than me? The grimoire is forever and so am I. Forever young and free. How you must hate that.'

Fire howled up, a swirling bright inferno bursting at the river's edge. Ships' masts plumed to burning crosses and rained flames on deck timbers and hissing water. The false dawn Adefina created filled with sounds of snapping ropes and splitting wood, but nothing could drown her voice.

'I will have my book from you! You're not fit to possess it; you never will be. You think you know so much but you know nothing! You didn't even know your father when he was right in front of you!'

Now it was Adefina who read the dread silence between them.

'That's right, your father, Benjamin Blake. *Benjamin Hazzard.* He was a night-creeping thief, forever on the run, just like you. He wanted so badly to find a way back to you, Benjamin, really he did. But he found me instead, and I snapped his neck like a twig.'

Through boiling rage, Benjamin sought the witch's lies but felt only scalding truth in her words. Struck mute and blinded by tears of rage, he rose against it and forced clamped teeth apart, with a roar to rip the night and announce the coming of his power.

Roof tiles exploded at his feet and windows shattered before his storm of light, punched from frames to a blizzard of glittering shards. Tree branches burst to splinters and flew like jagged hail to join the fires, as Benjamin's furious magic rolled to every hiding place in seeking Adefina.

'I'll give you nothing!' he vowed over it all. 'Nothing! I'll use the grimoire to destroy you with your own spells. I'll conjure from Hell and watch you burn!'

He raised his hand to offer another raging conjuration. But the finger combination was captured on the air and forced back as Juno hurtled forward to seize and push him to a chimney stack.

'No,' she commanded, *pleaded*. 'Don't give in to her.'

'You don't know what she did,' he cried, wrestling her grip through tears. 'She's evil, the worst evil.'

'And she's trying to make you the same. That's the way she beats you, by making you angry and twisted as she is. Don't let her do it to you.'

Benjamin fought a losing battle against Juno's touch and, with a groan, he hung his head in despair.

'You will give me my book.' Adefina's voice was soft, self-satisfied. 'I'll even trade you for it.'

'What can you give in return for the book?' he demanded angrily. 'What can you trade for magic?'

Time passed amid the alarm of fire bells and mortal cries and Benjamin watched Juno's fixed gaze of wonder for his renewed determination.

'I have a life you can save,' the witch said. 'Look.'

Benjamin overlooked the world below: a chaos of shadows dancing to the fire's manic rhythm. Together with Juno he searched for tricks, for enemies, until all at once the light betrayed a passing form in the lee of the tower. He blinked against the chance of mistake but saw how Juno reacted to it too.

'There's someone down there,' she said.

'My offering to you,' Adefina whispered as Benjamin recognised the pale face below weaving directionless and afraid.

'Brill,' Juno exclaimed. She darted unthinking to the edge of the tiles. Before Benjamin could urge caution, the girl hurled herself off.

She plummeted amid her fluttering cape to the up-rushing earth, reaching it softly and without sound. The moment feet touched roadway, she was gone, speeding beyond vision to the inky depths.

An instant behind, Benjamin was too late in reaching to prevent her reckless sprint for the trees. Unwilling to shout after, so dangerously exposed, he sought the safety of shadow.

The trees closed round with the promise of threats.

'You risk yourself for Juno,' Adefina observed from behind every shade, 'now that's interesting. Was she the one who made you? I thought Darach was the lonely one.'

Smoke rolled, drawing up from the river to dim his silver vision. Becoming one with his surroundings, Benjamin cast senses in all directions through the increasing veil. He spied wilful silhouettes moving to and fro, misshapen by firelight and murky clouds. Adefina would not be foolish enough to reveal herself so clumsily, he knew, and he reached deeper, daring to close his eyes as he searched. And there, in an unseen space *behind* the night, he caught her, matching his guarded pose and peering right back.

He perceived motion, a sharp advance from the right, and swung to meet it. Fingers poised, his lips moved, only to crush the spell as Juno appeared.

'Brill is somewhere close,' she whispered.

'But she's not alone,' Benjamin replied urgently.

A shape made wild and dark by the gloom rose from the undergrowth. Benjamin and Juno braced to meet the attack with magic and metal, only to see Brill facing them. Her eyes shone bright with fear where she stopped to regard them wordlessly. This time Benjamin was fast enough to catch Juno and, with a firm hold, he kept her from Brill and the silver blade that came to rest against the girl's neck. The dagger's reflected light fell on the face of Ilemauzar, half shielded behind her prisoner. From there the demon eyed Benjamin Blake nervously.

'Behind you,' Brill warned and the knife pressed more to silence her.

Benjamin did not turn to the heavy stomp of Rok's arrival. Even as Juno gasped, he held firm and looked to Adefina's smiling appearance through the smoke.

'Finally,' the witch said. 'I thought that was going to take all night.'

'It's not over yet,' Benjamin cautioned, though he watched her fingers so very closely.

Adefina masked her frustration with a weary sigh. 'Don't be foolish, Benjamin. It's over. Your freedom is a burning wreck; I have magic enough still to meet yours in a fight and Juno is outnumbered two to one. You have no hope.'

'There is hope in the Lord and He is my salvation.'

The voice carried on a new blade; a katana slipped between branches and darkness to chill Ilemauzar's throat and widen her eyes. Rising up, Varney forced a smile for his friends, through drawn and pained features, as the demon's teeth clicked furiously.

'You're dead,' she insisted, and with a sidelong glance of fear to her enraged mistress, 'I drove the blade deep. I killed you!'

Varney explained to Brill. 'I was not ready for Heaven,' he said. 'What would it be without you?'

Adefina fumed at the boy monk, at her idiot slave and at the one who still held her grimoire. Claws flexed to conjuring.

'Pulvis!' she shrieked with a stab of fingers for Benjamin.

The space between expanded, rolling with heat and light, and the witch's magic rushed forth.

'Fissilis!' was Benjamin's shouted answer with a palm pushed flat.

Magic met magic in a headlong crash of light. Flame erupted at the point of collision to dazzle the night, and crashed away to a nearby oak, bursting the trunk to a chaos of splinters.

In the moment's confusion, Ilemauzar abandoned Brill to strike Varney's sword. Blades clashed in a flowering of sparks to illuminate Juno's face where she thrust a hand towards the falling Brill, only to draw back as the passing breath of a Viking axe ended the rescue attempt and forced the Roman into a fighting retreat.

Adefina saw her opportunity and lashed to grasp Brill's hair. Hauling the girl up with a snarl, she held her fiercely as a shield against magic.

Thwarted in his building attack, Benjamin offered a muttered curse for witches and diverted his conjuring hands.

'Incendium!' he declared, snapping thumbs and middle fingers.

Ilemauzar, in mid-strike at Varney, howled to the sight of fire bursting along her dagger arm. Nearby, Rok gazed in mute horror between his axe-raising hands as his beard sparked to flame.

'Go!' Benjamin ordered, falling back as Juno obeyed and sped through concealing smoke. But Varney held, reluctant under Brill's terrified gaze, until Benjamin darted to seize him from a reckless attack on Adefina.

'Go!' And it was Brill this time, urging them both with her eyes on Varney. 'Trust Benjamin.'

The boys vanished.

Left behind, Ilemauzar and Rok thrashed to extinguish the last of tormenting flames from skin and hair.

'Never mind that!' Adefina railed. 'Follow them!'

Ilemauzar looked aghast at her mistress and was held from the chase by fearful doubt.

Brill spied her hesitation and smiled for the demon's conflicted emotions. 'Benjamin is strong as Adefina now,' she taunted, 'he'll destroy you all.'

The witch whipped a hand across Brill's smirking face with strength enough to send her flailing across the ground. The girl lay, stung but defiant, and watched while Adefina seethed, a wordless madwoman in the light of magic fire.

42

They ran until Varney collapsed.

Dragged down with a gasp of pain, he slowed to a standstill among the stones of a little churchyard. A steadying hand to a wooden cross did nothing to hold him and he fell heavily, groaning between earthen mounds until Juno and Benjamin raced to help.

Finding the wound he had concealed, Juno hissed for the damage done by Ilemauzar.

'Silver?' she half-guessed.

'My own blade and a demon's trick,' he admitted with a flash of anger he switched quickly to Benjamin. 'Why did we leave Brill?'

'To survive and give her the same chance,' Benjamin shot back.

Varney made to argue, but darting pain and Juno's calming hands held him back.

Benjamin cursed in frustration at his friend's torment. 'A whole book of magic and not one spell to heal wounds.'

'That dread book was not penned to be of help,' Varney reminded him weakly. 'You decoded it at last. I saw that much tonight.'

Benjamin nodded. 'Latin.'

'Latin.' Varney laughed for the solution and flinched at the anguish it caused.

'Moonlight is the only prescription for this,' Juno declared. Without hesitating, she tore the hole in Varney's clothing wide to fully expose his injury, and watched with Benjamin how the face of the holy boy eased to the touch of lunar rays.

'How long before it heals?' Benjamin asked.

Juno shrugged. 'A few nights at least.'

'I can still fight,' Varney promised with a hand to his katana.

'I believe you,' Benjamin assured him, 'but we need more than just the three of us and magic for our next meeting with Adefina.'

'What more?' Juno despaired. 'Darach is gone; Brill is held against us. And what if Adefina brings her hell-hound into the fight?'

'Darach?' Varney intoned sadly. He saw the truth in Juno's face and offered a whispered prayer for his friend.

Benjamin shook his head dejectedly and looked across the churchyard, searching for more than its cold, mortal rows. What was left to draw on now

Adefina had turned the fight? She could guard ships at port every night and hunt vampires every day. Worse, she could use all her cruelty on Brill to draw them out.

When the silent dead offered nothing but mist, he cast upwards to the moon. Despite his mood, he smiled for the caress he felt from the beauty above, where thin cloud interplayed with night light to form a halo encircling the pale disc. He tracked the rainbow fully around and back again.

And the moon in its glory offered an answer the dead dared not. It ran into his eyes so abruptly, he gave over for a time to perfect stillness, fearing to lose his first tentative grasp on the scheme of it. Only his lips parted in a soft gasp of wonder that slowly formed to words he barely believed he uttered.

'I can beat her.'

He said it aloud as much to convince himself as the others. After all, hadn't Darach warned that the vampire who looks too long at the moon goes mad in the end? And what if he *was* mad? But circles are ever protection and strength, wasn't that what Varney said? He ignored quizzical looks aimed by his friends to stare again on the burial mounds, perceiving the answer they too offered to the lunar glow.

'Incipe,' he intoned to bolster his conviction.

'Don't,' Juno commanded harshly.

Varney tightened. 'You have learned *that* spell?'

'Not in my language.'

'Let it alone,' Juno said.

'You don't understand. I can beat her. We can get Brill back and defeat Adefina and the others.'

'But at what risk, to you and to us? Find another way, Benjamin, I won't translate that spell for you.'

Varney filled the angry silence between girl and boy with his softly measured tone.

'Benjamin, understand Juno. Together we have seen magic used and only ever for wicked reasons. I want Brill back but I fear your plan. How can you reassure us you can use the power of the book for good and not let its evil use you?'

Benjamin eyed his friends keenly. 'I need only half of the spell to win.'

As Juno frowned for the answer, Varney crossed himself with a slow reverence. *'In nomine Patris, et Filii, et Spiritus Sancti. Amen.'*

'Latin,' Benjamin said with a moonlit smile.

43

The five symbols were at last complete.

For each corner of the grimy room Adefina had chosen, there was a single wicked shape traced in fireplace soot, and at the centre, an image of crossed arrows to link the rest in magic. Furniture and utensils obstructing her preparations lay broken and scattered through the room where she had worked in her frenzy.

Five shapes and as many hours in recalling them.

All for just five symbols?

'Shut up,' she hissed at her shoulder.

She had wracked her brain for them. With black fingers hesitating over the work, she had laboured near to tears in the effort to retrieve each scrawl before setting – and angrily resetting – the candles. But now, finally, all was... ready? Yes? She considered each corner again, unaware of how she bit her lip. Yes, everything was ready.

With a long breath, she stretched tired limbs in preparation for the next part. Anger had no place in her conjuring, and it was, she told herself, dangerous anger affecting her abilities. It boiled for the memory of her magic used so skilfully by another; her own magic turned against her.

By *him.*

She prepared now because he had used her magic again, just before dawn. His voice he sent to whisper as before, jerking her from slumber with offers of Brill for the grimoire, magic for freedom, safe passage to a ship, and a place to meet under the moon.

She flexed to control a wave of fresh rage.

Ah, but it's not just anger at Benjamin Blake, is it? Magic memory is such a fragile thing. Remember how two nights ago you could recall twenty-three symbols? Could you do that now?

'Shut up!' She rounded with blackened claws for the voice, finding Ilemauzar and Rok, with Brill secured between them at the far end of the space. None spoke but all stared, perplexed at her outburst.

'Mistress?'

'I said shut up. I need to concentrate.'

'But...' the demon made to try again but found wisdom in silence.

'Light them,' Adefina commanded.

A rush of air came as the obedient demon raced to illuminate the candles and, so quickly, they appeared to spring afire of their own accord and in a single instant. Her task complete, the demon retreated to await the next part.

To a click of Adefina's fingers, Rok approached. He carried with him a cloth bag, its material shifting to the movements of small life within. He handed the package to the witch with a bow and strode to join Ilemauzar.

With a sly smile for Brill, Adefina stepped to her arrows and knelt to begin.

'Benjamin Blake may have surprises,' she explained for the girl's benefit, 'so we must be more than ready.'

Drawing open the bag, she reached to produce the little captive, a puppy that came blinking into the light. The jet-black creature, bearing a single white patch on its forehead, regarded Adefina openly as the witch drew a long gleaming pin from her hair.

'Oh,' she cooed at the little creature, 'you're perfect.'

The sorcery began and, as the puppy yelped its distress, horrified Brill wrapped her arms against fear and held fast to her secret.

Benjamin had whispered to her, too.

'Be ready.'

44

Benjamin worked rapidly within the precincts of the ruined church.

At first of dark he had sped north, avoiding wall guards to leave London behind as he searched to find again the place from where first he had looked on the city.

The ancient site stirred itself to his arrival, sending a flight of bats through the blank round window of its western wall as he passed beneath. Pausing only to consider again the ranks of severed columns and the piled remnants they once held aloft, he had crossed the floor memorials to approach the altar. Up three broad steps to the platform, there he had turned round and round once more in a final assessment before getting to work.

He encircled himself.

With keen eye and sure strokes, he drew to the end of the tracing, his chalk stick tap-tapping on the stones towards the final symbol. When laid out, that one shape would seal the circles. But not yet.

'Are you ready?'

Benjamin tracked Juno's voice to silver eyes glinting in the dark among the rubble.

'Yes,' he said. 'I was waiting for you. Where is Varney?'

'Taking his place.' She mounted the steps, drawing into ghost light beaming through the high, round window. Though she hesitated at his circles, when he indicated the gap, she stepped to join him.

'Will she come?'

'What choice does she have?'

'But she'll expect a trap. She'll guess at your circles.'

'That's why she has to come. No dead army can reach me in here. But remember, when it begins, I cannot leave the circles. If I do, we lose.'

'I'm sorry.'

'Sorry for what?'

'This,' she said awkwardly with a look to the shattered surroundings, 'I brought you to this.'

'True.' And he smiled. 'I wouldn't be here if it wasn't for you.'

His kiss was all the explanation needed.

She gripped him tighter.

'Can your plan really work?

'After this, there'll be no more running,' he promised and eased her back.

'Stay within the circles,' she ordered and, with another kiss, she raced away.

He fought a sudden urge to follow her and bent over the final preparations. Closing the chalked arcs, he drew the final symbol with precise care. Stepping up from his work, he looked on all, recalling well the grimoire's dire warnings against error. Satisfied, he gave attention to the church and the land beyond its broken walls as he conjured.

'Nebula,' he intoned to a roll of fingers, little to index, and sought the result.

It came slowly and from all sides. Surfacing from the cold earth, mist flowed to his command to roll over stones and through the doorway until the ruin was flooded. Tendrils snaked up the altar steps and swallowed the circles about his feet.

And then for the last part.

Benjamin turned to London, distant and brooding. He offered crossed fingers to its skyline.

'I'm here,' he told her.

* * *

The night drew on; the moon grew bored. Alone in watchful silence over the ruin, it appeared to slow its course above, crawling through the heavens until, wearied by waiting, it lay back for a sleepy descent through scudding clouds. The leading edge of the arcing crescent finally touched distant woods and as it did, Adefina came.

A pale vision gliding among headstones, she criss-crossed Benjamin's line of sight. She used the very mist he had summoned, disappearing behind the veil in one place to reappear entirely elsewhere despite his efforts to track her. Skirting the church's exterior, she turned briefly towards him to offer a smile that was at once playful and filled with cruel promises. The hairs on his neck prickled fearfully for it as, an instant later, she vanished again.

Benjamin peered urgently about, seeking her on all sides and bracing for bolts of magic. But the world remained a silent void. Not a movement, no hint of sound or wind, came to shift the mist.

'Hello, Benjamin.'

Startled, he whirled to find her, within the church and dangerously close. She paced behind the columns around the altar and, from that safe distance, she examined the boy and his surroundings closely. A fresh smile lit on her lips as a notion occurred to her.

'A church, really?' she mocked. 'Was this to be your protection from me?'

'I am protected,' he promised her.

Her eyes narrowed for his daring, and fingers stroked thoughtfully. After some musing moments, she touched her lips softly. 'Aura,' she whispered to send a breath and nudge the mist from Benjamin's feet. His drawings were so perfect they displeased her.

'You have been busy.'

As Adefina spoke, Benjamin spied Brill's arrival. She walked slowly to the command of Ilemauzar's dagger, advancing along the aisle until the demon halted her with a jab. A moment later, from a side route, huge Rok appeared, a long sword held ready. Benjamin quickly read the negative signals that passed from the slaves to their mistress. They had not detected the other fugitives.

'All alone?' Adefina asked. 'Where are the other brats, I wonder.'

'Already on a ship at sea. I sent them ahead.'

Adefina offered a wry chuckle for that.

'Still a bad liar, Benjamin,' she chastised. 'I think they are closer than that. Let's see...' She turned abruptly and brought her hands together. 'In deepest shadow, perhaps!' Her spell launched, a blinding flash that punched to the recesses of the church. Sun-bright, it exposed all in a moment, yet found nothing but startled bats thrown into terrified disarray.

Shrugging off her failure to find Juno or Varney, Adefina peered once more at Benjamin and to the circles. 'I thought we were here to strike a deal,' she reminded him.

'It's best to be cautious when dealing with a witch,' he shot back.

She cast him a feigned look of offence.

'Why must you be so hurtful?' she asked. 'Have you been listening to fireside stories? You have nothing to fear from me. How could I not respect someone clever enough to learn the secrets of my book? In fact, you have more than earned your freedom by such intelligence.'

'I am free already,' Benjamin informed her. Ilemauzar bared angry teeth for the words.

'That being so,' Adefina countered, 'why don't you come and give me my book?' She held out one white hand and set her skull ring glinting in the motion.

'Why don't you come and get it?'

Adefina threw back her head and gave way to shrill laughter. Pressing a hand to her stomach to contain her amusement, she leaned against a column and took time to gather herself.

'Such a silly boy,' she tittered. 'Your plan is filled with holes, Benjamin. Did you really think I would dance into your circles and risk my doom at your hand?' She shook a finger at naughty tricks. 'Why would I take such action when all I need do is wait right here for the burning dawn to get me what I want?' Her smile demanded an answer.

'You don't have time to wait,' he informed her. It was his turn to weave a spell. 'Incendium!'

The effect was instant. Magic fire burst to his command and flowed at his direction. A single great tongue of flame swept skyward to find the peak of the western wall. It burst against the brickwork and endured, roaring furiously to massive orange streaks cutting the night sky.

'A signal fire,' Benjamin shouted over the fiery storm, 'visible from the city walls. The first alarm will be raised quickly. Soldiers will come to investigate and they will find circles of magic and a witch at her work.'

Adefina's face contorted and reflected the very fury of the flames. 'You whelp!' she spat, crashing her hands together. Power conjured to her snarled command and leapt across space towards the circles as Benjamin stood his ground. At the very edge of the outer ring, the witch's power was met by an invisible force and turned back, gouging a blazing track across the floor towards her. With a cry, Adefina threw herself to the cover of a pillar which absorbed the blow in a burst of dusty stone. Thwarted, she faced Ilemauzar and shrieked at her demon.

'Kill him!'

Unleashed by her mistress, Ilemauzar formed a dripping smile. Forcing Brill to her knees, she fixed Benjamin with her serpent's gaze and began to pace softly to the left, tracking about the headstones like a ravenous beast seeking a route to its prey.

Within his circles, Benjamin maintained a keen eye on her progress even as he flexed fingers to palms in readiness to repel the first attack.

Ilemauzar chuckled at the sight, reading in the boy's movements the agitation of a frightened child, and a malevolent glee pushed her smile wider. She halted, features unchanging as she straightened and flexed her shoulders in drawing a deep breath of preparation. All fell to stillness.

'Boo!' she snapped.

Startled, Benjamin conjured. Howling power cut towards the stones and ploughed furrows of scorched earth to a choking plume rolling to the boundaries of the church. Smoke spilled up the burning wall to reduce its fire momentarily to mere candle flicker, then fell away on the breeze. When the night cleared, Ilemazuar was gone.

Alarmed, Benjamin whirled all around, seeking the enemy before she could gain the advantage. She had surely avoided his clumsy spell, he reasoned, and cursed himself for it. He detected her then, slowing from a headlong rush about the pillars, and he met her malicious gaze where she stopped. He watched as she reached to trace a sword and dagger on the air, and mock him with clashing blades.

'Too easy,' she sneered with a slick of her lips. The demon braced for a sprint towards the circles.

The memorial stone at Ilemauzar's feet burst to a dusty eruption. An instant later, a second explosion blew upwards behind Rok. Confounded by the blasts and convinced of hidden magic, Ilemauzar fell back to take in the sight of Varney stepping from the grave, even as the Viking spun to behold the risen Juno.

'Let destruction take them by surprise,' the monk recited darkly.

'Don't waste my time, holy boy,' Ilemauzar sneered as she gathered her senses, 'your wound makes you half a swordsman.'

Varney merely grinned at the taunt and drew his Oriental swords.

'Yet I can be twice the warrior you are.' As though to demonstrate his claim, Varney reversed his waki-zashi and offered it to Brill. 'Complete me.'

Brill seized the dragon handle and rose boldly for the fight.

With a hiss of poison, Ilemauzar plunged in, her weapon spinning and wheeling against boy and girl. Varney responded and parried, metal singing to metal, and made room for Brill to draw sparks with her sword.

Rok took his cue and swung a blow at Juno. But the Roman anticipated the move and easily avoided the sword to offer a dangerous strike of her own.

Benjamin's attention was diverted by the sudden commencement of action, causing him to forget Adefina. When his senses howled their warning and turned him to her again, the witch's hands were already joined and her spell almost fully uttered. With no time to react with a spell of his own, Benjamin ducked as power assailed his position. Lightning exploded and sent painful daggers to his eyes. Though stemmed by the protective circles, the dazzling blast was enough to make him step back from the agony and throw hands against it. Far off in his mind, a tiny spot of calm warned against motion and urged balance as a foot scraped perilously close to circle edges. Still partially blinded, he shifted his weight and fought to prevent a fall into danger. He toppled, but the reaction was enough to send him crashing back onto the heart of his defences.

Through clearing vision, he detected a change in Adefina's position. With the battling vampires swinging nearer to her, she followed the arc of the pillars to ready an attack from behind. He fixed his target quickly and conjured.

The bolt of magic caught Adefina unprepared and tore her off her feet, sprawling the witch across a memorial marked by a high cross.

His next target.

A spell of destruction sent to its base ripped the cross's foundation to pebbles and the great weight toppled forward. Adefina cried out and desperately conjured. In mid-fall, the stone marker was obliterated and offered no more than a cloud of dust to her head.

The grey blizzard did nothing to mask the look of boiling hate she offered as she rose once more.

'Pathetic,' she hissed. 'You don't have the first inkling of the true scale of magic in your grasp, do you? You're not ready for it. You are a child playing with fire, Benjamin Blake. Let me show you real power.' Fingers and lips worked in time.

The sound of her spell came on as a crunch of stone on stone within the church. Benjamin sought the origin, bracing to deflect the assault. But the noise was everywhere at once, a wall of sound he struggled to locate. Only through a shifting of the fire's light above, and a lengthening of shadows below, did he finally see the dreadful scale of Adefina's conjuring.

The western wall was collapsing. Across its breadth, a massive crack ran to undermine that portion of the wall shouldering the round window. The gigantic form slipped on crumbling bricks, and jets of powdered stone whistled from the breach. The rupture swept on until a last supporting brick groaned and shattered, and the fall began. Speeding down upon the church, the toppling pyramid trailed its signal fire to a thousand flames, and their light caught Benjamin's stunned face as the avalanche found him and the altar.

It seemed a giant punched the earth. The blow rolled on a wave of destruction to carry witch and warriors along, flinging all indifferently across the aisle. A blinding storm of powdered stone filled the ruin and the church doorway belched it to the world.

From the first silence after, Juno sprang up, driven to a shrill cry for Benjamin. Rok prevented her advance with his arcing sword and, as she countered the attack, she caught sight of Adefina rising in triumph.

Winded, and blinded by dust, the sorceress offered a sneer for Juno's concern and advanced through billowing clouds. Behind, she heard Ilemauzar's cry of renewed effort against Varney and Brill, and the resounding clash of silver blades. She ignored it all and pressed ahead for the prize, swatting the foul air for vision in searching for her book.

But Benjamin was waiting. In the face of Adefina's look of wonderment, he stood unharmed on the altar platform, a grey-smeared phantom hemmed by the frame of the fallen window. And standing boldly yet within his circles.

'Pulvis!' he roared.

Only Adefina's reflexes prevented her destruction in the instant. She offered a desperate counter-spell and fell again before an explosive collision of power. A blow at her back stunned her and she found herself in the protection of a shattered pillar. Safe from Benjamin's magic, and concealed from his examining gaze, she searched her hands frantically for inspiration. Dismissing combinations that could not hope to penetrate the circles, her mind locked onto one possibility among the filthy digits, and she prepared. If force could not move Benjamin Blake, perhaps fear would.

'Do you ever have bad dreams?' she called to him across the stones. Her hands were already working in time to a whispered command as she slowly regained her footing.

Benjamin watched her rise and he braced for the strike. At first, there appeared to be no effect from the spell she cast. No onslaught of power leapt towards him, no fiery light, though he kept his hands ready for conjuration in reply to hers. Only when he cast his sight to the spaces between the rubble did he finally perceive the result of her spell-weaving. Around the full circumference of his position, the floor seeped oily black as the sneaking dank creatures of the night came crawling. Muddy insects, bloated worms, spiders, snakes, rats, all manner of nightmare beasts in their thousands, emerged at Adefina's behest to seek out her enemy. Her army slithered along the church walls and over rubbled peaks, their very presence swamping Benjamin's magical abilities with childhood fears. A million hungry eyes regarded him and surged closer, waved on by Adefina, whose malevolent leer was framed by tumbling hair and illuminated by the fires.

The witch-vision broke Benjamin's moment of fear in an instant. Peering at her, he found his answer to the crawling horror under her command. Steadying his mind, he scanned keenly across the skittering ranks and chose his best weapon.

'Levitas,' he called to a fat, mangy rat.

With a squeal, the fleshy rodent was snatched upwards from among its fellows and thrown perfectly on target.

Into Adefina's face.

The witch shrieked hysterically against the mass of fur suddenly raking at her cheeks and eyes. Staggering back, she reached instinctively for the wriggling attacker and, in her terror, her confounded mind lost control of the spell. As one, the mesmerised creatures broke ranks and fled back to darkness while she wrestled with the scrabbling rat.

* * *

Amid bricks and burning, vampires locked in combat.

Again and again, sword met wakizashi and katana as Varney and Brill worked against Ilemauzar.

'You are tiring,' Ilemauzar jeered Varney. She slashed at the boy's throat but struck nothing as Brill distracted and Varney circled deftly away.

'When I have destroyed you,' Varney retorted, *'I will lay me down in peace and sleep, for the Lord makes me dwell in safety.* I can last until then.'

A crash from above announced the fatal weakening of a column and the opponents were forced apart as a block plunged to the aisle. With a frenzied howl, Ilemauzar leapt over the obstacle into a renewed attack.

Distracted by the explosion, Rok wavered in his own assault, and once again Juno ducked the slicing arc of his sword to thrust her weapon at the giant's belly. The Viking was quick enough to slap down the thrusting arm, but too late in meeting the Roman's onward charge. Juno's head drove into its target, folding the Viking at the stomach and butting him clean off his feet. Rok crashed onto a debris pile and lost his weapon to the shadows as his opponent bore down. He dug quickly through the folds of his ragged clothing to bring forth his war axe. With a sweep, he struck the Roman blade aside just in time and scrambled back to his feet.

Juno was forced to change tactics as the shorter Viking weapon swung furiously at her through unending arcs. Ducking and rolling, she avoided the axe-head, sometimes by mere inches, and sought an opening for a counterattack. Rok brought both hands high for a crushing blow and she moved, slicing at the open target he presented. But the bearded warrior sensed the tactic and shifted back. The blade sang wide and Juno was exposed. Rok offered a ferocious battle-cry and hammered downwards. The girl raced one move ahead, blocking upwards with her arm to halt the axe at its handle. She followed through again with her head, crunching brutally into Rok's nose to send him reeling.

* * *

At the circles, Benjamin watched as Adefina finally cast the rat aside with a disgusted sound and refocused on him. He waited for her next spell to blast his position. But all at once, the witch showed her back and strode purposefully to the edge of the ruin, there to throw her arms wide to concealing night.

'Show yourself!' she demanded of what lay in the dark and raised her arms higher. 'Come now!'

Prepared for some fresh horror, Benjamin watched as a human figure rose at the church wall to wipe the smile from Adefina's startled face.

Matthew Hopkins levelled a cocked pistol to the witch's heart.

'What Hell is this?' the witchfinder demanded of the scene before him. He gazed in horrified wonder on circles, on the silver-eyed Benjamin, and on demons dancing in battle about the ceremony of evil conjuring. Through his amazement he fumbled into his tunic to bring a pocket Bible with shaking fingers against all evil.

'I confess,' Adefina cried suddenly between her arms, her face brimming with tears. 'Oh, have mercy, sir, a measure of pity on one led astray by Lucifer and his servants.'

'You are a witch,' Hopkins snarled.

Adefina wept for the accusation. 'No, sir, please. Not a witch. A slave. Captured by false promises, I was. My head was turned by lies.'

'I saw what you did to John Stearne.'

'Not I, not I,' she countered with a frantic gesture to the circles. 'Your friend burned in fire summoned by the demon Benjamin Blake. The demon who stands now at the heart of this gathering and controls what you see here. I am a slave to him. Free me, I beg you.'

'Shoot her!' Benjamin howled at the addled witchfinder.

But the command and the opportunity were already lost, obscured by a dread shadow that fell on Matthew Hopkins as another, larger form rose to the witch's call. The witchfinder turned and looked up in terrified bewilderment to the slavering features of Adefina's hellhound, jet black save for a white patch on its forehead.

The creature's blow was sudden and brutal. It took Hopkins off his feet as though he were weightless and cast him reeling among the debris. The man cried out for mortal limbs crushed against unyielding stone, and he fell broken in the dust to Adefina's cold amusement.

Chilled by the sight, Benjamin met the creature's hungry stare as it shifted to him. Claws raked deep gashes across a wall where it entered the ruined arena in expectation of softer prey. Through his fear, Benjamin dug deep for magic combinations. He knew the hideous creation approaching would endure many spells for Adefina before it succumbed, buying her more than enough time to strike.

'Do you like my puppy?' she teased, stroking the creature's fur like a valued pet. Keeping eyes on the boy, she leaned to speak directly into one huge, pointed ear. 'Tear his circle apart.'

So ordered, the werewolf rose, and stomped its hind legs as it offered grasping front claws for Benjamin's consideration. Its snarl of hungry anticipation presented rows of slavering fangs as the advance began.

The hound's mammoth shape filled Benjamin's vision and grew with every lumbering step. He watched claws spark on fallen blocks to dazzle and distract as he worked to keep the witch carefully in sight, knowing she would take the first opportunity to strike at a weak opening. The creature reached the columns and, after a wary pause to sniff the air, it stepped past to examine its prey more closely, savouring with its dull brain the possibility of smashing through the circles' magic to reach its prey.

Partially concealed by the beast's form, Adefina's hands drifted towards one another again and Benjamin watched the seed of a new spell growing in her eyes. He held fast, torn between blasting the hound and defending against the magic she prepared to set in motion.

A far-off cry rolled across the land, a lone jubilant war chant piercing the night. Surprised by it, all turned in search of the source and beheld a dark horse and rider rearing against the sinking moon. Benjamin dared hope for an instant that it signalled the first soldiers from the city. But this lone horseman was strange to his vision, misshapen in the saddle. The figure did not seem to be human at all, but, by the shape of its head and furred covering, appeared somehow hound-like.

The snorting horse was spurred into its charge, and the 'werewolf rider' cried out furiously again for battle. The wind of galloping sent the bizarre form to a flapping in the race and, tugging at the head, the gusts peeled back the covering, the hood of an animal cape. Darach was revealed beneath, already drawing his broad sword.

Adefina's black hound roared against the advance of the werewolf-killer. Abandoning Benjamin, it sprang a wall to meet the attack despite the witch's raging protests. It clawed rapidly towards warrior and mount and, with a sweep of one paw to catch the horse's thundering legs, it brought all to earth with a resounding crash.

Darach tumbled away but pulled up unharmed to tear free of his monstrous cloak. 'I see you began without me,' he said to everyone. He swept his sword as though to test its weight and took up a battle stance under the manic glare of the hound. The warrior smiled in return and flung down the werewolf skin like a challenge. 'You'll make a better cloak than your cousin,' he taunted.

Vampire and hellhound roared into battle.

Darach leapt back as massive teeth smashed together barely inches from his throat. Ahead of the werewolf's next bite, he side-stepped and channelled his movement into a powerful swinging of his sword. The blade found the beast's shoulder and cut past thick fur to a spray of yellow blood.

Howling its agony, the hound retreated and stabbed its razor-sharp claws at the vampire but clutched only air in the effort.

Darach launched into another sweeping advance, both hands driving his sword on. His blade travelled towards the animal's exposed neck but at the last instant, monster fingers clasped the metal and stopped it short. Darach faced rows of glistening teeth as the werewolf faced him down. His sword useless, the warrior selected the next best weapon.

His head.

Surging forward, he smashed his forehead against the broad, dripping nose of the hound. As pain flared in the creature's brain, the warrior used the diversion to slide his blade harshly from the gripping fingers, slicing through them to bring anguished whines from the beast. He continued the movement and spun fully about to plunge his sword deep into the creature's belly, forcing the creature higher on its legs through the force of the blow. With pitiful howls, the tormented werewolf clawed a moment at the fatal wound and toppled forward, its massive weight bearing down to flatten Darach as the silver blade ended its monstrous existence.

Across the ruined floor, battles raged on. Ilemauzar fell back before a merciless hail of blows from Varney and, for the first time, it became clear the demon was beset by fearful doubt. A slash offered by Brill's shorter blade passed her defences and ripped foul skin. Darts of silver-laced pain raced into the demon's wicked mind.

Varney bellowed to the night. *'Blessed be the Lord my strength, who teacheth my hands to war and my fingers to fight!'*

Made terrified by the monk's words and yet more afraid of Brill's speed, Ilemauzar scrambled backwards, swinging frantically as she tried to make room for attack or escape. But boy and girl appeared at every turn, striking against each strike she offered and driving into every opening presented. Ilemauzar worked desperately to avoid a killer thrust.

Juno and Rok careened violently between the demon and her opponents as the separate battles collided. Weapons clashed and sang on all fronts at once until, spotting an opportunity, Ilemauzar jumped aside and fled. Varney quickly broke from the duelling vampires and gave chase, leaving Brill to join Juno in her fight.

Once more a target for Rok's axe, Juno was forced to roll from another strike, kicking out at the Viking's legs as he travelled. The blow flung Rok from his feet and Juno struck down with a slicing attack at the giant's neck, only to find the strike blocked by the axe handle. In a flash, Rok kicked Brill away and seized the Roman blade. With a crushing hold, he used all his strength to launch Juno overhead and away, disarming the Roman in the process. Rok tested the feel of the captured sword and, pleased with this new weapon, he bore down on Juno, shouldering Brill aside as he plunged on.

Juno fell back from a lethal onslaught of sweeps and stabs. The Viking laughed at what was becoming a game, and one where the outcome was certain and only a short time away. He sliced left; the Roman ducked right. He stabbed right and the girl jumped left. He let fly with both weapons at once and Juno moved boldly to block. The Viking was left exposed for a great kick that sent him reeling.

Crashing backwards, Juno felt her wrist strike a solid object fallen on a layer of ash and dirt. Her fingers identified it and hope grew with the touch. She watched Rok recover for a move into a fresh charge and she timed her action to coincide with his. As the giant hurtled forward, she drew the Viking's fallen sword and launched it.

Spinning to find its mark, the blade tore into Rok, forcing the Roman sword from his hands as he was lifted and carried back. A pillar received him in a rattling crash and the cutting blade sang deeply into the stone. Firmly pinned, Rok looked in horror on his silver wound and slumped, held to standing by the pinning sword.

Adefina staggered back, confounded by the turn of events against her slaves, by the turning faces of Juno and Brill, so defiant in regarding her. Held by those looks so unafraid, she realised too late that Benjamin was still in the fight and forming a spell.

'Ventus,' Benjamin uttered, summoning up a tearing whirlwind. At once Adefina was battered by the force of the storm. Under the boy's guidance, the spout of rushing air moved across the ground and dragged the screeching witch along, hauling her steadily towards a dancing fire.

Perceiving Benjamin's plan with a start, Adefina frantically sought a defence, thrashing about for a weapon, any weapon, to counter him. She found nothing but the fire and discovered her answer there. With fingers wide, she flicked her thumbs inward to ring fingers. 'Levitas,' she commanded.

Benjamin was slow in predicting the move and reacted badly to the blazing mass that came hurtling at him. Forced to conjure a blocking defence, he battered the sailing fire down, but lost his grip on the witch in the same instant. And though she landed hard, she was quickest to the next spell.

'Pulvis.'

The blow followed a second after the flames, and though the protective circles diverted the worst, it smashed the fire to an explosion of countless scorching darts. The force of the blast took Benjamin's balance, and as he toppled with a cry, the grimoire slid free of his satchel to tumble across symbols, smudging lines in its passing to an opening in the dust! He clawed desperately to retrieve the volume but his legs failed and he tumbled headlong after it down the altar steps.

'Pulvis!' Adefina repeated quickly, and the fresh spell swept Benjamin to crash heavily against a pillar, far beyond the grimoire.

With a hideous shriek of triumph, Adefina advanced.

45

Benjamin dragged at the earth towards the grimoire.

Another powerful blast from Adefina dashed hopes of regaining the book as he was thrown brutally back against the brickwork.

'Rest easy, Benjamin,' the witch mocked, drawing closer until she stood over him. 'When I have the grimoire, I will make all things well again. And then you *will* sleep with the dead.'

A savage war-cry announced Darach's attack. The warrior sprang forward, his sword already drawing high for a massive strike at the witch. He had barely closed the distance when her conjuring hands punched him aside with invisible power. The same magic was instantly turned on Juno and Brill, hurling both cruelly away.

'At last, the rebels fall,' Adefina sighed wearily. 'Your freedom lies in ruins.' With a consoling stroke for Benjamin's face, she stepped past the ring of pillars, drawn smiling to her book's glittering where it lay beyond the boy's drawn circles. With tender care, she knelt and clasped the source of her power to herself as a lover, touching it fondly and taking time to blow a layer of dust staining its cover.

'Incipe,' Benjamin whispered, finally, and at last.

'What did you say?' Adefina asked lightly, her gaze still lingering on the grimoire.

'Audite,' he quoted, the second line of the spell.

Frowning at the boy's words, the witch looked questioningly towards him. She frowned yet again on catching the knowing look in his face, and her own features began to twist in slow recognition of an awful truth. She glanced urgently to the split circles where Benjamin had found his protection, and only then to the ring of pillars that encircled them all.

'Ventus!' she uttered in rising alarm, aiming her power at the base of one.

The obedient wind sprang up and tore at the stone, scattering aside concealing dust and mist. The symbol Benjamin had chalked there at sunset was revealed, just one of the many he had drawn and hidden on the stones in this third, wider and secret circle Adefina now knelt inside.

'Nox,' Benjamin called, his trap closing fast.

'You whelp!' the witch screamed. 'You treacherous little dog!'

Adefina pushed fearfully to her feet and made to escape the circle. But the ground under her was already shifting to the first cracking of memorials, already lifting to the force of that rising beneath. She staggered on uneven ground; her arms wound tightly around the grimoire.

'Ex sepulcrum venite!' Benjamin cried, finishing his command on this, the middle line of the spell.

Adefina took another step as a patch of earth burst up by her foot, pushed violently aside by the thrust of a long dead hand from the grave below. The parched, spindly fingers gripped keenly at her ankle and locked tight. Another leathery hand erupted, this one snapping to clutch the hem of her cape, followed by another, and yet more, until a crop of grasping hands flexed in jostling for their share of the wailing sorcer-ess. As quickly as she kicked or battered one dusty claw loose, another bony limb took its place. She was dragged to her knees by the hauling dead, and mottled hands fought in reaching for her belt and next her blouse. Such was her panic now, Adefina released her grip on the grimoire to slap hysterically at the spindly fingers upon her. But her shrieking efforts were futile and she was pulled harshly onto her back. Snagging digits entwined arms, neck and hair, and by degrees, the screaming witch was pulled into the cold, choking earth. The end came in a final wail of terror that rose through clay filling her mouth, and Adefina Corvus was dragged underground to her dusty death.

The mist tumbled back and the whole world fell to a horrified silence.

At last, pained by the witch's strikes, Benjamin pushed slowly to his feet and surveyed the quiet circle of his making, where all limbs save one had fully vanished back into the earth. Bearing that shining skull ring on one finger, Adefina's hand hung lifelessly in touching the cover of her beloved book. Benjamin moved to ease the volume from her reach for the last time.

In a flash the witch's hand snapped shut on his, and Benjamin cried out in fear and pain as nails held and bit spitefully through immortal skin. But the attack passed quickly, and Benjamin pulled free to regard crescent-shaped cuts on his hand, the witch's parting gift in her death spasm. With a final slackening of fingers, her hand fell to eternal reaching for her grimoire.

Benjamin heard a sound, a low rising moan of protest, and with renewed fear looked to Adefina's grave, expecting her return still. But the sound came from farther off, and he looked between the dying fires to find Rok staring back. Still speared to stone, the Viking's anguish for his dead mistress became a scowl of hatred for Benjamin and he struggled furiously to be free. Only the sudden pressure of a warrior's sword laid against his neck stopped his wrestling efforts. The Viking glared at the grinning Darach.

Juno came between the fires to watch Benjamin dutifully work the grimoire back into his satchel. She returned his smile as Brill pressed through smoke to survey the destruction with satisfaction.

The friends stood in smiling silence until one dared say it.

'Freedom,' Darach whispered.

'Freedom,' Juno agreed, 'thanks to Benjamin.'

'Circles within circles,' he said, and they smiled together.

And as they smiled, it happened.

The joy washed abruptly from Juno's face as she perceived movement behind Benjamin. She lunged forward instinctively, grabbed defensively, and spun into a turn with him. For a bare moment in time, Benjamin saw nothing but the girl's determined features, heard nothing but the gentlest whistle on the night air as something travelled swiftly.

The dagger meant for him struck her deeply.

She lurched under the blow and staggered with a gasp, catching his hands in falling. Pulled with her, Benjamin cried out and sought the attacker. Gravely wounded, Matthew Hopkins tumbled forward with his throw to land with a pained cry in the dust.

Juno's whisper of knowing called Benjamin back.

'Silver,' she said, and smiled sadly as her eyes fixed on him.

'No,' he protested, and he desperately searched his mind. 'There's a spell, there must be a spell for this.'

She hushed him with a touch. 'There isn't one. The grimoire was not made for good. That's why it needs someone good to keep it from the world.'

Her words did nothing for his pain.

'Why did you do it?' he demanded bitterly, feeling the shift in her now.

'No greater love, Benjamin,' she reminded him, and her tears were silver.

It ended in a moment that would burn for an eternity. Benjamin felt the strength leave her grip and watched her features become peaceful. The silver fire in eyes that held to his dimmed slowly and the natural colour washed in. And even as he watched, she became indistinct to his sight, altering to become shaped by silver vapour dancing and sparkling on the air. Benjamin heard sword and dagger chime free and fall to earth. The last of Juno was caught on a shifting breeze and the shimmering vision closed on him, her lips passing to his as smoke. And she was gone.

Benjamin looked on empty hands as his ears filled to Brill's sobs, and to a Viking's mocking laughter.

Reaching for the fallen sword, he worked slowly and calmly through the sound. He tested the unfamiliar weapon in his hand, carefully gauging its weight and balance. Finally, and no less slowly, he rose and faced the chuckling Rok.

And he roared!

He filled the area between with all the rage and hate a vampire can feel, and the strength of it shook the stones and wiped the vampire's idiot smile away. In a flash of fearful knowledge, Rok understood what approached was no longer a mere boy to be toyed with, and what he carried along would be no quick spell of death. This punishment would take much, much longer.

Benjamin strode forth, leaving Brill and Darach aghast, and bore down on Rok where he clawed desperately for release. The Roman sword drew high for the strike and Rok cried for pity.

Benjamin sensed the racing movement too late. The enemy darted across his vision and her blade thrust coldly to his neck. He halted, caught at the mercy of glaring Ilemauzar.

The demon jabbed a warning finger at the others. 'Don't you move!' she barked. 'His head will be off before you reach me.'

'Your mistress is dead,' Benjamin said, twisting to offer Ilemauzar a defiant stare. He saw the demon's sickly gaze scan for the truth of it and heard her gasp for the dead hand in the earth.

Anger and bewilderment overcame Ilemauzar. Unable to reason this outcome in the battle, she was reduced to clicking inaction, her slavish mind behind blinking eyes unwilling to decide the next move for itself.

'The boy killed her,' Rok croaked bitterly. 'He used trickery and lured her to destruction.'

Ilemauzar weighed up the information and slowly pushed confusion aside in favour of crystal visions of torture and vengeance. Bony fingers tightened on the handle of her sword and once again she found Benjamin and her murderous intent.

A moment's silent communication between boy and demon was broken by a distant cry, fearful and repeating directly to the rear of Benjamin's stilled head. Its urgency drew others to it and he looked for some reaction in the faces of Ilemauzar and Rok. What he found in each was a rising tide of cold terror.

'Ilemauzar!' Rok began to howl. 'Release me! Have mercy! Release me!'

Ilemauzar ignored the Viking's pleading and reeled from the horror she beheld. Her sword fell from Benjamin's neck, forgotten, as she faltered with quivering lip as the approaching voice grew clearer. It was Varney's voice raised in the same cold fear visible in Ilemauzar's face. The demon spared a last glance for the boy, her plan for revenge thwarted. 'Another night, Benjamin Blake.'

The demon fled from sight, and the whimpering Rok, still struggling in his place, was abandoned with his pitiful cries after her.

Benjamin whirled in confusion to locate the source of the demon's fear. He found Darach, visibly afraid even as he moved with urgency to sheath his sword, and Brill, already stepping back, shaking her head in voiceless terror. Beyond, racing ever closer, Varney charged on with his dire warning. Benjamin at last made out the boy's words, and he too was made afraid as he looked to the eastern horizon.

'The sun is rising!'

46

Exposed in the open beyond the walls of the city, the onset of dawn's first fire had caught them. Even as Benjamin looked on, rays of sunrise glittered distantly in a greying sky.

'Run!' Darach commanded, and he followed his own advice in a blinking.

Turning from the eastern glow, Benjamin felt the wind of Varney's passing as the boy gathered Brill to him. He made to follow, pausing just long enough to secure the satchel and its dread contents about his shoulder. As he did, his vision met with Rok's, the warrior's features twisting to a mask of terrified pleading. He stretched out a hand to the boy, begging for release from the terrible fate spilling nearer.

'I will serve you,' Rok promised, 'I will serve you.'

Benjamin tucked Juno's sword away and Rok found his fingers clawing at empty space left by the boy's flight.

The vampires sped between light and dark, in pursuit of remaining night, fast retreating from the unstoppable radiance now tumbling over the edge of the earth.

London! They crossed field after field towards the city, the colours about already rising distinctly from the night hue. On they raced, past sleeping cottages and animals that noisily protested their passing. On, until they saw city walls rising boldly against a sky-line of failing dark.

The wall of light burned after and, in its relentless advance across the ruined church, it found Rok and Hopkins together.

The Viking screamed against the dawn.

He threw up hands against blinding light but its rays fell scorching on vulnerable skin, blackening it to dust in an instant. The warrior's filthy beard and cloth rags burst to flame and exposed his vampire flesh to punishing beams. Before the witchfinder's unbelieving gaze, sharp nails clicked in anguish on burning skeletal fingers and vampire teeth bit at scalding air even as they crumbled. Melted eyes dribbled down running cheeks and flowed to choke shrieks escaping liquid lips. The daylight left noth-ing, not even his bones, and Rok fell to wind-blown ash on a groaning Hopkins.

Hungry for more, the light swept on.

Varney led the climb up the sheer city wall, hand over hand in pursuit of salvation. When first he, then

Brill and Darach after, disappeared above, Benjamin doubled his efforts, fearing to lose sight of them among the chimney pots and roofs beyond. Gaining the top, he searched for his friends, quickly spying Varney where he waved for greater speed. Benjamin plunged after.

Leaping roof to roof, the vampires' escape followed the line of the river, its waters sparkling with the first reflected light. Benjamin cast a glance back urgently to gauge the sun's progress. The border between night and day lay just behind, pushing rapidly across the fields stretching to the base of the city walls.

Momentarily hypnotised by the dawn's onward ferocity, Benjamin's foot snagged on a jutting tile and he pitched forward, directly towards a roof's edge. With only shifting waters below, he flung out his arms and dug nails into a passing chimney stack. He held firm but his body twisted sharply in the fall. With a gasp, he watched the satchel tear away and carry on, speeding across the tiles to the lip of the roof. He lunged after but clawed short. He could do no more than watch as the satchel struck the river's surface and carried the grimoire to deep waters.

Waters that glimmered in welcoming dawn's relentless advance.

He hurtled on, refusing to look back again for fear the ever-gaining light might burn out his eyes as he ran. Further ahead, his companions steered a route away from the river and Varney pointed quickly to the spire of a church rising amid bustling houses.

Sanctuary.

Benjamin followed hard on their trail, springing across street-gaps to race up pitched roofs and skate down their rear sides, working to close the gap to the others.

Leaping to street level, Varney's speeding form gained the dark side-door of the church and plunged into lingering shadow. He caught Brill's hand and pulled her along. A second later, Darach reached the spot. With a look for signs of Benjamin's approach, he gestured for his friend, drew quickly into the dark and was gone.

The edge of the roof loomed. Benjamin gave himself to space, launching as far as he could. Treetops slapped at his feet and an instant later, headstones in the little churchyard threatened to upset his landing. But he cleared all to reach ground and resume his pace without pause. Leaves filtered the sun's rays. Straining hard, he used the last greying shadow of the doorway to dive through.

Soft earth gave way to marbled floor and he slid between pews, beneath the mute welcome of statues. Gaining the centre of the aisle, he looked desperately for his friends. But there was no sign on any side.

Turning around and around, he looked for evidence of their passing, finding nothing. With growing desperation, he was drawn to the high arched windows over the altar. A multitude of colours in glass began to shine, responding to the day's first touch, and the windows seemed to become the waking eyes of a great beast. Their light, blazing with vivid hues, crept down the wall beneath and began to seep along the aisle towards him.

'Benjamin!'

The urgent call tore his attention to a recess where the shadows still hung over the large marble tomb of some fallen warrior. There, in the deepest black remaining, Darach summoned him on.

Benjamin leapt for the dark, his feet clear of the floor in a headlong dive as the sunlight raced to deny the last hope of refuge.

Down he tumbled, falling into the depths of darkness and on down a flight of stone steps after the crashing Darach. Together they reached the bottom in a heap of limbs, just in time to see the light of day send blinding daggers through cracks in the tomb, to form the fiery bars of a daytime cell.

47

enjamin, are you all right?

Juno.

Her voice was a phantom whisper in the mind. Her face, pale and untouchable as the moon where she appeared to him. He sought her again and again, finding her in the dark. She was a twinkling silhouette on the bridge wall at Ravenhill, clear and close in a smuggler's box, ferocious in the fight, and gentle in piercing his defences to reach the heart of magic.

'Benjamin, are you all right?'

Darach's face was drawn and his voice was made hollow by the vaulted ceiling.

She slipped away in a blinking, and Benjamin found the warrior close to his side. Nearby and watching tearfully, Brill clung to Varney where he knelt in silent prayer for the fallen. Benjamin offered them all his mortal misunderstanding.

'We were supposed to have forever.'

His own tears came, numerous and stinging as wicked spells, but without magic to stem them. He grasped Juno's sword to fight the pain as Darach's arms and Varney's words became a shield against the worst.

'*Where can I go from your spirit? If I go up to the heavens, you are there, if I make my bed in the depths, you are there, if I rise on the wings of the dawn, if I settle on the far side of the sea, even there your hand will guide me, your right hand will hold me fast.*'

'She was the best of us,' Darach assured his friend.

'That's true,' Varney said. 'In Juno all things became possible, remember? Who was it held thoughts of escape for us all? And when the opportunity came, when we feared to act, who but Juno had courage enough to seize the moment and spur us on? Most important of all, who but Juno created our magician, our mighty witch-killer, Benjamin Blake?'

Benjamin laughed weakly for the description but shook his head.

'Not so mighty,' he said. 'I lost the book, remember.'

The vampires considered this news quietly.

'Well,' Darach shrugged finally, 'we could never hope to destroy the cursed thing. Perhaps the river is the best place for it, hidden from the world.'

'Let the tide have the book,' Brill agreed with a dismissive flick. 'The only place to find its magic now is in your head, Benjamin. That's the best outcome. Varney and Darach are right. You were created by

Juno, who had strength against evil for us all. When Juno saved you from death, she gave the best of herself to you. No greater love.'

Benjamin wiped his tears, thanking his friends with his eyes as he found her again, smiling still.

Benjamin, she whispered, it's time to go.

'Look,' said Brill. She gestured to the steps where the light of day was steadily fading. 'Night is coming on. The world is ours.'

***

'One decision remains.'

In the quiet interior of the church, as colourful windows ebbed with the dusk, Darach paused. Standing deliberately at the junction of the crossed aisles, he gestured in turn to the four points of the compass to prompt the others. 'What is to be our destination?'

The question stalled all to an uncertain silence as the truth sank in. They were truly free, free at last to choose, though none wished to be first in breaking the happy moment.

'Europe or the New World,' Benjamin recalled at last.

'Precisely,' Darach replied.

'Or beyond,' Varney added. 'Jerusalem.' He caught Brill's sharp glance. 'By way of Paris. Brill can earn some money while I recover.'

'What about you, Benjamin?'

The boy pondered 'When we first met, Juno told me you favoured crossing to the Americas.'

'And still I do,' the warrior agreed. 'I have long desired to see the shores of the New World.'

Benjamin pondered his choices, considering the warrior's idea as he followed from the church and once again up to steal across the rooftops of sleeping London. Between puffing chimney pots, they aimed for the distant river and the renewed promise of ships bound for foreign lands.

East to Europe or west to the New World? It was a heady decision. Barely accustomed to the reality of the capital, Benjamin's head swam with thoughts of further journeys. Just nights ago, only his imagination roamed beyond the edge of paper maps; now he was faced with the reality of following even farther.

'You see?'

Darach's question pulled him abruptly from wistful thoughts and he caught a breath for the sight before him. Beyond the rooftop, a fleet of great ships arrayed, rising in such numbers their towering masts formed a forest of rope and canvas, and all within a vampire's leap.

'I have never seen a sight like this,' Benjamin said, overawed.

'Vessels offering passage to all parts of the globe,' Darach said, no less in wonder. 'Brill and Varney are below, scouting destinations. Time to choose, Benjamin.'

'Why the New World?' Benjamin asked, still filled with uncertainty. 'Why did you choose there and not Europe as Brill suggested?'

'Poor Brill,' Darach smiled. 'She forgets the great advantage of the New World over the old. There are no witches and no hellhounds.'

Benjamin laughed for the explanation and nodded at the sense he made. 'The New World it is, then.'

Darach clapped hands to a delighted cry. 'You will not regret it, Benjamin, I promise you. The New World is a trove of wonders. I have read of them, such sights to behold, and all bigger than here. The night there is wider and longer and... and even the moon is bigger.'

The warrior's enthusiasm set Benjamin to chuckling, and from there to laughter until his merriment caught Darach and they filled the night with the sound. Sailors' lanterns far below swung in search of ghost children and they laughed harder at that.

Here I am.

The hairs on Benjamin's head prickled as the voice rose silvery from dark waters to reach the deepest part of him.

I'm waaaaiting.

He peered towards the voice, on the dark water of the Thames, flowing soundlessly through the heart of the city.

Find me, the grimoire whispered on the river's muddy floor. In his mind's eye, Benjamin saw it, its pages flowing to the water's movement, turning and turning back, endlessly straining for the light of the moon. Those ever-rolling pages would mark the slow passage of time, counting the hours, days and years to come, waiting to rise again on a tide to bring up its secrets.

'Benjamin!'

He almost cried out at Brill's voice, such had been the strength of the trance. Trembling, he forced his eyes from the water to find her where she stood boldly on a ship's mast-spar, Varney at her side.

'Benjamin!' she repeated, gesturing urgently to the vessel. 'Darach! Our ship. This is the one for us all. Bound for the wine ports of France and on to the New World.'

Even as she spoke, mortal shouts were raised for all hands to the mooring ropes, and the ship creaked free.

With a cheer, and a hearty slap for Benjamin's shoulder, Darach led. His leap was long and true and took him confidently to the mast and its ropes.

I'm here.

Benjamin's ears filled again with the chilling dreamlike voice and he drew back from the roof's edge in fear.

Concerned at the action, Darach stepped to the limit of his perch. 'What is it?' he asked, scanning about for danger.

'The book,' Benjamin whispered in dread, 'the grimoire is calling.'

'Then the sooner we are far out to sea and beyond its call the better,' Darach replied. He offered his hand. 'Quickly now, join us and we are under way.'

But Benjamin shook his head. 'You don't understand. It's not just speaking to *me*. It's calling anyone with the power to hear.'

Waaaaiting.

'What if they find it, Darach? What if it is pulled up by someone else who is able to use the symbols and power?'

The others considered his words grimly as canvas unfurled to seek a driving wind.

'It might not be found for a thousand years,' Brill argued, 'or ten thousand.'

'And then we will be slaves again,' Benjamin warned.

'Curses,' Darach muttered. 'You are right. Oh well, the New World must wait.' He braced for the jump to his friend.

But the spell was already cast.

'Ventus,' Benjamin whispered. Performing the correct finger movement gently, he conjured a wind to fill the sails, strong enough to nudge the great ship farther into the river's flow.

The vampires looked back helplessly on the tide that carried them.

'Benjamin, what are you doing?' Varney called.

'I'm staying,' he replied. 'Don't you see? My path is with the grimoire, for a thousand years or ten thousand. I unlocked it and took its power and the same will happen again, unless I find it or stop others finding it first. Darach, you go to the New World because there are no witches there. I stay because there are witches *here*.'

'You may face worse than Adefina,' Darach cautioned, his form fading into the night. 'Will you be ready?'

Benjamin threw back his head and laughed again.

'More than ready,' he called. 'I learned well from the grimoire but I learned more from my friends. Juno taught me never to let it rule me for evil. Brill, you taught me to watch always for unexpected enemies. From you, Darach the hunter, I know that no matter how fierce those enemies seem, they have weaknesses for me to find. And, Varney, I know I can walk among mortals without fear of detection. You *all* prepared me for this. Let witches or demons come. They'll learn a hard lesson.

'I am Benjamin Blake and the night is mine!'

FINAL PROMISES

nd there, with a bow, I conclude my tale of the great Benjamin Blake.

No applause, please. It was my joy to share with you, truly, and a delight to answer your questions. But oh, I don't think I *have* answered all of your questions, not really. I've just replaced the old with so many new ones, haven't I?

Did Benjamin ever see his friends again? Did Ilemauzar escape the burning dawn? And, across all of the nights to this one, what other creatures of darkness crossed swords – and magic – with Benjamin over the many years from then till now?

Now, *there* is a question worth answering! Oh my, the adventures he has shared with me down the centuries. 1777, 1889, 1940, and just last night, that strange incident of the ship striking Tower Bridge; that was certainly him. Just recalling the escapades makes me dizzy, quite honestly.

But, goodness, look at the time. The house lights came up long ago and I have a matinee tomorrow.

All right, all right. I'll tell you what, hold all your questions for just a short while. Tomorrow night, I promise, I will arrange tickets for you at the stage door. The very best seats. Come afterwards and we'll talk again. Who knows, perhaps Benjamin himself will join us before the end.

He won't be far away, of that I'm certain. Since his arrival in 1645, Benjamin has never left London, not even for a single night.

'Why would I?' he often jokes. 'Landscapes change and seasons turn but wherever you go in the world, night is the same.'

And when he says it, I realise how Adefina Corvus was right in one thing: Benjamin is a bad liar. Something more than familiarity with London and its dark streets holds him to this city. I believe there is purpose in his staying, just as I believe I know what you want to ask next. The most important question of all.

Did the grimoire stay at the bottom of the river?

I asked that of Benjamin after our first meeting all those years ago. Like you, I simply had to know. The question stopped him in the doorway, and for the longest time he offered no answer. I supposed that naturally, or rather, supernaturally, he was reluctant to say too much about the fate of such an evil book. Best to leave it lie, perhaps, wherever that might be.

But then he spoke and his words were like a clue to everything. In a simple rhyme that washed his silver eyes briefly to blue as he remembered, he said:

> *'Close thine eyes and sleep secure,*
> *Thy soul is safe, thy body sure.*
> *He that guards thee, he that keeps,*
> *Never slumbers, never sleeps.'*

22ND APRIL, 2022

ACKNOWLEDGEMENTS

Writing is described as the 'loneliest craft' but, in truth, no book is written alone.

Benjamin Blake would never have seen the light of the moon were it not for those working quietly in the Riley Realm, and who deserve more thanks than I can offer – even in a vampire's lifetime.

Ciara O'Hara of Purple Crayon (www.purplecrayoncopy. com) whose editing skills and patience with me were tested to the full on 'Project Silver'.

Mags Gargan, ever watchful test-reader and editor, and enduring friend.

Alba Esteban (Instagram @alesturadesign) who gave Benjamin his look, and whose magic you hold in your hands now.

Erin Fox, spooktacular fellow traveller beneath the full moon, my ideas guru and social media queen.

And, of course, Ita, who started it all and knows Benjamin better than anyone.

Thank you, each and every one.

Benjamin Blake
will return in
*The Revenge of
Billy Buckler*

9 781739 371807